I0760073

E.L. RHODES

THE MEETING PLACE

A Novel

THE MEETING PLACE

ISBN 978-0-210-00003-4

Book Cover By: Glenn Williams and Walter Brinkley

Author Photo By: Glenn Williams

Edited By: Jean C. Hsu-Lupo and Unice Y. Hsu

For Vera

And in loving memory of

Leah Tilman

Joseph M. Belger

Yvonne "Popcorn" Mosley

Kenneth "Sam" Powell

Chapter 1 - Viola

Her hand, small and petite, covered by the soft, blue, thick cotton glove gripped the metal pole as she stood still waiting impatiently. The icy cold of the metal pole cut deeply and painfully, piercing through her glove like the blade of a razor-sharp knife. She quickly removed her hand and wrapped her arm around her body. Her other hand was wrapped firmly around the thick rope handle of the shopping totebag which contained her precious items. Barely moving, she stood as if she had already been frozen solid by old man winter himself. Staring in the same direction for over twenty minutes, she wanted only to see just a glimpse of its nose peeking over the horizon. Now swaying from side to side, she remained focused on its expected sight. She was at its mercy. The bitter cold made her seek its refuge and she was now longing to snuggle comfortably in its warm bosom.

The cold, wet bead of moisture crept slowly from the corner of her eye down the front of her face as the frigid wind forced its way through her layered garments chilling her small bones. She wiped her face then tightly folded her arms together and tapped her feet against the cold pavement in an alternating succession.

Finally, creeping slowly toward her from off in the distance was the vision of that which satisfied her desire. Her anticipation grew stronger as it advanced nearer. Now upon her, after slowly settling to a complete stop, the doors of the #4 bus opened. It had just completed its run through Main Street. The thin small woman hurried aboard.

"Morning Vy!" greeted the driver while looking out at her from under the brim of his hat.

The young woman quickly dug into the pocket of her coat. Just as fast as she retrieved it from her pocket, she dropped the coins into the small, oblong glass encased receptacle. She then sashayed down the aisle without uttering a word. As she maneuvered toward a seat, the heads of the other passengers turned and faint whispers began. She held firmly onto her bag while keeping her nose pointed toward the ceiling of the now moving transport. Just as she was about to slide into the blue, vinyl bench seat, she turned and placed herself on display for the snobby and snidely remarking spectators.

"Take a picture why don't ya?" She declared loudly. She looked at all of them with her sassy but angry look then turned and faced the back of the bus. She reached around to the bottom of her blue and gray plaid coat and not only did she pull up her coat, she raised her coat and dress high above her waist. She bent over and smacked her bottom while yelling as loud as she could, "YOU ALL CAN JUST GO STRAIGHT TO HELL AND KISS THIS ON YOUR WAY DOWN!"

The rude stares and snide remarks were what she had to contend with daily; ever since everyone in her small town of Emporia, Virginia found out that she had been impregnated by none other than Willy Sims. Willy Sims, also known as the Honorable Reverend Sims, was the pastor of The Mount Calvary Baptist Church of Emporia. This tidbit was the talk of the town and everyone had something to say about it. Everywhere she turned, the words whore, harlot, or home-wrecker was whispered from the lips of some self righteous sinner masquerading as a holy saint.

After adjusting her clothing, she placed her large bag on the seat and cautiously lowered herself down. She grabbed onto the chrome bar that was attached to the seat directly in front of her before leaning back against the backrest. The heat blew from the small holes along the bottom of the windows. It wasn't cozy, but just warm enough to help take the chill out of the air. She folded her arms and closed her eyes. She was tired; tired and cold. If it wasn't for her son who had taken ill with the flu, she would have never left the house. He needed to be cared for and they were running out of food and medicine. She would have walked to town if she had to for him.

After resting her head and closing her eyes for a quick nap, her small pleasure was quickly interrupted.

"Vy! Hey Vy!" The voice whispered.

She ignored the voice and continued with her resting.

"Viola!" The voice whispered once again.

"What in the hell do you want? Don't you see me trying to get some rest?"

"Does Jessie know?"

"Does Jessie know what?"

"Does he know about the baby? I mean, it being the Pastor's and all."

Without opening her eyes or turning her head, she answered. "Why do you want to know about me and Jessie's business? So you can only have more rumors to spread around town about me? I'll tell you what, I'm gonna answer your question but only after I bust you in your big, loud, gossip tellin' mouth so you can't spread no more of your filth!"

A cold, dead silence rushed throughout the bus cabin. Viola piled all of her belongings snugly against the wall then rose from her seat and turned toward the woman who was now looking terrified. She removed her high heeled shoes and balled up her hands into two little fists. She stood up tall and erect then inched toward the back door of the bus. Moments after, the vehicle slowed and then came to a stop.

"Viola, now you settle down back there. We'll be havin' none of that today. You leave Miss Thelma alone. Miss Thelma, you go on now, this here is your stop. Leave her be Viola, you just leave her be. I won't have to call the sheriff again will I?" yelled the big, husky bus driver from his seat.

With that, Viola relaxed her hands and lowered her head. Thelma having realized the impact of the bus driver's statement, noticed the affect that it had on Viola. She slowly rose up from her seat all the while never taking her eyes off Viola. She inched between the angry little woman and the seat closest to the rear exit then hesitantly started down the steps to the double doors.

"Go on Miss Thelma, she ain't goin' to harm you none." Once again the bus driver reassured the trembling woman. Thelma reached for the long chrome handle of the doors and began to push. As she turned to exit she looked back at Viola and produced a snobbish smirk over her face. She turned up her nose then mumbled under her breath, "Just shameless."

Viola's hands once again returned to their balled position. As Thelma turned to lower herself down on the last step to exit, Viola quickly took hold of the shiny bar secured tightly to the back of the seat in front of the exit doors and the long vertical chrome pole that was located just at the top of the steps. Bracing herself, Viola pulled herself off the floor and raised her foot.

"Viola no!" yelled the bus driver.

The unsuspecting, snobby Thelma looked over at the driver who had now risen from his seat. He was waving his arms and gesturing like a policeman stopping traffic. Just as Thelma began to turn toward Viola, she could feel the hard boney heel of the little woman's small foot wedge between her shoulder blades.

"Noooooooooooo Viola!" yelled the driver.

It was too late and Thelma knew it. Without warning the tiny woman delivered a powerful jolt to Thelma's back. The passengers could hear her yell out loudly as they watched her head whip back toward her shoulder blades.

"Iiiiiiiiieeeeeeeeeemmmmmmmmmm!" Thelma screamed. Before she knew it, Thelma felt herself lifted up and out of both high heeled shoes and soared through the air. As her body began to crash through the rear double doors, her head wasn't as lucky. During her short flight, her head was quickly greeted by the metal threshold just above the doors. The top of her forehead scraped against the metal during her forced exit. As she was spit from the exit-way, every item in her handbag scattered through the air as the bag itself took flight. Her knees made impact with the awaiting ground after which she slid about four feet across the cold pavement. With her hands down by her sides, nylons ripped down to her ankles, scratches across her forehead and shoeless, she swayed forward then slowly back to the rear before slamming face first into the pavement. As she lay on the cold concrete covered with earth she uttered the remaining half of her statement, "Sor-ry," then passed out.

"Now smirk at that you self-righteous hypocrite! If it wasn't so cold out there I'd come and whup you some more!" Viola yelled as Thelma lay face down on the pavement.

Everyone on the bus rushed off to Thelma's aid.

"Y'all better get back on this bus for y'all get left. She'll be alright. I gotta get home so let's get movin'. I got a sick boy at home so come on now. I said she'll be alright. She'll have a headache and maybe a mild case of the 'next time I'll just shut the hell up' but other than that she'll be alright, so let's get goin'," Viola said.

The crowd didn't budge. They ignored Viola as they continued assisting the young woman who was still sprawled out on the cold pavement. The bus driver had even joined in with the revival of poor Thelma.

"Ben, now you get back on this bus so I can get home. Anybody else who wants to stay can just get left!" Viola screamed.

Still, everyone remained focused and tended to Thelma. Angry and frustrated even more now, Viola walked up to the driver's seat and pulled the metal switch down to the "close" position. The doors to the bus closed. The group of passengers all rushed over to the door yelling for Viola to let them back on board. Ben, the driver rushed through the crowd and began banging his hand against the glass of the door.

"Viola, now you open these doors, right now!"

Viola just sat quietly, looking around at all the different controls. "You goin' to take me home then?" Viola asked calmly.

"If you open the door, sure," Ben replied.

Viola pushed the switch back to the "open" position. As the doors began to open, Viola immediately pulled the switch back down and the doors re-closed. She stood while leaving the crowd standing in front of the door. Thelma had managed to pull herself up and was now sitting on the freezing curb. Viola walked across the aisle and lowered one of the windows. She leaned her head out and yelled as loud as she could. "Thelma, you'd better get your nosey ass up off that cold ground, pretending to be more hurt than you really are, before I come out there and turn that pretend into reality! You'd better be up by the time I get there or else!"

Viola stared at the woman for a moment before closing the window. Before she could make her way to the back door, Thelma jumped up and staggered as fast as she could down the sidewalk. After slamming the window shut, Viola walked back over to the driver's seat and once again pushed the switch to open the doors. The driver and all of the angry passengers rushed back on to the warmth of the transport. As they returned to their seats, Ben picked up the handset of his two-way-radio. He looked back at Viola angrily as she slowly sashayed back to her seat still mumbling to herself.

"Viola, I'm afraid I'm gonna have to ask you to leave the bus!"

Viola, now lowering herself in her seat, calmly replied. "Well, I guess I'm afraid that I'm gonna have to ask you to kiss my ass, Ben."

"Now Viola, don't make me have to call the sheriff. Come on now, let's go!"

Viola slowly raised her head and continued to speak in her calm voice. "Now Ben, why you wanna go and do that? Aint no cause for you to call the sheriff now is it? You know that busy body Thelma was instigating me. Now I don't want no trouble Ben, but you know I aint scaret! And besides, it'll be pretty hard drivin' this here bus with only one eye to see out of. How many days will you have to take off from your job before your vision comes back, huh? So ask yourself, is it really worth it? Besides, you wouldn't want me to call and tell Luke that you called the sheriff on his dearest and most favorite cousin now would you? He'll ram his foot so far up your ass your farts will smell like shoe leather for six weeks!"

Luke was Viola's first cousin. He, like Viola, was as mean as a snake, maybe even meaner. He was so mean that he once beat a man to near death just for touching his new car after Luke had just run him over. That's right, after he had hit the man with his car. The young man was only crossing the street with his bag of groceries; Luke drove up and failed to stop at the stop sign at the intersection. He struck the man and knocked him to the ground. The poor guy's groceries flew in every direction. Luke remained in his car waiting for the man to collect himself and remove himself and all of his belongings from out of his path so that he could continue on his way. He revved his engine as the man struggled to pull himself up from the ground. Having become more agitated, Luke began yelling at the man to move while blowing his horn at him.

Spectators stood and watched but said nothing as the man helplessly tried to maneuver himself to an upright position. No one said a word to Luke for they all knew how crazy he was. Two of the male spectators finally walked over to assist the young man. As they lifted him to his feet it appeared the leg that was struck by Luke's car was broken. Not able to apply any pressure on the leg, the young man lost his balance and before either man could catch him, the young man placed his hand on the top of the hood of Luke's new car in an effort to steady himself. This infuriated Luke.

"Hey, get off the car!" Luke shouted at the man. He climbed out of his car and rushed around to where the young man stood wincing.

One of the spectators assisting the young man backed away slowly from the car while the other held firmly on to the young man's arm for support. Luke walked up and slapped the young man's only crutch. The Good Samaritan let go of the young man's arm and held the side of his face. He looked at the young man and said, "You're on you own!" and then ran off.

Luke stepped closer to the young man who now was balancing himself on one leg. Without saying a word, Luke slammed the young man to the ground and beat him for over five minutes. When he was done, he walked back around to the driver's side of his car, climbed in and sped off running over whatever groceries that remained in the brown paper sack.

Yes, Luke was crazy and none of the residents of Emporia wanted any dealings with him. The only person he had any respect for other than his father, was Viola. His father was just as mean as he was and as for Viola, well she was the only other person ever to have whipped him. He never forgot when Viola laid into him. She hurt him pretty bad. That was when he, as she had put it, "took part of my virgin."

Viola had injured Luke so intensely that he walked with a slight limp from that day forward. Luke rained down havoc and hell on all of Emporia. Nope, Ben wanted no part of Luke, not in this lifetime. He wanted only to drive the bus for another day and he knew if Viola called her crazy cousin and told him that Ben had given her a hard time on the bus, Luke would come calling. As he returned from his deep thought he could still hear Viola's voice in the distance.

"How much money will you loose for not being able to work 'cause you know Luke's gonna tear your ass up?! You'll be walking around with a tin can and cane by the time he's done with you." Viola then became silent as she slowly rose to her feet once more. Once again her hands transformed into little tightly balled fists. "Now why don't you just put that radio back in that cradle, Ben?"

Viola inched closer and closer to where the big burly man sat. He slowly placed the handset of the radio back into the cradle and pulled the switch down to close the doors. He looked at the little lady in frustration. "You know, you're more trouble than you're worth. I'll be glad when Jessie gets back home. Somebody needs to settle you down."

"Well it won't be you, so just drive FAT BOY!"

Ben shook his head and sucked in his gut before slowly pulling away from the curb and down Main Street. After reaching Viola's stop, the bus slowed before coming to an abrupt stop. Viola stood and picked up her belongings. Then she sashayed down the aisle toward the front of the bus. Just as she was about to step down on the stairs, Viola turned and faced the driver and stuck her finger in his face. "Ben, if I hear that you spit one word of this to the sheriff, I'm gonna find you! You hear me? And as far as the rest of you go…" At that moment, Viola lowered her shopping bag to the floor of the bus and turned and faced the clean, wide windshield of the bus. She bent over and pulled her dress up over her backside flaunting her nylons and undergarments. She then reached back and gripped on to the fleshy part of the right side of her buttocks. Before looking back at their squinted and disgusted looks, she yelled out the remaining portion of her statement. "IT'S STILL HERE FOR ALL OF Y'ALL TO KISS!"

The little lady smoothed her dress, grabbed her bag then strutted off the bus and onto the road. The doors quickly closed and the vehicle sped off. After a short walk, Viola reached home. She walked up the few steps which led to her front door. She stepped inside while snatching off one glove and then the other. She pulled off her coat and hung it on the hook beside the door. In an effort to warm herself, she rubbed her hands together to unthaw her little fingers and ran them up and down the sides of her still chilled arms.

Grabbing her bag, she rushed into the kitchen. Pulling her apron from the hook next to the pantry, Viola slipped it on and washed her hands in the kitchen sink. She quickly pulled out her pots and pans, her seasonings and vegetables to begin preparation of her son's supper. After getting the meal started, she stepped into her son's room.

Inside, she could see him lying in his bed quiet and still. She pulled up the chair which sat in the corner of his room and placed it next to her son's bed. As she sat next to him, she placed her hand across his forehead then gently slid it down to the right side of his neck. He was burning up. His skin was warm and wet from perspiration. His fever had still not broken.

Viola pulled the towel hanging from the side of his bed to wipe him dry then rushed into the bathroom to retrieve a bottle of rubbing alcohol from the medicine cabinet. She pulled the already damp wash cloth that was neatly folded across the towel bar above the basin and ran cold water over it. The excess water vanished quickly into the dark opening as she twisted and squeezed the cloth before returning to her son.

He lay there, now moaning and feeling helpless. Viola placed the damp cloth across his forehead then began pouring small quantities of the clear alcohol into her hand. Rubbing it between her hands, she wiped the liquid across her son's neck and over his arms. She was worried about Cecil, her only child. He was a good boy. Named after his grandfather Cecil Barnes, Jessie's dad, Cecil was his dad's everything. Cecil had been ill before, but never like this, that's why his mom worried so. She knew that it would kill her and her husband if anything were to happen to him.

Viola returned to the kitchen to check on her soup. The chicken emitted a wonderful aroma which met her nose as she approached the kitchen. It was almost ready. Viola began preparing the tray by carefully placing a small glass plate and then a small glass bowl in the center with a neatly folded napkin on the side, on top of which she put a soup spoon. She placed the crackers on the plate and retrieved the ladle in preparation of filling the bowl with the hot liquid that she surely knew would assist in her son's recovery. She had just stepped over to the stove and turned down the flame when she heard the thunderous explosion. The booming sound repeated. She removed her apron and walked into the hallway and up to the front door. "Who is it?"

"It's Beau. Can I talk to you for a sec?"

Beau was the sheriff in Emporia. Viola slowly opened the door. Peeping from behind the wooden structure, she could see Beau standing on the front porch of her home.

"Beau, what are you doin' out here in this weather, car break down again?"

"Howdy Vy. Nah, car's runnin' just fine."

"Well come on in. You know Jessie's still up in Richmond. He won't be back 'til next Friday. They're workin' him a might much up there but the pay is good and Lord knows we could use the money. So what brings you out here? Wait, don't tell me it's about that mess on that ole bus today. So Ben called you did he? I tried to warn him, now I'm tellin' you Beau that he's…"

"Now hold on, it wasn't Ben and he wanted me to let you know that too for some strange reason. You must have raised the roof on that bus did you?"

"Beau, now you know me and you know that I only get riled up when I have cause to. All I want is be left alone is all but folks around here seem to just feel compelled to pry into my business."

"Well, it seems that Miss Thelma done gone and filed a complaint she did. Says you kicked her and tried to run her over with the bus after you forced everybody off the bus with a knife. She said you just went plum crazy. She says that nobody knows why you went crazy. She said that all she remembers is complimenting you on your hat and the next thing she knew…"

"WHAT?! Complimenting me about my hat my ass! A knife? Run her over? No she didn't say that I kicked her. She's gonna need pallbearers after lying on me like that! Now Beau you know I never use weapons, well maybe a stick here and there but normally you know I handle my business with these right here," she said while extending her little fist toward the officer.

"She says that she has witnesses, too. Says they'll back up her story. She said that you kicked her so hard she thinks she might even have brain damage."

"Damn right she's got brain damage, and she's gonna have more than that when I'm finished with her! Her and all of those lyin' ass witnesses! Who are they?"

"Now settle down, Vy. Now you know I can't tell you who they are and besides, I haven't spoken to anybody yet. I wanted to talk to you and hear your side of the story."

"Well thank you Beau, at least somebody around here has some decency. Ok, I walked onto the bus minding my own business like I always do. I spoke to Ben and to everybody else on the bus. I saw Thelma sitting near the back of the bus and asked her how she was doing. She asked me about Jessie and I told her that he was doing fine and would be home soon. She said that that was good because then I could stop acting like a WHORE! Now Beau, you know that was uncalled for, even for a slut like Thelma. I got out of my seat and told her that what she said was uncalled for and she needed prayer. She stood up and told me that I could cram my prayer up my ass. When the bus stopped, I stepped aside and as she went to exit the bus, I believe her purse got caught on the door and she slipped off the bottom step and tumbled onto the ground. It might have looked like I kicked her to some people but you know I would never do anything like that."

"Did you lock everybody off the bus out in the cold?"

"No, they all got off and the doors closed and jammed. I was trying to un-jam the doors so they could get back on. See, I was only trying to help."

"Vy, I'm probably gonna need you to come down to the station tomorrow if Miss Thelma wants to proceed with this."

"I understand Beau and you know I don't want any trouble. Can you please excuse me for just one second? I've got something on the stove that needs tendin' to. You hungry? You had your supper yet?" She asked as she headed toward the kitchen.

"No thanks, I ate over at the diner before I came out here."

Beau stood waiting in the living room with one of his hands placed on his hip just above his gun belt. He held his big rimmed cowboy style hat in his other hand and hummed to himself as he strolled leisurely through the room looking at old photographs. He reached up and slid the zipper halfway down on his fur collared insulated jacket which was emblazoned with a blue and gold embroidered star. He stopped at each table looking at generations of old family portraits. He picked up a small picture frame from off of the mantle directly above the fireplace. He smiled while admiring the couple in the picture. His attention quickly shifted to the muffled voice which had now become clearer after stepping into the hallway.

"I'll tell you what Missy, if I have to go through any trouble because of you and your big mouth...Beau is here now. What do you mean it wasn't you? Beau said you filed a complaint! Oh you didn't huh? Well I'll tell you this, when I find who did, and you know I will and if I have to go down to the jail, ooooooooh I'd hate to be that person. I'm gonna be pretty mad when I get out, especially since my boy is sick and all. Aint no tellin' what I might do when I see who was responsible! Somebody's gonna get it though, I guarantee that! What?...Uh huh…Uh huh….I see…Yeah, he's right here…Ok, hold on. Beau? Beau!"

Beau entered the kitchen looking at Viola strangely. Viola was standing just beyond the entranceway leading into the kitchen with one hand on her hip and the other holding the telephone handset. Her arm was extended toward Beau.

"It's for you."

"For me?"

"Yeah, for you, take it."

Beau accepted the telephone from Viola and placed the receiver to his ear. "Sheriff Daily speakin'. Uh huh…Uh huh…Uh huh…Are you sure? Yeah, but you said…I know but…Sure, I understand…Nobody's gonna kill anybody…No, I wouldn't want that either…You're sure about this? Ok, that's fine. Yes, I can do that. Ok, you have a good evening then."

Beau walked over and placed the telephone handset back on its resting place before looking over at Viola who was now nonchalantly stirring her big pot of soup.

"Well it looks like Miss Thelma has decided not to press charges after all."

"Mmmm, go figure," Viola replied as she continued to stir her steamy mixture.

"Yeah, go figure. She also wanted me to tell you that she wasn't in her right mind when she filed the complaint. She said that she thinks she was in one of those 'walkin' comas' and had a case of the amnesia, you know, one of those split personality things. Yeah, that's what she said; she said to tell you that it was the other person inside of her so you really shouldn't be mad at her."

"Ah I know she wouldn't have done that deliberately and I'm not going to bother Thelma if that's what you're thinking. As for that other 'split personality bitch', well I guess I'm just gonna have to beat Thelma across the head until she comes out 'cause she's got some explainin' to do!"

"Viola, leave Thelma alone. Please don't make me have to come back out here to run you in, Ok? "

"Sure you don't want no suppa Sheriff?"

"Yeah, I'm sure but thanks kindly."

Beau pulled the zipper of his jacket up until it reached just below the collar. He slid his thick leather gloves on, one after the other and headed for the door.

"You have a good evening Sheriff and say hello to Sarah for me."

"I sure will and thanks for the encouraging words."

"Encouraging words, what encouraging words?"

"Not to me, but to Miss Thelma. I hate paperwork! Now go on and tend to your supper. Oh Vy, one more thing. Is it true, are you really pregnant by…?" Beau paused for a second while looking down at the floor. He looked back up at Viola and smiled, "Never mind. Just forget about it. You take care Viola and you call me next time somebody goes prying into your business. I'll have a talk with 'em."

Beau popped his hat on top of his bushy hair and waved to Viola before stepping out through the door and down the steps toward his squad car. Viola closed the door gently after watching Beau climb into his car.

"He's just as much of an ass as the rest of these folks in this town," she thought, then walked back into the room and checked on Cecil. After wiping his perspiration again she returned to the kitchen and continued with preparing his meal. She dipped the long handled ladle into the hot soup which she had prepared. She filled the bowl and then she pulled a slice of bread from its wrapper and spread cool creamy butter across the surface. The bread was placed onto the small plate next to the steaming bowl of soup. She carried the tray into Cecil's room and placed it on the table beside his bed.

Cecil lay sleeping. Viola called quietly to her son, "Cecil honey, wake up Sweetie, it's time to eat. Come on Dear, you need to put something on your stomach. It's your favorite; some of Mom's specially made chicken noodle soup."

Cecil opened his eyes and Viola began to help him sit up in his bed. She fed him the hot soup but after taking one bite of the butter covered bread, he would not eat any more of it. Cecil placed his hand over his stomach. After a few seconds he removed his hand and continued to slowly sip the broth from the spoon his mother held. Viola placed the bread up to Cecil's mouth and once again he refused to eat.

"Come on Sweetie, I want you to try to eat some of this. Just put a little something solid on your stomach, Ok Sweetie. I promise it'll make you feel better," Viola said while still gently pressing the small piece of bread against his lips. Finally, Cecil gave in. He opened his mouth and took the food from her fingers. He chewed it very slowly. After a few minutes had passed, Cecil swallowed the bread and seconds later his hand returned to his tummy. This time he was wincing and moaning. This was the first bit of solid food he had eaten since he had become ill. Cecil rolled over onto his side with his back to his mother. He began to gyrate and heave as if he was about to vomit.

Viola quickly grabbed the small trash container near the bed. As she leaned over Cecil, the bowl of soup emptied as it tumbled to the floor with the remaining pieces of bread soaking in its puddle. Cecil became quiet and his jerking motions ceased but he remained on his side. Relieved, Viola kneeled down and began to wipe up what was left of Cecil's meal.

After she had completed wiping up all of the food, she placed the soup soaked towel into the trash container. As she began to pull herself off the floor, she looked at Cecil. He still lay on his side and had drifted back to sleep. On her knees, she leaned over and pulled his pajama top down to cover his exposed back.

The blast nearly blew her face off. It was loud and lasted for a few seconds. Viola revved back as the wicked wind left his body. She began to smile, "Poor baby just had gas that's all." But her smile quickly dissipated as the stench crept up into her nostrils. The smell was awful. It was strong and foul. Viola stood over the son she loved and looked at him with her eyes watering and a shriveled up frown formed across her face. "No more bread for you young man, not now, not ever. That's just disgusting!" she thought.

Viola, still gagging, reached over and adjusted her son's blanket. While tucking him in, Viola thought that she'd better check the rear of Cecil's underwear for she was certain that he had defecated on himself. She slid her finger just inside the top of his pajama pant and pulled it away from his flesh. She leaned closer and gave his backside a thorough check for stains. "Skirurrrrrrrr-RIP!" was the next sound that she heard. That's right, with her face buried down near his rear, Cecil had released another loud blast from his opening. It was as if an alarm had gone off from Viola getting too close; as if his buttocks had fired a warning shot. Viola didn't stick around for the aftermath of this one. She yanked the blanket up over her son's exposed body and ran out of the room.

Several weeks later, Cecil had fully recovered and returned to school and Viola returned to her normal routine. She did any and every thing to keep herself occupied. It was all she could do to keep her mind off Jessie. How she missed that man. She worried about him constantly. You see, Jessie wasn't the smartest man in the world but was probably one of the luckiest.

He always seemed to be in the right place at the right time. Actually, that's how he met Viola. There were plenty of men who wanted Viola, that is, before they found out what a handful she was, but Jessie just happened to stumble right into matrimony. Jessie had just been hired on along with two other young men to help Viola's father with the construction of their new barn. Jessie was a carpenter by trade but took on odd jobs to make ends meet when there was no other work available.

One particular morning, Jessie reported early to her father's home so that he could rope off the area for the new barn. As he passed by the old barn he heard a loud high pitched scream followed by Viola rushing out in a panic. She was running so fast that she ran into Jessie and knocked him flat on his back. She tumbled to the ground then slid across the dirt. Jessie jumped up and rushed over to her aid. He bent over the small, frail young girl and attempted to help her up. He looked at her and was immediately attracted to her beauty. With concern he calmly asked, "Are you alrigh…"

Before Jessie could finish his question or give an apology Viola rolled over and "POW!" she socked the apologetic young Jessie in his eye then jumped up and ran off. Jessie fell to the ground and in love with one punch. With his eye swollen and his nose wide open with love, he began his pursuit of the young Viola. Every day he would try to say something sweet or charming to her but as I said, he wasn't the smartest man in the world. He just couldn't quite communicate his thoughts the way he would have liked. Once as she headed over to feed the pigs, Jessie had decided to take a chance and walk over for a chat. He knew that this may be his only chance to make an impression on the young Viola. He decided that it was time to give it his all. He slicked his hair back and stuck out his chest and walked right up to the demon seed he adored.

"Mornin' Viola!"

"What do you want?"

"Oh nothin'. I just wanted to come over and talk to you is all."

"Talk to me about what? You need to be workin' on that barn," she said as she struggled to hold in her laughter from viewing the sight of the shiny black ring under his eye.

"Nothin' in particular."

"Ok, well you've talked to me. Now you can go on back to work."

"You goin' to feed those pigs, huh?"

"Looks that way don't it?"

"Well yeah, I guess it does. Well maybe you're right, maybe I should be gettin' on back to work here."

"Yeah, I guess you should."

"By the way, that sure is a pretty hog feedin' dress you're wearin'."

Viola looked down at her dress then balled up her hands into fists as she looked back at Jessie. "Are you tryin' to get your other eye closed? My aunt made me this dress and you're saying that it's only fit for feeding hogs?"

"No, no I'm just sayin' that you look pretty is all. I'm just sayin' that you're probably the only girl in the world who can make that dress look good while sloppin' hogs. Wait, that didn't come out right."

"Shut up, just shut your mouth and leave me alone!" she yelled.

"I'm sorry, I didn't mean it that way. I guess I'm only trying to say that you are the prettiest girl I've ever seen and I li…" Jessie stopped in mid-sentence. Realizing that it was no use, he lowered his head. He turned and started heading back up toward the barn. Viola knew that he was only doing all he could to compliment her and that he was really a nice guy. She realized at that moment that she too, was attracted to him. She lowered her fists and then looked at her dress once again. She picked up the bucket of slop and headed toward the pen.

She looked back at as she watched Jessie drag himself up the hill before yelling, “Hey, how’s your eye doing anyway?”

Jessie looked back at Viola and smiled. “Well, the vision’s coming back slowly but surely,” he yelled.

“Sorry I hit you so hard.”

“Oh that’s ok, I guess I’ll live. You sure can pack a punch for a little thing,” he said now walking back toward her.

“Yeah, I guess. It’s from fighting with my brothers.”

“I’ll tell you what, how about we bury the hatchet by letting me take you for a soda later?”

“I gotta check with my daddy, but if he says it’s alright then that would be just fine.”

From that day on, the two of them were inseparable. One year later they were married. As for Jessie’s eye, it never did heal completely. It seems that Viola’s punch had damaged his eye socket so that his eyeball could never sit properly again which made his eye look crooked. I guess from the day that she punched him, they never saw eye to eye again (sorry, I just couldn’t help myself).

That was just the beginning of Jessie’s injuries from Viola. She once broke his jaw while giving birth to her son. After she punched him in the jaw, she screamed, “NOW YELL PUSH AGAIN, DAMN IT!” The doctor said he had never seen anything like this before in all the years he had been delivering children, both the mother and father moaning in pain during childbirth.

Over the years, through all of the broken bones, burnings, biting and unconsciousness, Jessie hung in there with his wife. He did everything he could not to upset Viola. After all, by this time he was convinced that she was made up of three parts. She had the structure of a woman, the strength of a man and the mean streak of a rattle snake.

If Jessie stayed out too late, Viola would surely give him a piece of her mind. If he came home intoxicated and unruly, she would not say a word. He would spend the following morning nursing his wounds while she sat quietly in the kitchen soaking her hand in a bowl of ice.

This went on until the day Jessie snapped. It was on this day that Viola opened her mouth and released the sharpest daggers that her tongue could construct. She spoke the only words that could push Jessie over the edge. On this particular day Jessie and Viola sat at the dinner table as they always did. Viola started in on Jessie about him being out with some woman. Jessie denied the accusation of course. She didn't ease up.

"I'd better not hear anything about you with some tramp!"

"Vy, I just ran into her at the drugstore, that's all."

"Well I heard that you spent a lot of time talking with her. What was that all about?"

"It was only two minutes!"

"Two minutes? You say that as if that's a short while. Hell, I got pregnant in less time than that! How well do you know this slut anyway?"

"We used to go to school together."

"Did you ever kiss her?"

"Well yeah, we used to see each other but that was a long time ago."

"See each other, what's that mean?"

"Don't mean nothin'."

"Did you two do it?"

"Do what?"

"I will come over there and break my foot off in your ass if you're temptin' me. Do IT! Damn-it, you know what IT is and you'd better tell me the truth 'cause you know I know when you're lyin'."

"Ah Vy, c'mon it wasn't like I was a virgin or nothin' when we met."

"Oh, so was she your first?"

"No Vy, she wasn't."

"Oh so you do admit that you did it with her huh Mr. Nasty-I-want-be-sleeping-with-my-old-sluts-again!"

"I don't want to sleep with her. Don't you think that you're taking this too far? I told you that she wasn't my first."

"Is that a fact? Well good, because you weren't my first either!"

"WHAT? What did you say?"

"You heard me, I said that you weren't my first either. I had plenty of men and most were better than you, too. As a matter of fact I..."

Each shoe slowly slid off both feet and onto the floor. The huge vein bulged from her forehead and her eyes began to roll toward the back of her head as she no longer had any air intake.

His grip was so tight around her neck as he hoisted her into the air. She just knew for sure that she was going to die. Her only saving grace was Cecil. He began to cry from the other room. The sounds of the young infant crying pulled Jessie from his jealous rage and he released his grip. Viola fell to the floor coughing and gasping, trying to force breath back into her lungs.

"The baby's cryin', you want me to get him or do you?" Jessie asked calmly. He spoke as if nothing had happened. Viola looked on in disbelief. She couldn't believe that her husband of all this time, who never would as much as lift a finger against her, had almost in a split second taken her life without a second thought. It was as if he was someone else, someone she didn't know. This was someone, for sure, she definitely didn't want to ever see again. From that day forward, Viola never raised her hand to Jessie again.

Several days after Cecil regained his health and had returned to school, Viola was summoned to meet with the principal. Cecil had gotten into a fight with one of his classmates. Viola rushed down to the school which was only a few blocks away. As a protective mother, her only concern was Cecil. After climbing the steps of the large brick building, the tiny woman reached for the large metal handle and snatched open the door. With her purse clutched tightly under her arm and a cigarette stuck between her lips, she paused. She reached up and pulled the thin wrapped tobacco stick from her lips and plucked it down the stairs then quickly returned to her marching.

After passing several classrooms, the concerned mother had reached her destination. The large opening was winged by two oak doors that swung open on each side. The word "Principal's" was painted in black on one of the doors and the word "Office" was painted on the other. This was only the second time Viola had visited the principal on Cecil's behalf. She had come down once before to discuss Cecil's absences due to his illness with the principal.

Viola quickly stepped inside the office and walked up to the long wooden counter. Sitting just beyond the counter surrounded by old grey file cabinets was an older woman. She sat in her wide-backed, cushioned, rolling desk chair typing on the keys of an old black Remington. She pushed on the keys quickly and with every low ring of its bell she would push the small metal lever over to the opposite side and then repeat the sequence. Viola cleared her throat to get the woman's attention. Ignoring Viola, the woman continued with her typing.

"Excuse me!" Viola yelled. "Is Principal Burmer here?"

The woman paused from her work and looked over at Viola snidely. "Yes, he's in, your name Miss?"

"It's Mrs. Just tell him that Mrs. Wiley is here. Tell him I've come to see about my boy Cecil. Is he alright?"

"Just one moment, I believe he's on the telephone."

The woman went back to her typing, the keys now clicking faster than before. Viola slowly eased her way around the long counter and up to the woman's desk. The woman continued pressing on the keys of the large black machine. As soon as the muffled sound of the small bell rang out, Viola reached over and placed her hand on the lever of the typewriter.

"Can you check to see if he is available please?" she asked.

"I'll check in a minute. Now Miss can you please wait on the other side of the counter?"

"You're new around here aren't you? No, you don't look familiar at all. In fact, I'm sure that I've never seen your face around here before."

"Why yes, my husband and I have only been here for two months. We're originally from Richmond. Now please, I still must ask you to wait for Mr. Burmer on the other side of the counter."

"Un huh, I see. You enjoy typing?"

"Why yes, yes I do. I'm pretty proficient at it and it's my job. So yes I do."

"Well if you don't get Mr. Burmer out here right now, I'm gonna break those fast little fingers of yours and jam them RIGHT UP YOUR ASS!"

With that, the woman looked over the rim of her black framed eyeglasses at Viola then placed her hands on her hips. "Well, I never!" she belted.

"Well you will if you don't get it in gear, sister!"

"Well I must say you won't get any assistance here with an attitude like that."

"Missy, you must think I'm playin' with you."

Viola placed her purse on top of the woman's desk and inched closer. Just as she was about to pounce on the defenseless woman, Principal Burmer called out to Viola, "Mrs. Wiley!"

The woman, sitting covering her face and head beneath her arms in preparation of an onslaught of knuckles, slowly peaked through the small cracks between her arms at the woman that she now deemed insane.

"Sorry for the delay Mrs. Wiley, please come right in."

Viola looked at the terrified woman for a second then turned toward Mr. Burmer's office. Before she walked off, she reached down and snatched the neatly typed paper from the woman's typewriter and ripped it into shreds. "Type it again, Bitch. As a matter of fact, how about you type something like, 'I must be more polite to the parents.' I believe one hundred times should be good enough but just know that if it's not done by the time I leave Mr. Burmer, I'm gonna finish what I was about to get started!" Viola slowly raised her fist then walked away leaving the woman looking puzzled and shocked.

Viola walked around the desk and stepped inside Mr. Burmer's office.

"Where's Cecil, is he alright?"

"Yes Mrs. Wiley, he's fine. He and another young man got into a small altercation; it was more like a little tussle that's all, but he's fine. Both boys have been disciplined for fighting."

"Wait, my Cecil fighting? He wouldn't have been fighting unless he was being picked on. Why is he being punished?"

"Well, it seems that Cecil threw the first punch in the fight, Mrs. Wiley."

"Why, what did the other boy do to him?"

"My understanding is that some of the kids were picking on Cecil and the young man that he struck just went too far, but we still do not condone fighting here. After all, they were just words."

"Too far? I taught my son not to fight unless he has to. What did the boy say? What was he teasing Cecil about?"

Mr. Burmer walked over to the window of his office. He picked up a small yellow metal canister from off of the window sill and removed the lid. He slid his thumb and forefinger into the canister and pinched into the small pile of flakes that covered the bottom of the container. He walked over to the small table near the grey file cabinet next to the door leading to his office and dropped the flakes into the clear glass basin which was filled with cloudy fluid. Their lips protruded from the water as they fed off of what they considered their daily meal. The goldfish continued to feed as Mr. Burmer rubbed his fingers together before hesitantly speaking. "You, they were teasing your son about you."

"Me?"

"Yes Mrs. Wiley. It seems that one of the young men called you a name and your son retaliated with force."

"Called me a name? What name could a young child have called me that would enrage my son to fight, knowing that I'm going to beat him for that? No, it had to be something else. Maybe the other boy tried to hit him and no one saw it."

"No, I asked Cecil if he had hit the young man first and he confirmed that he did."

"Well what in the hell did the other boy call me?"

"I uh…I…I believe it was 'whore'."

Viola's eyes lit up. She stared at Mr. Burmer as if he had called her that terrible name himself.

He could see the anger building on her face. "Now as I stated before and can assure you, the boy has been disciplined for his actions," Mr Burmer added.

"Has his ass been whipped?"

"He has been dealt with Mrs. Wiley and his mother has been contacted as well."

"Well where is she? I'd like to know what she's been teaching her son at home."

"Well Mrs. Wiley, sometimes these kids hear and get things from sources other than the home."

"Well in this case, my Cecil should have knocked the hell out of him. To say something that hateful about somebody's mother, well I know that I would have probably done the same thing or maybe even worse."

"Mrs. Wiley, I'm sure there are alternatives other than fighting. We try to teach the children how to control their tempers because at the end, fighting solves nothing."

"You don't see how Cecil's reaction was justified and why? Enough of that 'Mrs. Wiley' crap. You know me, so speak to me like you do."

"Well, no Viola I don't."

"You of all people, Wesley, should know how that feels."

"Why do you say that?"

"Now don't play stupid with me Wes. You remember how the boys used to tease you about going parkin' with your mom? How they use to say that you were born with the cooties because your mom was such a slut. You remember, sure you do. They used to say that your mom was such a whore that she used to let the dog pump her. How about when they said that the milkman always left extra milk at your house because your mom was giving him all of her cream. Oh yeah, you remember don't you?"

Mr. Burmer's face was turning beet red and steadily getting redder by the second and he too was now displaying great anger. "Vy, that was a long time ago!"

"Yeah it was, but I see you still know how that feels. So take my son off this foolish punishment. He was only defending his mother's honor, same as you did back then. You got your ass whipped but hey, you still fought. They were only just words back then, too."

"I'm sorry Vy but he was fighting and rules are rules."

"Is that you final answer?"

"I'm afraid it is. The rules apply to every student here, no exceptions."

"Fine! I'll just be taking Cecil home then. Oh and by the way, the milkman wasn't poking your mother, it was the mailman and everybody knows it! You knew it too didn't you? Is that why you go visit him every Christmas? He's your real daddy isn't he? You look just like him, you've got his eyes. You ever get the urge to just go lick some stamps? What kind of woman would lay with every man in town and when she gets pregnant, she blames it on the guy who treated her nicest. That would be her husband. I would have said your dad but we both know that your mother's husband is not REALLY your dad, right? You know, your mother really was a tramp!"

"My mother was a saint!"

"Just because you heard her yelling for God at the top of her lungs every night while you were supposed to be asleep does not make her a saint, more like a slut than a saint but I guess since they both start with the letter 'S' that's close enough."

"You evil bitch!" Mr. Burmer yelled.

"What, what did you call me?"

"Oh I'm terribly sorry Vy, I humbly apologize. You just pushed me too far."

"Now can you see how Cecil felt?"

"Yes, yes I guess I can. I'll remove his punishment immediately."

"Thank you Wes. I'll just be collecting him now. I guess you can also see how some of us just can't control our tempers when we're pushed the wrong way."

"Yes, you're right."

"That's exactly right. I guess you also know that you should be expecting a return visit from me to come and whup your ass for callin' me a bitch! You have a good day 'til then but I'll see you soon Wes. I'll be seein' ya real soon."

Viola turned around and walked out of Mr. Burmer's office. He stood there with his mouth wide open staring at the little woman as she exited. He immediately stepped outside his office and instructed the secretary to remove the recess restriction for Cecil Wiley. The young lady acknowledged then stood up from her desk. "Uh, Mr. Burmer?"

Mr. Burmer slowly turned and looked at the young lady still with a blank stare in his eyes. "Yes?"

"I couldn't help but over hear the conversation between you and Mrs. Wiley."

"It's Vy, we all just call her Vy around here."

"Well, yes sir, do you think she's really coming back here for you?"

Mr. Burmer looked at the woman and then smiled. He spoke calmly and confidently to her. "I've known Mrs. Wiley since we were kids. I know everyone in her family. When we were kids, she was meaner than a rabid dog, never backed down from anybody. I saw her once bite a dog just for licking her hand. That was a long time ago though. We're all grown up now and we've all matured. We're adults now with families and responsibilities."

"She's coming back isn't she?"

"You can practically count on it!"

With that, the young lady rushed out of the room. She ran down the hall and through the front doors of the school into the bright sunlight. In the distance she could see Viola pulling Cecil along the sidewalk.

"Mrs. Wiley!" The woman yelled. "Mrs. Wiley!" She repeated, still yelling at the top of her voice. After finally hearing her name being called, Viola stopped and turned. The woman quickly advanced toward Viola and her son. As she neared she began to slow down and approach Viola and Cecil cautiously. Viola let go of her son's hand and stepped toward the huffing woman with her purse clutched tightly under her left arm and her right fist pressed tightly into a small ball.

"Well what do you want?" Viola asked.

"I just wanted to apologize for my actions earlier. I didn't mean to be rude."

Viola looked the woman up and down from head to toe then turned and began to pull her son down the walkway.

"Mrs. Wiley," the woman said.

Viola turned in the woman's direction. With her eyebrows angled downward over her eyes, her upper teeth grinding abrasively against the lower group of teeth, and her nostrils flaring, she angrily shouted, "I heard you!"

The young lady slowly extended her arm toward Viola. Viola looked down at the woman's trembling hand. The white papers rustled as the woman's hand shook with fear while she cautiously pushed them closer to Viola's hand. "I typed it just as you instructed, '*I must be more polite to the parents.*'."

Viola snatched the papers from the woman's hand and reviewed each sheet. She returned the papers to the woman and smiled. "That's impressive, guess I won't have to come back and kick your ass after all!" She said then quickly turned, grabbed her son by the hand and hurried off.

Viola and Cecil made their way up the sidewalk and continued for the few blocks that it took to reach their home. As they approached the front of the house, Viola noticed the front door to her home was ajar. She stopped. Looking puzzled, she glanced at the entrance to the house but could not come to reason with how or what could have caused the door to be in this position. "Maybe I didn't shut it while I rushed out," she wondered. She took Cecil tightly by the hand and approached her entranceway with reservation.

As they entered the house, Viola released her son's hand and pushed the door completely open. She peered around the entire room but saw nothing. "Wait right here Cecil, don't you move from this spot, Mother will be right back." Cecil froze. Viola advanced deeper into the house checking every room. Everything seemed to be in place. "I must have not closed the door completely when I left," she mumbled.

Just as she reached for the door knob to close the front door, the massive dark silhouette appeared in the entranceway leading to the kitchen. Viola quickly pulled Cecil behind her then angrily balled up her fists. Her boney knuckles protruded like dull daggers. She lifted up her fists and took her fighting stance. Now bouncing on her toes and brushing her nose with her thumb.

"What are you going to do with those except come in here and cook me some supper?" Viola slowly lowered her hands. She knew this voice. She stretched out her arms and ran into his arms. It was Jessie. Viola held him tight while Jessie embraced her and laughed loudly. "Come on over here son and show your dad how big you've gotten," Jessie said proudly.

"I'm so glad you're home Honey!" Viola screamed out.

After finally prying Viola off him, Jessie went and sat down in his favorite chair. Cecil followed. Viola went into the kitchen and retrieved a cold glass of iced tea for her man. She started back toward the kitchen.

"Wait Honey, come sit down and talk to me. I want to hear about everything that's been going on around here. You can start by telling why little man here is not in school today," Jessie said.

Viola stopped in her tracks then looked back at Jessie. "Why, what have you heard?"

"I haven't heard anything, but I'm sure something's been going on in this God forsaken town."

With a look of relief, Viola started back for the kitchen. "I'll be there in one second Hon, I just have to make a quick telephone call."

Viola went into the kitchen and placed her call. The call ended just as quickly as it started. She returned to the living room with her family then sat beside her husband, smiling. She took him by the hand and looked deeply into his eyes. "So what are you doing home so soon anyway? You weren't due back for another couple of days."

Jessie looked down at the floor then back at his wife. "I got laid off."

Viola's smile slowly disappeared. "Laid off?"

"Yes, laid off. You know as in let go or although you worked your butt off and came to work everyday on time, we don't need you anymore. Yeah you know, like we know you have bills and a kid to take care of, but that's not our problem and oh yeah, we'll call you if we need you. That kind of laid off."

"I can't believe that after all the time you've worked there and all the sacrifices that you've made."

"I guess that wasn't enough huh? With most of the lines at the station operational now, I guess they didn't have much use for us laborers anymore. Don't worry Honey, I'll find something else."

Viola stood up and walked out onto the porch. Slamming her hands down as hard as she could against the railing of the banister she yelled out, "WHY?!"

Jessie rushed out from the house to comfort her. He embraced her as they stood on the porch for over an hour.

The kids piled out of the building to awaiting automobiles and parents; some headed in different directions in small groups. The building emptied quickly as it did at the end of each day. The loud yells and screams from the playful children slowly dissipated as they vanished over the hills and around each bend. Walking out of the now vacant school with the last remaining staff, Mr. Burmer looked in every direction for the little terror. He looked across the street, down both sides of the building and even behind the bushes that led up to the front entrance. He was unaware that her husband had arrived home unexpectedly and Viola was not about to leave his side, not even to get her revenge. Mr. Burmer had no clue that he was now the least of her worries. He was the last thing on Viola's mind. With Viola nowhere in sight, Mr. Burmer smiled while digging in his pocket to retrieve his keys.

The punch to the side of his jaw came from out of nowhere. His face whipped from left to right and froze in that position. Just as he started to turn, the thunderous slap to his face forced his head to snap down and crash onto the roof top of his 1942 Chrysler New Yorker. His head bounced off the roof and was then slammed once more against the side window. As his face slid down smearing the glass, it then returned up the path from which it came. Up and down it slid caused by the repeated constant and swift onslaught of kicks to his buttocks. Finally, after tiring from delivering the brutal beating, Mr. Burmer's attacker watched as he fell slowly to the ground. Mr. Burmer passed out cold and was left hanging halfway out of the trunk of his car with both of his eyes blacked and his necktie tied around his forehead and draped down the side of his face.

Weeks had passed. Jessie was still unsuccessful in finding employment of any kind. He tried everywhere. With Emporia being as small of a town as it was, there was just nothing available.

That evening while eating supper, Jessie sat staring down into his plate. He looked broken and defeated and Viola sensed his despair.

"What is it?" Viola asked.

Jessie continued staring at his now cold food. "Vy, I need to go back up to Richmond and look for work. That's the only place that I'll find a job. There's nothing here; not in Emporia."

"Jessie dear, I know you have your pride Honey, but Richmond is just too far for you to be away from your family. I worried so much while you were away, not just for you but all of us. Me here with Cecil alone and you so far away, it's not the way a family should be. Surely we can come up with some other way, some other alternative."

"What would you have me do Woman, watch us all starve and the bank take our home? That's not going to happen. I have to go where the work is."

"I could get a job."

"Doing what? What do you know how to do that would make enough money to pay our bills? Well I guess you could be a deputy, you're good at bustin' heads." Jessie said smiling trying to lighten the subject.

"I can wait tables or something like that and you know that the only head I like to bust around here is yours!" Viola said jokingly.

"No! No wife of mine is going to work and besides, who's going to hire a pregnant waitress anyway?"

Viola looked down at her barely noticeable bulging stomach and smiled. "Oh I can make somebody give me a job!"

"You know, my cousin has been tryin' to get me down to Carolina. He says he could get me on the job with him. Its good work and good pay, too. I could make a good living there. We could be happy."

"Now Jessie, you know I can't stand your cousin John. The last time he came up here I had to punch him in the throat for brushin' up against me."

"Ah honey it was just an accident."

"An accident my ass. How many times have you accidentally brushed up against somebody with an erection?"

"He said it was his smokin' pipe. He said that he had just started carrying it in his front pocket, up high and just a little to the left."

"Yeah, well he sure had a hard time apologizing with his Adam's apple smashed, didn't he? He is just a nasty bastard and I don't want to go."

"Well Vy if I don't find something soon we'll have to."

Jessie continued to look for work in the weeks that followed but still had no luck. Some letters from the bank started arriving and were soon followed by letters from other debtors. Seeing no end in sight, against Viola's wishes, Jessie decided to pack up his family and move to North Carolina where his cousin was holding a job for him.

They arrived in Fayetteville on a Sunday. Jessie's cousin John and his family were still in church when the bus arrived. Jessie, Viola, and Cecil waited for over an hour for John to pick them up. Through the dust cloud, the black 1940 Ford pickup rattled up the road leading to the bus depot. It was covered with mud and dirt. The high pitched whining noise grew louder as it neared the terminal. After the loud contraption coasted to a slow halt, the short round figure of a man climbed out. Jessie walked out and embraced his cousin. Viola and Cecil soon followed Jessie. As they neared the two, Jessie turned and placed his arm around Viola's neck. "John, you remember Vy?"

John placed his hand on the front of his throat and smiled, "Yes how could I forget cousin Vy? Woman, you're still prettier than ever."

Vy didn't speak, instead she quickly turned her head in the other direction and just grunted.

"And this here is Cecil, my big man," Jessie continued.

"Hello Cecil, I'm your cousin John. I've got a boy bout your age, too. I think you'll have plenty of fun with him. Mary's at home cookin' supper, hope y'all hungry."

Jessie and John loaded the back of the truck while Viola and Cecil piled in the front seat. Once the men were done with the loading, Jessie hopped into the back of the truck bed. John climbed into the truck, looked over at Viola and smiled. He started the engine and the loud whining noise returned. "Hold on back there Cousin!" He yelled and sped off heading for home.

Jessie started work the very next day. He was a laborer for a construction company. He kept that job for three months before obtaining another job with the railroad as a porter. Viola and Cecil continued to stay with John and his family until Jessie returned home from a six day train run only to find John with a taped up nose, two blackened eyes and a cold ice pack resting in his lap. Viola had stomped him in the face after knocking him off from on top of her. He had been drinking and snuck into her room after his wife had fallen asleep. Viola was nine months pregnant. His nose was broken and his pelvis was badly bruised from the constant stomping that Viola had delivered to his crotch.

"What in the hell happened to you?" Jessie asked.

"Ah weren't nothin'. You know how I get when I've had a little too much to drink. I musta been kinda sleep walkin' I guess and walked into the wrong room by mistake. I guess 'ole Vy musta thought I was a burglar or somethin' and boy, she let me have it! It was cold and I was only tryin' to pull the cover up over her."

"Burglar my ass!" Viola interrupted. "Yeah he was a burglar, he was tryin' to steal some of my stuff! Sleep walkin'? This snake came slitherin' into the room with his pipe in his front pocket again. He got on top of me smellin' like swamp dust and cheap liquor talkin' about let him just put the tip in. So I tell him no, let me put the tip in but instead I tried to ram not just the tip but my whole foot through his ass! Sleep walkin' my ass! You ought to be ashamed of yourself you bastard, I'm nine months pregnant! When this baby is born, I'm gonna have him whip your ass for tryin' to put a dent in his head!"

After that night, Jessie was asked to leave which he did. He moved his family to a small house in Hopewell just outside of Fayetteville. That's where Carrie, Viola's daughter, was born. They remained there until the early 1960's. After receiving numerous promotions, Jessie and Viola purchased a new home in Fayetteville. Jessie retired from the railroad in 1984 at the age of 63. Viola and her husband continued to love and enjoy one another until the day he died.

Some say that she was so angry at him for leaving her alone that she slapped him while he lay peacefully in his casket. No one ever saw her cry at Jessie's viewing or funeral. Every time someone would ask her "how do you feel?" the sound immediately following would echo throughout the church. "POW!" She would slap that person hard across the side of their face with the back of her hand and yell, "With my hands!" and then break out into a loud, high pitched laugh. She did this throughout the viewing to all who asked without exception. She smacked women and children of all ages. She slapped friends and family. She popped everyone who asked, everyone except cousin John. John, who was now just as old as Viola, walked up to her using a cane to assist him. He leaned over and offered his condolences then asked the million dollar question.

"How are you feeling Vy?" He asked with a weak and trembling voice.

The entire row sitting behind Viola braced themselves in preparation for the electrifying wallop that they knew John was about to receive. Viola didn't strike him. Remembering the bad terms in which they had departe, Viola couldn't bring herself to slap her husband's cousin who probably was in just as much pain and grief as she. Instead, she affectionately placed her left hand on the side of his face and gently caressed it. John moved in closer to give Viola a kiss on her cheek.

"Oh hell no," she grunted and with one quick jolt, she shoved the handle of his cane upward into old cousin John's crotch. "I think I've got a handle on it!" She whispered and once again broke out into laughter. With a shocked look on his face and teary eyes, John fell to his knees and fainted. Viola continued to laugh and yell. "I was only trying to pull the covers up on him. Hey, does he look cold to anybody?" She continued grunting.

This was when Cecil first realized that his mom was losing it. Losing her husband had affected her mental state.

After the funeral, Cercil discussed their mother's situation with his sister Carrie. Carrie, married herself and now residing in Palo Alto, California with her husband and three children was not in a position where she could let Viola move in with her. Besides, she knew that Viola would never leave the east coast and be too far away from Jessie's grave.

So three months after the funeral, Cecil moved Viola in with him. She now resided in a place that somehow would always remind her of struggle, Richmond, Virginia. She lived with Cecil and his family. She originally thought that it would be nice to be around her son and her grandkids but she felt like a burden to them; she felt out of place and homesick. Returning home from work one day, Cecil was met by his mother on the front porch.

She sat him down and spoke the words that he knew she would soon say, "I want to go home, Son."

"Mom, your home is gone. We sold it, remember? This is your home now."

"Yes, I remember, but that's not what I mean. I want to go back to Fayetteville."

"Momo, what about California? What if you went on an extended visit with Carrie and your other grandchildren?"

"Cecil, that would be nice, but I'm homesick. I want to go home to Fayetteville."

After several repeated requests from his mother, Cecil took Viola back to Fayetteville and visited several retirement homes there. She fell in love with Hayfield Streams Retirement Facility and moved in two weeks later.

"Now that you've finished telling my life story, you can take your ass on up the road!" Viola said.

"Wait, don't go, I'm enjoying this!" Lizzy yelled.

"Hell Lizzy, you can take your ass with him!" said the grouchy Viola.

"Vy, let me get this right, you actually slept with the pastor of your church?"

"Hell no! That old, fat, ugly, toothless bastard, no way in hell would I have done that! I just told folks 'round town that."

"Why in the world would you do that? Stepping on ducks can lead to happiness, though," stated Lizzy.

"It was my way of getting back at him. Well you see, when my daddy died, well he actually committed suicide. Well anyway, that old bastard reverend wouldn't preach at his funeral because he said that my daddy had committed the deadliest sin or somethin' like that so I told him that I'd fix him, and I did. By the time I was through with him, he couldn't collect two cents on Sundays. He finally came to my house beggin' for my forgiveness. I never told anybody the truth until I was about to move down here. I figured the damage had been done by then so I let him off the hook. I told that nosey ass Thelma and I'm sure she passed it along to the entire county. Don't know what happened after that. Son go home, I'm tired now."

"Ok ladies, I was just instructed that I have to leave. I'll see you all in a couple of days. Keep an eye on her for me..."

"Ah leave already will you?!" Viola grunted.

"You see what I mean? Ok Mom I'll leave now but I'll see you soon. Call me if you need anything. I love you."

"Yeah, yeah, I love you too, now git!"

Cecil stood up and as always gave his mother a kiss and embraced each of her friends before leaving. Although Viola would always send him home before he was ready, she still always hated to see him go. She would always seem to act a bit solemn and even a little depressed after his departure but would soon snap out of it and return to her aggressive and quick tempered self.

Chapter 2 - Rose

"Yum…everything smells soooo good." Wheezing slightly and holding on tightly to her father's hand, she took a few steps forward and stopped. She gazed into the thick, warm glass which held a view of promised sweet, baked goods and treats. Tugging gently on her father's arm and looking deeply into his eyes, as innocently as she possibly could, she pressed her short, chubby, index finger firmly against the almost transparent shield. "Can we get that one, Daddy? Can we?"

Her father looked down at her and smiled at his precious sweetheart of a little girl who was now pointing to a large, pink iced, chocolate cake and replied as sternly as he could, "No Baby, we can't get one today." Her head lowered slowly. She looked as if she had just lost her dearest friend. He hated seeing her so disappointed. He knelt down on one knee and placed her small thick hands inside his. "Ok, how about just a slice today?" he whispered softly in her ear. Her sadness and disappointment vanished as quickly as that slice of cake would as soon as she got it home. Her smile reappeared and she began licking her lips and rubbing her hands together in anticipation of the sweet, delicious treat. They only rode into town once every two weeks, and the highlight of the trip for her was always the bakery.

Rosetta was only seven but had the appearance of a ten year old. Her squat, thick, tubular shaped legs and round torso gave her the facade of a short, water barrel filled to capacity. Her neck and arms weren't much different either. They were chunky.

To say the very least, she was an overweight child. Rose as everyone fondly referred to her, since birth had been fighting unpleasantly with asthma. Her dad kept her inhaler close by at all times. Over her young life she had battled with many asthma attacks which were all very scary to the girl. To her father, Rose was the short, chubby apple of his eye and he spoiled her rotten.

Rose loved her father just as much. She had never known her mother as she had passed away when Rose was only seven months old. Some suspected Rose's father of killing her mother. They say that her father had come back early from town one afternoon and caught Rose's mother fooling around with one of the hired hands. The hired hand ran off and never returned. Just three days later, Rose's mother was accidentally run over by a tractor with the driver being, you guessed it, her father. Well, I guess I can see how that could happen, can't you? It was probably the first case of a "drive by killing" in the county. They say that she had a "closed casket" funeral due to the tire tread marks that were embedded deep into her face.

Anyway, Rose's father raised her up to be a fine little girl. She was polite, hard working, and respectful. Everyday after school she'd rush home to do her homework and daily chores. She would feed the chickens and pigs and sweep the porch before assisting her father in the kitchen. She loved her father's cooking and since they raised livestock, there was always an abundance of meat and Rose loved meat! They had a good life together and a wonderful farm. The farm was located in Calhoun County just outside the city of Camerona, a small town in South Carolina. The small two story farm house was surrounded by acres of land and livestock.

Everything had been going well for Rose and her father. That is, until just weeks after her sixth birthday when Rose cried more then than she'd ever cried before. That day was one of the saddest days of her young life. It was the day her father married her new step-mother Sarah-Ann. Rose hated her and was extremely angry with her father for bringing Sarah-Ann into their home. Sarah-Ann and Rose were no strangers to one another. She taught at the school Rose attended and was known as a witch by all the school children. You can imagine just how frustrated and embarrassed Rose must have felt. Her father Sam had only met Sarah-Ann five months prior. She quickly charmed Sam into matrimony. No mention of the wedding had been revealed to Rose until her birthday. That was an historical event in Rose's short little life; it lay claim to Rose's sixth birthday as the worse birthday ever.

After the wedding, Sarah-Ann immediately moved into the house and began making changes. The change in her personality seemed to transform overnight as she became very demanding. There was now a new woman receiving much of Rose's father's attention and affection that Rose had not had to share since her mother's passing.

Years passed and Rose blossomed into a beautiful, young butterfly; a butterfly too heavy to fly. Not only had she gotten taller over the years, she was now wider as well. I guess you could say that there was more of her to love, a lot more. Unfortunately, Sarah-Ann didn't feel that way. Throughout the passing years, Rose and Sarah-Ann had developed an even more hate filled relationship. They could not seem to resolve their differences which kept her father stuck right in the middle of every disagreement. Rose resulted to not doing much around the house, nothing except eat.

If it didn't move or wasn't nailed down, Rose ate it. Her father had once put her on an eating restriction courtesy of Sarah-Ann's recommendation. This only forced Rose into a deeper rebellion and resulted in her sneaking food and putting on even more weight. She would wait until her father and Sarah-Ann were fast asleep before going on her food finding missions. She would pull out all the leftovers from dinner and whatever else caught her eye and gorge until she was stuffed. If she heard somebody coming, she would waddle as quickly as she could back upstairs to her room and climb into her bed. Sam and Sarah-Ann would walk into the kitchen only to find a half empty refrigerator and a table full of dishes. Sarah-Ann would stand at the bottom of the steps calling out to her. "Rose! Rose! You get down here right now and clean up this mess!"

The only response that she would receive was a few muffled burps and the sounds of Rose's uncontrollably loud gas.

"Sam, I don't know what you're going to do with that girl but you'd better do something quick!" Sarah-Ann would grunt then return to the bedroom. Sam as always, stayed behind and cleaned up Rose's mess.

Of course, instead of Rose losing weight, she gained. She was now at her heaviest weight. Her head was huge and her eyes bulged from their sockets with each breath. After only walking up a few steps, she'd wheeze and gasp for air. She now looked like the love child of Porky Pig and Mrs. Potato Head and she didn't care. All she knew was that it was a way to make Sarah-

Ann angry and to get attention from her father. He had become extremely worried about her health but said nothing to Rose about it. Still, Rose could see the concern in her father's eyes.

Rose had also become quiet and cold toward both Sarah-Ann and her father. She no longer received the attention or the affection that she had once felt from her father. Sarah-Ann had stepped in and changed everything, including Rose and her father's close relationship.

The most memorable change and damaging day occurred when her father spanked her. Before that day, he had never even raised his voice to Rose. It was another day that she would never forget. Rose, still only wanting to win the attention of her father, had decided to prepare his favorite meal before he returned home. Her father and Sarah-Ann had gone into town earlier that afternoon. Rose worked in the kitchen the entire time that they were gone. She cooked for hours. She made pork chops, green beans and mashed potatoes. She had even made her special cornbread for him. It was special to both Rose and her father because it was her mother's special recipe that had been passed down by her grandmother and her father loved it.

Ever since Rose was old enough to cook, she would use recipes from her mother's cookbook. Rose's mother had started putting the cookbook together from the beginning of her cooking years. She continued to compile and add other recipes she obtained from close friends and relatives of dishes that she or Sam enjoyed. Although she never knew her mother, this was always something that made Rose feel close to her. She later made changes to most of her mother's recipes by adding other ingredients to either spice up a dish or just to make the dish taste more to her liking. Rose experimented with cooking quite a bit. There were pencil markings throughout the old folded and worn pages of the cookbook from both Rose and her mother, through almost every recipe, every recipe except the cornbread. Rose would prepare the sweet cakes just as her mother did. She would use all the ingredients prescribed by the recipe and her father loved it.

After Rose had completed the dinner preparation, she rested the warm cherry pie she had so lovingly baked out on the window ledge to cool. As she put the hot tin pan down she could see her father's dusty black Ford pickup truck moving up the dirt road that led to the house. She quickly set the table, placing each piece of her mother's good china cautiously and tenderly upon the table. She meticulously arranged the silverware and napkins perfectly in their proper places then positioned a shiny glass next to each setting. Rose then stepped onto the porch as her father and Sarah-Ann were stepping out of the truck.

"Well don't just stand there girl, come on over here and give us a hand," her father yelled.

Rose waddled out to the truck, stepping proudly like a young mother duck. As she approached, Sarah-Ann and her father began to hear the muffled crackling. The rumblings were that of mashed thunder trapped beneath a seat cushion. With every step, Rose's uncontrollable flatulence would be released. Their frowns slowly appeared on their faces before they rushed by her. They wanted no parts of that. The two stood at the top of the steps and watched as the heavy young girl dragged each huge thigh closer to the truck. Her buttocks rolled like a puppy ensnared in a sleeping bag.

"Just grab those last two bags honey," her father yelled.

Rose snatched up the bags of groceries then leaned against the truck for a quick breath of air. After collecting herself, she pushed off the bed of the truck and used the momentum to gain two quick steps. She soon slowed to her dawdling waddle.

"Come on Rose, we only have four hours of sunlight left. If you keep that slow pace up, it'll be dark outside by the time you get in here."

The mouth-watering aroma filled the air and her father was smiling brightly when Rose finally made her way inside.

"What's all this, Baby Girl?" he asked.

"I just felt like cooking, that's all. It's all your favorites, too. We've got pork chops, mashed potatoes, green beans and I even made cornbread! I made it from Mama's old recipe just like I used to," Rose said smiling as she looked over at Sarah-Ann. She knew that this would anger Sarah-Ann.

Sarah-Ann didn't disappoint Rose by no means either, her eyes became like piercing daggers through Rose's heart and her jaw bone bulged from the sides of her face as she pressed her teeth tightly together. No one was entitled to any of her husband's attention, no one except her; not his mother, his friends, his daughter and especially not the memory of his dead wife. Sarah-Ann dropped her package onto the floor, turned and rushed out of the house.

"Here comes the drama," Rose mumbled just loud enough for her father to hear.

Sam's eyes widened and he tilted his head while extending his hands out to his daughter, "Rose, show some compassion, ok?"

Rose knew what her father didn't. She knew that it was only Sarah-Ann's juvenile acting in an attempt to pull her father away from her good doing. And he did just that. Rose looked her father in the eyes then over to the table that she had lovingly prepared. She looked back over at him. Sam lowered his eyes and rushed out the door to Sarah-Ann's side. He spoke quietly with her, trying to calm her down.

"She didn't mean anything by it honey, she was just trying to do something nice that's all."

"She hates me Sam and you know it. She did this just to throw her mother in my face as being something that I could never be to her. 'I made Mother's cornbread just the way you like it."

"No, no, that's not what she meant, Dear. Come on, let's go inside and enjoy the meal that she prepared."

Sarah-Ann looked at her husband and smiled. She knew she had won him over and that the meal had now become secondary to her pretentious hurt feelings. "Ok, I guess you're right but… I'm switching plates with you and I'm not drinking anything unless you drink it first. I don't trust that girl, Honey. She might try to poison me. It's bad enough that I think she's going to try to kill me in my sleep. My only saving grace is that she's so big, I'll hear her coming before she gets out of her bedroom."

"Honey, you've got Rose all wrong, she loves you."

"Uh, excuse me but in what house have you been living since I've been here?"

The couple chuckled and walked into the house arm in arm. Sarah-Ann's smile vanished as soon as she looked into Rose's eyes. Rose found it amusing that Sarah-Ann was angry with her. She had finally gotten to her. Rose walked back into the kitchen and grabbed the pot from the stove. She emptied its contents into a large glass bowl and placed the pot back on the stove. She then put the bowl on the table. Rose watched as her father continued to console Sarah-Ann even more as they stood in the hallway. She watched as they embraced before entering the kitchen where she continued to work diligently.

"Ok, let's enjoy this good meal," Sam said cheerfully.

"Everything looks so good Rose," Sarah-Ann added.

"Yes, everything is good," Rose replied snobbishly.

The family sat down and started in on the feast. "These pork chops taste great, Hun," Sam said.

"Thanks Daddy, they are pretty good if I may say so myself. I can't remember the last time I had a really good meal like this." Rose said as she looked directly in Sarah-Ann's eyes.

Sarah-Ann cut into the pork chop on her plate and put the small piece of meat from her fork inside her mouth. After chewing purposely for a while Sarah-Ann looked back at Rose.

"Um Rose, this IS tasty. It's kind of tough though but nice and tasty. Maybe I'll just cut a few small pieces and suck the flavor out of them because I'm getting a headache trying to chew it."

"Aw come on Dear, it's not that tough," Sam interrupted.

"Oh, so you do admit that it's tough, huh?" Sarah-Ann replied.

Once again Rose knew what Sarah-Ann was up to but today she was ready for battle. She was not going to tolerate her conniving, wicked step-mother today. She was not going to just sit and watch her manipulate her father into saying or doing something that he didn't want to or at least so she thought.

Rose looked at Sarah-Ann with such disgust then turned her attention to her father who was still stammering, trying to spit out his answer to his still jealous wife's truculent question. Sarah-Ann was beginning to become frustrated with her husband. She needed his answer to further prove to Rose who was truly in control of the household.

"Well Dear is it tough or not?" Sarah-Ann asked forcefully.

Sam stared down into his plate then slowly looked at Rose and smiled, "No, no Baby it's not tough. The chops are fine and they taste great!"

Rose quickly pushed her chair back away from the table and lowered her head to look underneath. Sam and Sarah-Ann both looked on strangely as they awaited the reappearance of her head. "What are you looking for down there Baby?" Sam asked.

"Nothing Daddy, I was just checking for something. It's nothing."

Rose sat back upright in her chair then pulled herself back up to the table and began eating. Sarah-Ann began tapping her fork against her plate as she regrouped from the unexpected answer from her spouse. She picked at the food on her plate before continuing her attempt to devour Rose's moment. "You don't think the meat is tough, huh?"

Sam shook his head, smiled at Rose once again and continued with his meal.

"Aw, isn't that sweet. Daddy thinks that he's going to hurt his little girl's feelings if he says that his meat is tough."

Sam swallowed his mashed potatoes then mumbled, "No, I mean it, it's not tough at all. It's the best, Sweetheart."

Rose smiled and continued eating. She looked over at Sarah-Ann who seemed satisfied with her husband's answer and nodded her head at her. Rose soon found out why Sarah-Ann was satisfied with Sam's answer. It was her opening.

"The best?" Sarah-Ann interrupted. "I've made you pork chops plenty of times, so you're saying that you like these better?"

"No, I'm only saying that these are the best Rose has made, Dear."

"So who's do you like the best?"

"I like them both; Rose's and yours taste great!"

"Surely one tastes better than the other."

Rose sat quietly. She continued eating her meal. Watching as Sarah-Ann attempted to trap her father into saying that her chops could not compare to her own. "How silly," she thought.

Sarah-Ann wasn't about to give up. She leaned closer to Sam and glared into his eyes, "Well?"

"Well what?" Sam replied.

"Well whose chops are better?"

"I said I like them both now let it go Sarah-Ann. Come on, we're having a good meal here that Rose spent a lot of time preparing, let's not mess it up." Sam's smile had dissolved. He spoke calmly but somewhat sternly to Sarah-Ann and this surprised Rose. Once again Rose slid her chair away from the table and peeked under and once again the couple looked at each other strangely. A few moments later she returned to the table.

"What are you looking for Rose?" her father again asked.

"Nothing Daddy, its nothing," she replied and started back in on her food.

The room became quiet for only a few minutes while they all ate before Sarah-Ann's final vulgar attempt for attention was performed. Just when things seemed to have calmed down, "Plop!" Sarah-Ann leaned over her plate and spit out a mouth full of already chewed green beans back onto her plate. She grabbed her napkin and began wiping her tongue with it. Still spitting and frowning, she looked over at Rose. "Why Rose darling, why I believe you put a little too much salt into these green beans. They taste…well for lack of a better word, they're disgustin'."

Sam looked over at Rose apologetically. He scooped a mouthful into his mouth. "They taste just fine to me."

"And these mashed potatoes, I declare, tastes like you dug them right out of the ground. Did you clean the potatoes, Dear? They're a bit soggy, too."

Rose continued with her meal. She looked at her father occasionally and smiled. Rose knew that her father was not buying into Sarah-Ann's attempted ambush of her meal. He was for once, actually sticking up for her. Sarah-Ann on the other hand was becoming even more frustrated with her husband. Her plan was backfiring until…

"This is the worst cornbread I have ever tasted. Where did you say you got the recipe? Whoever gave you this recipe must have been a dreadful cook."

That was all Rose could stand. She looked over at her father. He lowered his head and said nothing to his wife. He knew those words spoken by her had really upset his little girl and yet he said nothing to stop her. Sarah-Ann continued with her attack on Rose's cornbread. "It's too thick and gummy. I'm sorry I just can't eat this, any of it. Would it upset you if I gave my plate to the dog?"

Rose somehow managed to keep her composure. She slowly lifted herself from the table and walked toward Sarah-Ann. Sarah-Ann placed her hand around her throat and swallowed deeply. Rose walked right by her. She was still determined not to fall into Sarah-Ann's trap. She was not going to yell and have a fit and get punished by her father for speaking to her disrespectfully. She had decided to kill her with kindness.

Rose retrieved the cherry pie from the window sill. "My cherry pie will shut her up, Daddy loves my pie," she thought. Rose then took the pie over to where Sarah-Ann sat, walked over to the cabinet and pulled out three small plates. She lifted the sharp knife from the drawer and returned to the pie. Just as she began to cut a portion of the pie for Sarah-Ann she heard the only words that could push her over the edge.

"Girl, you need to burn that recipe book. Whoever wrote those disgustin' recipes ought to be run over!"

Rose looked over at her father and once again he lowered his head. Rose couldn't believe that he was going to let that wicked woman get away with talking about her mother like that. Rose's jaws tightened. She began to shake and her father knew that she was about to explode. Sam jumped up from his seat but before he could rush over to Rose, the pie was on its way. "Oh hell no!" Rose screamed as she jammed the pie hard against Sarah-Ann's face. "Nobody talks about my mother that way, nobody!"

Sarah-Ann's head whipped back causing the two front legs of her chair to rise. Rose kept jamming and twisting the pie deeper in Sarah-Ann's face. Suddenly, Sarah-Ann went flying, slamming brutally onto the hard wood floor. With her face full of cherries, Sarah-Ann screamed out for her husband. Rose kneeled down beside Sarah-Ann and whispered angrily in her ear. "How's the pie now? You like it? That recipe's in the book, too. It's called 'slap-a-bitch pie'. It's an old Indian recipe that I thought you might like. It's quite easy to make. First you need a bitch, then you add some… oh never mind, I'll show you how to make it when you're feeling better," then she took a puff from her inhaler.

Sam kneeled over his wife and began to help her up off the floor. "Rose didn't mean it Dear she really didn't, did you Rose?"

Rose leaned over and took Sarah-Ann by the hand. She peeled her balled fingers opened then nodded. "That's where they are! I kept checking under the table because I thought you had found them but I see Sarah-Ann still has them."

"What? What were you looking for under the table? What does Sarah-Ann have?" Sam asked puzzled.

Rose turned and slowly headed for the steps leading to her room. Once she reached the bottom step, Rose turned and sadly peered into the eyes of her father and whispered just low enough for them not to hear, "Your balls." She then turned and leisurely climbed the stairs.

Up in her room, Rose was basking in the thought that she had won the battle. All was quiet until Rose overheard Sarah-Ann yelling at her father, telling him that if he didn't whip her that she was leaving him because she was not going to live in a house with an undisciplined child. Rose's thought of winning the battle had quickly caught the 8:15 bus from her mind when she saw her father enter her room with his belt in hand. Her father gave her the first whipping that he had ever given her, courtesy of Sarah-Ann of course. He whipped her and told her that she was never to speak to Sarah-Ann in that fashion again and if she ever struck Sarah-Ann again she would receive an even more severe whipping.

From that day forward, Rose's relationship with her father was nonexistent. It was never the same again. She barely spoke a word at home after that day. Sarah-Ann still continued strolling around the house, always with a smug attitude toward Rose. Rose didn't mind, she accepted her defeat. She often thought of ways to kill Sarah-Ann, but instead she just sat in her room counting the days until she would no longer have to stay in a house with the woman she hated. Her father tried to make things right between them but she knew that as long as Sarah-Ann was in the house, he could never commit to their relationship. Rose continued trying to eat her pain away but was unsuccessful.

Two years had passed and Rose was now a senior in high school. She had now taken up a new hobby, drinking. She would often come home from school reeking of alcohol and would stumble up to her room and pass out. Sarah-Ann spoke to Sam about Rose's drinking on several occasions but knowing how much damage he had caused in his relationship with his daughter, he left her alone. He knew how he had contributed to her loneliness and misery.

Rose was now riding the border of obesity and drinking wasn't helping matters. The rolls of fat around her midsection and the knotted bunches of flesh which gathered around her buttocks was a true indication that she was just one thin mint cookie away from exploding. She could no longer wear socks because the elastic gathering would cut off the blood flow to her feet. The fabric would press so tightly around her ankles they would create dark indentations in her flesh, which also caused her feet to swell up like balloons. The huge bunions and nail fungus didn't help either. Her feet looked more like three day old road kill than a precious part of the human anatomy.

With her weight increase, Rose began to run into more and more problems. She couldn't walk up a short flight of stairs without perspiring. Actually, she would begin to perspire just from the thought of walking up a short flight of stairs. She needed some type of daily motivation just to walk up the stairs to her room. Everyday Rose would stop by the kitchen on her way to her room and grab a moon pie or a hand full of cookies from the large glass jar, wrap them up in paper then toss them up the stairs. Her greed would force her up the stairs after them. After reaching the treats she would go into her room, sit quietly and devour the sugary snacks. She repeated this process every time she needed to climb the stairs, sometimes up to five times a day. If there were no snacks readily available, Rose would use whatever was in the refrigerator. Once she threw a whole barbecue chicken up the stairs. This was the only time she ever ran up the stairs.

Rose continued to eat and drink herself deeper into depression. Her hygiene regimen consisted of waking up and rolling out of bed. She stopped bathing and usually wore the same clothes daily. Her hair was never brushed and lay matted to her scalp and always smelled like old liccorice. Her teeth were developing a greenish pasty residue on them. Of course, the stench emitted from her body didn't smell like her name either. Her soul was now a deep, dark, empty hole and she cared about nothing, not her appearance, not her father and definitely not Sarah-Ann.

One day, Rose arrived home from school drunker than a retired hooker. She waddled up the front steps and fell into the front door only to be met by Sarah-Ann and her father.

"My God Rose, you're drunk!" Sam yelled.

"That would be a yes my dear testicle-less father or as the Indians would call you 'Man With No Balls'," she slurred.

"How dare you speak to your father that way, Young Lady!" Sarah-Ann grunted.

"Oh I'm sorry Daddy, I forgot, you do have a pair. You hide them in the coffee can in the pantry, right?"

Rose picked herself up off the floor and swayed in multiple directions trying to reach the sink. Sam took her by the arm and helped her to the kitchen table where he lowered her into one of the chairs. Sarah-Ann walked over to Rose and knelt down beside her and started in on her.

"It's bad enough that you have to disgrace yourself but do you have to disgrace your father and me, too? Look at you, drunk, filthy, and smelling like an outhouse. You're so fat that you can barely make it up the steps! You're disgusting, that's what you are, just disgusting. How long are you going to keep hurting your father like this, how long?"

Rose sat there wobbly and quiet. She realized that as much as she hated Sarah-Ann, she was actually making a valid point for once. Rose realized at that moment that maybe it was time to finally end this silly war with Sarah-Ann. She looked into Sarah-Ann's small squinted eyes and realized that it was time to let everything out. She was tired of feeling this way. Rose leaned forward and placed her arms around Sarah-Ann's petite shoulders. She held her tightly and softly. After only a brief moment of this sweet caress, Rose then pressed her fingers tightly into Sarah-Ann's flesh and with one swift jolt, Rose unleashed everything that had gathered in the pit of her stomach that was ready for departure.

Sarah-Ann screamed out for Sam once again. Rose laughed uncontrollably as she pointed at Sarah-Ann and wiped the remaining warm chunks from her mouth. She had successfully covered them both with vomit.

"She did this intentionally honey, I know it. It was no accident!" Sarah-Ann yelled angrily. Rose continued to laugh. Sarah-Ann stood up and shook the thick mushy liquid from her hands. She was so angry you could begin to smell the stench steam from the top of her head which caused her to heave chunks, too. She covered her mouth and rushed into the bathroom and Sam followed.

Rose wiped her mouth then stood up, "Whew, I feel much better now." She broke out into laughter again as she listened to

Sarah-Ann in the bathroom still heaving. After climbing the stairs, Rose yanked off each piece of the stained garments from her body. Her dress reeked of regurgitated hamburger, alcohol and other unidentifiable stink resulting from the residue that had been ejected from her insides. She carried her clothing into the bathroom and dropped them into a neat but malodorous pile in the bathtub. She washed her face and hands then scooped a handful of water from the running faucet and washed out her mouth. Her breath still smelled like a freshly stepped-in pile of dog shit and was beginning to make her feel nauseous once again. Rose quickly rinsed out her mouth again then brushed her teeth.

Now feeling much better, Rose sat on the side of the bath-tub and turned on the hot water. She lifted the dress from its resting place and began running the hot water over the garment forcing the small chunks of food and thick liquid to drop into the small drain opening of the bathtub. She reached and grabbed the pure white bar of soap from the dish resting on the side of the tub and began scrubbing away the stains that she felt were sure to ruin the garment.

"Rose, you'd better wash that dress out and hang it up outside. I don't want that smell in my house!" Sarah-Ann yelled from thc bottom of the steps.

"Her house, what makes her think that this is just her house?" Rose, wearing only her birthday suit was beginning to become agitated all over again with Sarah-Ann. Two hundred and sixty three pounds of angry pure flab was staring at itself in the mirror. She couldn't believe the gall that Sarah-Ann had. She gathered all of her clothing, some that she had been wearing for weeks. One of her gray braziers that was white when purchased, was sitting at the top of the pile, it too stank of back fat and armpits. She carried the items over to the bathtub, dropped them into the hot soapy water and began washing them.

"Did you hear me Rose? Wash that stench out of that dress. I don't want that nasty thing smellin' up this house!" This infuriated Rose. With her jaws clenched tightly together, Rose gathered up each piece of the wet clothing and stormed down the stairs. Sarah-Ann was sitting in the kitchen as the table in her robe sipping a hot cup of tea and ginger trying to sooth her stomach while yelling at her husband Sam who had retreated to the bedroom. Sarah-Ann continued on about how uncontrollable Rose was and how she was in need of more discipline.

The sight was unbearable. Rose stood in the entranceway of the kitchen stark naked and holding a pile of dripping wet clothes. Sarah-Ann placed both hands on the table. With her mouth flung open and her eyes opened wide, she gazed at what appeared to her as the most ungodly sight she had ever seen. She stuttered as she tried to get her words through her widely opened mouth. "Wha, wha, what are you you you you uh uh doing Rose? You you you'd better get back up those stairs and put on some clothes before your father sees you like that."

Rose said nothing. She stood there in the doorway just staring at Sarah-Ann then without warning, Rose charged over to Sarah-Ann. She was like a raging bull, well more like a raging bull with a pile of wet clothes between its hooves. "Ooooooooooh Saaaaaaaa," was all that Sarah-Ann had enough time to scream out.

"SLAAAAAAP!" was all that was heard afterwards. Rose had rushed over to Sarah-Ann and with both hands slung the soaking wet clothing and half cleaned under garments across Sarah-Ann's face. It made a loud slapping sound as Sarah-Ann's head once again was snapped back. Her chair rose up and over and the back of Sarah-Ann's head was kissed in the most unaffectionate manner by the hard wood floor. "How's that, are they clean enough?" Rose shouted then turned and giggled back up the stairs to her room. Rose got dressed and sat waiting for her father to come upstairs to give her a scolding. She sat nervously thinking about life after death because she knew that her father was going to kill her for certain this time. She took a puff from her inhaler and began to breathe deeply. Shockingly, her dad said nothing. In fact, he never came up the stairs.

Rose lay across her bed in the dim light, thinking about life after school since it appeared that she wasn't going to die that day. She daydreamed about having a family of her own and how she was going to be the best wife and mother ever. She wanted twins, a boy and a girl. She wished for a husband with a nice job who would love her and care for her and who liked food just as much as she did. As she began to drift off into her slumber, her thoughts of family crossed over into her dreams.

Rose's dream continued with her living in a nice house with very well mannered kids. They were clean and intelligent. Her husband was a very prestigious lawyer and he always took her to the finest restaurants to eat. As she sat looking through the menu, her husband blew her a kiss before excusing himself. As he exited, the waitress walked over to the table. "What will you be having today ma'am? The steak is very tender and seasoned to perfection and the trout is magnificent!"

"Oh my word, they both sound so good. Let's see, steak or trout. They both sound too good. What side dishes do you have?"

"We have fresh steamed green beans. We also have…"

The waitress was suddenly interrupted by Rose's husband. "So how we doing?" he asked Rose.

The waitress placed her hand on his shoulder and looked at Rose. "She is out of control and I want her out of here!"

Rose looked up at the waitress oddly wondering why she would say something like that to him. The waitress continued, "All she does is eat and shit and EAT AND SHIT!"

Rose's husband walked over and placed his hands on his wife's shoulders. "She's still young, that's all."

The waitress tossed her pen and pad on the couple's table then placed her hands on her hips. "Either she gets out of here or I do!"

"She'll be leaving soon anyway."

"I'm not sure I can wait that long."

"Calm down honey. It won't be long."

"Damn her, and look at her dress, it looks like a pair of drapes! How big is she going to get anyway?"

Rose sat there quietly until her husband and the waitress completed their conversation. They both looked over at Rose as she sat still in her seat. With her hands clasped tightly together and placed neatly on top of the table, she spoke calmly to the irritated waitress.

"I'll have them both, the steak and the fish, thanks."

The young woman stormed through the dining room followed by Rose's husband. Rose could now hear them talking in the distance. Their voices grew louder and clearer with each word spoken. It seemed the farther they traveled in distance, the louder they spoke. Soon the volume of the voices pulled Rose from her fantasy back into her dreadful reality. She rose from her bed and walked over to her window where she could see Sarah-Ann and her father standing. Sarah-Ann was standing in front of the clothesline folding the dried bed linen while yelling at Sam. "I don't care Sam I want her out of here!

"Ok, ok, you know she's heading off to college right after she graduates, can't you hold on 'til then?"

"After she graduates? That means I'll have to deal with that girl and her attitude for the whole summer! NO WAY!"

"It's only a few months, Honey."

"Well, in those months maybe I can find me another place to live, FOREVER!"

"Now hold on Sarah-Ann, maybe Becky could look after her during the summer. Rose always liked her Aunt Becky. Now you know she'll have to come home for at least a week before heading to school."

"One week, for what?"

"Well, she'll have to pack."

"She can take everything to Becky's"

"She has friends that she'll want to say goodbye to."

"She can call them."

"I'm sure she'll want to see me before heading off to school."

"She can call you, too."

"Sarah-Ann now that's just ridiculous and besides I will want to see my daughter before she goes off on her own."

"Well then you can drive to Becky's to see your daughter. Just in case I'm not making myself perfectly clear, please listen carefully. Once Rose graduates from high school, I want her gone. I want her gone for good and if you can't see to that then you can find yourself another wife!"

Sam stood glaring into space. He couldn't believe what he was hearing. This woman wanted him to push his only daughter away from him so that she wouldn't have to deal with her. He knew how Sarah-Ann was, how jealous and manipulating she could be. After returning from his gazing, Sam returned his attention to his wife. She was standing with her arms folded across her chest and looking at him as if she was in control and knew what his answer was going to be before he had even spoke it. "Well?" she grunted. Sam looked up at the window. He could see Rose standing there looking out at them. "Well, is she going or what?" Sarah-Ann asked impatiently.

Sam too, placed his arms across his chest and folded them. He stepped closer to his attitude filled wife and answered her. "Yes Dear, I'll see to it."

Rose stepped away from the window and walked back to her bed. She couldn't believe what she had just heard. She couldn't understand what power Sarah-Ann had over her father. Now she hated them both. Although she couldn't wait to leave that house, she was saddened by what she now knew to be her worth to her father. Rose's sadness soon turned into anger. She stormed downstairs and did what she always did during these times, she ate.

Sarah-Ann and Sam entered the house just a few minutes after Rose had entered the kitchen. To both their surprise, Rose was fully dressed. She stood over the opened oven door placing her next victim inside for heating. No one spoke a word. For the first time, Sam could not look at his precious daughter. But Rose looked at him. She looked at him with such shame and disgust.

Rose continued with her preparation. She prepared another pan of cornbread from her mother's recipe and placed that too, in the heated oven. Sarah-Ann and Sam went to their room and Rose sat at the kitchen table thinking. After her food was ready, Rose gathered the pan of cornbread and the pot of greens and placed them on the kitchen table. She poured herself a large glass of milk before lowering herself onto the plastic seat cover of the kitchen chair. She began to dig into her meal. She ate directly from the pot and dug into the cornbread pan with her fingers. Both the collard greens and the cornbread were quickly devoured.

Sarah-Ann returned to the kitchen only to find Rose slumped over the kitchen table. Her body lay still and solid. The muffled high pitched squeals of flatulence which forced its way through Rose's exit way were the only sign of life detected. Rose had eaten herself into unconsciousness.

Sarah-Ann tried waking Rose. She nudged and pinched the huge lump of woman. She then tried lifting the large girl up from the table but could not manage to even budge her. She called for Sam. As always, Sam rushed to his wife's side. He couldn't believe what Rose had done. With Sarah-Ann's assistance, the two pulled and tugged at Rose but still were not able to budge her. Finally Rose opened her eyes and without hesitation, Sarah-Ann started in on her. "Girl what have you done? You're gonna eat yourself to death!" Sarah-Ann walked over and sat down. She was gasping for air and perspiring heavily. Trying to lift Rose was surely a task for a fork lift or maybe even a mule and some rope. "Get up and go to bed Rose, you've got school tomorrow. You can't afford to mess up in school, so go on," Sarah-Ann said while looking over at her husband.

Rose knew exactly what that meant. She knew that Sarah-Ann wanted to make sure that she graduated from school so she could be sent away from home. Rose slowly pulled herself up from the table. She walked even slower toward the steps which led to her room.

"Goodnight, Baby," her father said.

"Yeah, goodnight!" grunted Sarah-Ann.

Rose walked between Sarah-Ann and her father and she too grunted. "Goodnigh….."

The vapor of rotten collards, curdled milk, and something indescribably disgusting quickly filled the air. The stench traveled like a biblical plague. It was deadly, and since Sarah-Ann was sitting in the direct line of fire, she became the first casualty. She placed her hands over her face tightly but was unable to fend off the savage beast. Her eyes began to water and Sam watched as his wife gasped for air. As her hair began to wither, Sam did the only thing that he could, he ran. Sarah-Ann was trapped. She sat slumped over the table coughing and gagging uncontrollably.

"Sam! Sam! Help me Sam!"

Sam did not answer. He had rushed outside in an attempt to save his clothing and lungs from the devastation which lurked inside his home.

"Sam! She's got to go, Sam!" Sarah-Ann screamed.

At the end of the school year, Rose was ordered by Sarah-Ann and her father to pack up her things in preparation for her trip to her Aunt Becky's. After her summer with Aunt Becky, she was off to Alabama State University. She would be pursuing her dream in becoming a nurse.

Rose spent the summer at her aunt's and just as Sarah-Ann had instructed to her husband, Rose returned the week prior to her scheduled departure to Alabama State. She didn't speak a word to Sarah-Ann for the duration of her stay. Rose knew she would never return home. She was off to meet new friends and a new life.

The campus was active. There were so many new faces and so many things to do. After being a freshman for only a few months, Rose still had not made many friends. She tried being as friendly as she possibly could, but for some reason the students were not receptive to her. It was not until she had her altercation with Stewart Fillmore, another freshman on campus, that she came to know her plight. Stewart was a self proclaimed genius. There was no one who knew as much as he did. At least that is what he had established in his mind.

Rose and Stewart attended geometry class together. They both sat in the front of the class. Stewart would always be the first to yell out the answer to any question that was presented to the class by the professor. Rose too, always knew the answer but would remain silent. Her test scores would always reflect that she, in fact, was the smarter of the two. Stewart would smirk or speak very condescendingly to any of the other students who asked questions.

On one particular day, the professor drew a parallelogram on the board. He followed his drawing with the following question: "Who can tell me what 'g' equals?"

Stewart immediately raised his hand.

"Yes Mr. Fillmore?" said the professor.

Stewart rose to his feet proudly. He looked around the room smugly. He walked up to the board and wrote: "*g=sqrt[a2+b2-2ab cos(A)]*". Then as quickly as he stood, Stewart seated himself.

After a short study of Stewart's answer, the professor responded. "I'm afraid that's incorrect Mr. Fillmore."

"Professor sir, with all due respect, I do believe I'm correct."

The professor looked around the classroom, "Would anyone else like to try?"

"Sir, my answer is correct. If you would only go back and check your…"

"Miss, would you like to give it a try?" the professor asked Rose.

Rose looked around the classroom. She didn't stand. She sat quietly, feeling almost embarrassed that she knew the answer. She cleared her throat before gently speaking. "Yes sir." She walked up to the board and wrote: "*g=sqrt[a2+b2-2ab cos(B)]*" then quietly returned to her seat.

"That's correct!" The professor shouted, "Well done Rose."

Stewart turned up his nose and followed Rose with his eyes back to her seat. After she was seated he leaned over in her direction. "That isn't the right answer, you're both wrong."

"Let it go Stewart, you're wrong, face it. Besides, nobody's right all the time," Rose replied.

"Wrong? The professor just feels sorry for you, that's all."

"Feels sorry for me, why would he feel sorry for me? You're the one that he should be feeling sorry for 'Mr. I can never be wrong'."

"He feels sorry for you because your ass is as wide as the door! Let's face it, it'll take more than an average geometric equation to figure out the circumference of that ass! So you see, no one is going to hire someone like you. You're too big! They'd have to buy an extra large desk and chair and expect less people to ride the lift when you're on it. So many people would be late for work just because of you. So if I were you, I'd try to figure out what other talents I might have or I'd kill myself. Maybe you could join the circus as 'the fattest woman in the world!' Yep, that's what you should do, figure out what else you're good at."

Rose was crushed. This was the first time since she had left home that she had heard those kinds of tasteless remarks made to her. All this time, she thought that Sarah-Ann was the only person on this earth capable of such rudeness and negativity. Suddenly her eyes welled up with tears and she lowered her head.

As the professor continued with his lecture, Rose slowly lifted herself up from her seat. She began gathering up her books in preparation to leave.

"Uh, is there a problem Miss Sterling?" the professor asked.

Rose said nothing, stood still, afraid that if she uttered one word the entire class would witness her falling apart.

"Miss Sterling!" called the professor.

Rose remained frozen, still unable to speak. She looked down at Stewart who was looking around the classroom displaying his always pompous smirk. Rose slowly turned to the professor. She felt the first of several teardrops slide down her cheek then she closed her eyes. She began thinking about Sarah-Ann and how she always told her that she wouldn't amount to anything. She thought about her father and how he turned his back on her for his evil wife. And now, after finally thinking she was free from all negative comments, there was Stewart. Rose slowly opened her eyes. She stepped back and looked around the classroom at all of the expectant faces. Slowly returning her focus on the professor, she spoke calmly. "I am good at this. I will succeed and people will respect me because I'm smart."

Professor Atley looked on strangely, and then before he could speak, Rose grabbed onto the back of Stewart's head and slammed it downward hard against the top of his desk repeatedly as she shouted, "I will! I will! I will! I will succeed!"

After Stewart's head was slammed on his desk with each "I will", it didn't quite bounce back after the fourth time as he was knocked unconscious. Professor Atley rushed over to assist him and Rose returned to her seat. In a panic, she reached into her small brown bag and pulled out the small plastic device, held it to her mouth and puffed from it. Stewart moaned as he slid slowly back into consciousness. Rose looked over at Professor Atley and gently said. "He's Ok Professor, he was just thinking of his next answer." Professor Atley smiled and headed back to the front of the classroom. You could hear faint chuckles from the other students throughout the remaining class time.

As the years passed, Rose had matured and taken up new interests. Among these new interests were boys, bathing, and "Little Debbie" cakes. She soon realized her two new interests were definitely in conflict. The boys were interesting but the cakes satisfied her so much. She would soar through heaven with every bite of a Little Debbie, but every bite also brought along more calories which soon turned into more weight. Sometimes it seemed as though she could feel her buttocks expand with each bite. Her thighs rubbed together so briskly at times that the friction alone would cause her nylons to smoke.

Rose hated being big but she could never give up her passion…eating. Food was still at the top of her list. It was her way of life and she related everything to it. This was how she possessed her uncanny gift of remembering people's names. She associated them with food. There was Paul who was tall, pale, and lanky; Rose related his name to pasta. Rose's friend Debbie who always wore a white ribbon around her dark hair, reminded Rose of "Little Debbie" cakes. Rose wanted to be her best friend. Then there was Randolph who she related to sausage. Yes, that's right, sausage. It seems he constantly rubbed his hands between his legs during class. By the end of class he would have completed his preparation and it was always in plain sight for Rose's viewing. Although she knew that it wasn't really a sausage in there, for some strange reason, it still made her mouth water. That was her talent, relating items and names to food. Let's see, so you've got pasta and Paul, Debbie to Debbie and Randolph to

...well he was just the nasty guy who was always the last one to leave the classroom.

Rose remained in school. She never returned home. During the holidays and other breaks, Rose would stay with Aunt Becky. She had worked extremely hard for four years and was graduating with honors. Needless to say, Aunt Becky was the only person to attend the graduation. This hurt Rose deeply.

After graduation, Rose stayed in Montgomery. She explored and sought employment. She was hired at Jackson Hospital in Montgomery as a nurse. She had moved into a small apartment that was within walking distance from the hospital. Rose enjoyed her job very much. Caring for those who couldn't care for themselves was all she wanted. Rose soon found out that her job had its fair share of ups and downs. She cared for Mrs. Billingsley, who suffered from chronic stomach pain, but was always so pleasant. She also attended to Mr. Schmeling, who was relentlessly constipated and required regular warm salt water enemas. He was a very unpleasant fellow but I guess you really couldn't blame him much. I mean, being full of shit everyday can take its toll on a person.

Everyday that Rose walked into Mr. Schmeling's room, he would greet her the same way as he did all the other nurses, "Hey! I'm full of shit, what're you going to do for me? Hey, help me over here!"

Half the time he really didn't need an enema, the nursing staff believed he just liked getting them.

Rose had been working at the hospital for over three months before being transferred to the coma ward. For some reason she was terrified. What would seem like easy duty somehow had Rose scared to death. Her first day on her new job was pretty depressing. There were no patients to talk to, no pills to hand out and looks or gestures of appreciation to receive. All of her new patients did nothing but lay in their beds quiet and motionless. Rose making her rounds, had nothing to do but turn her patients, bathe them, change their I.V.'s and check their vital signs. This was her routine with each of her patients.

Rose was continuing making her rounds when she came to a young man's room. Of course, he was lying still in his bed. His eyes were closed and a young lady sat quietly in a chair next to the window.

"Hello," Rose said pleasantly.

"Hi," the young lady replied.

"I'm Rose, I'll be his nurse today."

"You're new aren't you?"

"Well not new to the hospital but today is my first day in this ward."

The young lady sat with her legs crossed staring at the floor then shifting her eyes quickly up at Rose. "You take good care of him, ok?"

"Is he your husband?"

"No, he's my brother. He was in a car accident three days ago. He's been like this ever since. Please help him."

"What's your name?"

"Tammy."

"Well Tammy, I'm going to do everything I can to make sure that he's comfortable. I promise."

The young lady rose to her feet and walked over to Rose. She attempted to wrap her arms around the big woman but settled for patting her arm instead.

"I believe you will," she said.

Rose began her new routine by slowly raising the young man's head and then lowering it. Rose repeated the motion several more times. Young Tammy gathered her things and started for the door.

Just before exiting she looked back at Rose and smiled. "Thank you Rose, thank you."

Rose nodded and Tammy stepped out of the room heading down the hallway. Rose turned and looked down at the young man. She gently stroked the side of his face with her hand and then she realized that she had to catch his sister before she left. Rose rushed out into the hall and hurried down to the corridor where she found Tammy stepping onto the elevator. Rose called out to her.

Tammy stepped out of the small enclosure and walked over to Rose with concern pasted over her face. "What's wrong Rose?" she asked.

"Not to worry Tammy, I just wanted to know what his nickname is. Does he have a nickname or do you have a pet name that you call him?"

"No, his name is Ralph and everybody just calls him Ralph."

"Ok, then Ralph it is. I'm sorry if I worried you, I just thought it would help to know his name. That's all."

Tammy smiled then stepped back in the awaiting elevator car. Rose returned to the room and went back to attending to Ralph. She turned his hands from left to right, raised his arms and his legs up and down. She turned him over on his right side then rolled him back over to his left. This was one time when being a big woman actually came in handy. After Ralph's rotation was complete, Rose checked Ralph's temperature and took his pulse. Rose made the proper notations on his chart and then walked over to the storage cabinet located over the sink. She pulled the small square white paper block from off the shelf. She then retrieved a clear bottle and the large chrome bowl from under the cabinet. She turned on the hot and then the cold knobs on the faucet. As the water flowed forcefully, Rose placed her hand underneath the clear liquid and adjusted each knob until the water temperature was sufficient.

Once the desired temperature had been reached, Rose positioned the bowl under the flowing water and filled it halfway with the clear liquid. The cautiously moving woman made her way back to her patient's bedside and set the metal bowl on the table next to where he lay. She walked back over and gathered the small block and the bottle of solution and returned to the table. After pouring a quarter of the solution into the bowl, Rose removed the white paper from the small block. She placed the paper on the table next to her and submerged the unwrapped sponge into the liquid. She squeezed the mixture out of the sponge until it was damp. Rose wiped down her patient's face and *neck. She raised each of His arms were raised as they were washed. The top of his gown was untied and lowered so that nurse Rose could clean his torso. Rose returned the sponge to the liquid. She lifted one side of the sheet to expose his right leg. It too was washed along with his right foot. The sheet was draped back over his leg and Rose stepped around to the opposite side of her patient's bed. She repeated the same process on the opposite leg until it too was cleaned.

After covering the young man's leg, Rose walked back to the table where the bowl rested. The sponge was submerged and the excess fluid was drained once more. She lifted and rolled Ralph to expose his backside. While propping him up, she carefully cleaned his rear. She placed the sponge on the top edge of her hand and slid it between his buttocks from bottom to top and then repeated the process. She lowered her patient back down and Rose threw the sponge back in the bowl.

"Whew, you're a heavy one aren't you?" She said to her patient. Ralph lay there still and lifeless. "Ok, let's get you finished up. I'll turn the radio on for you when I'm done ok? You like music don't you?" Rose reached into the water and retrieved the soapy sponge once again. Using one hand, she applied enough pressure to force the unwanted liquid from within. She reached over and pulled the sheet down to just below Ralph's knees. Realizing that she had never really ever seen a young man's privates up close, she froze. She had tended to children and elderly men but never a young man her age. She felt pretty strange for a moment. Even though she was a professional with a lot of training she still felt more embarrassed than anything else.

Rose collected herself and looked outside in the hallway to see if anyone was watching. She couldn't take her eyes off it. She reached down hesitantly and slowly slid the bottom of the young man's gown upward. His thighs were muscular and smooth. She looked up at his face and now realized that although his eyes were closed completely he was still an attractive young man. Rose continued. She pulled the gown farther up until the young man was completely exposed. She glanced back over at the doorway once more.

"Oh my," she whispered. Rose stood and stared at the young man for a few seconds allowing herself to regain her composure. "I will definitely take care of you. Your sister has nothing to worry about."

Rose began wiping and washing the young man's private area. As she washed him she began to perspire and her hands began to tremble. She must have washed him in that one area for over ten minutes. She couldn't stop herself and of course she had to stop for a brief moment to take a puff from her inhaler. Rose dipped the sponge in the liquid and wrung it out and returned it to her joyful place. She watched the door and the hallway as she slowly stroked his member with the soapy sponge. She was now beginning to pant heavily and was getting light headed. Suddenly her joy was interrupted by the sound of the medicine cart being wheeled towards the room. Rose quickly adjusted Ralph's gown and pulled up the sheet.

The wobbly front wheels cast a high pitched squeaking sound which increased in volume as the cart drew nearer. The small shadow increased in size as it approached the door. "Are you almost done with him?" It was Nurse Randall, the head nurse. "He needs to have his I.V. changed. It's just saline."

"Yes, I'm done. I've turned him and I've just finished bathing him. His vitals have been checked, too."

"Ok good, can you hook up this I.V. then?"

"Sure."

Nurse Randall removed the bottle of clear liquid from the cart and handed it to Rose. As she turned to leave the room Rose could hear nothing but the deep gasp from her supervisor. "My goodness! What…I mean…how long has he been like this?"

"Like what?" Rose replied.

Nurse Randall, with her mouth wide opened pointed down at the young man's crotch. Rose turned only to be met by the erected white cloth. Both women stepped back and looked on and could not believe their eyes. In a flash, Nurse Randall rushed out of the room. Rose remained by young Ralph's side staring at his face in astonishment.

As Nurse Randall entered the hall she called out for the doctor. "Dr. Webber! Dr. Webber! I need the doctor in here. Has anyone seen Dr. Webber?"

The young nurse at the desk quickly lifted the handset to the phone and pushed the button marked "intercom". "Paging Dr. Webber…Paging Dr. Webber….Dr. Webber, please report to ward 'C'….Dr. Webber please report to ward 'C'."

After three minutes, a tall, gray haired man wearing wire rimmed eye glasses and a long, white lab coat stepped inside young Ralph's room. He was met at the door by nurse Randall who immediately took him by the back of his arm and escorted him over to the young patient's side. Dr. Webber looked at young Ralph then quickly snatched the sheet down below his knees. "How long has he been like this?"

"We're not sure," Nurse Randall replied.

"Wow! That thing looks like it's been 'spit shined' and buffed!"

"Well I had just finished bathing him sir," Rose said while trying to hide her embarrassment.

Nurse Randall stepped in for a closer look. "Yes, it does look pretty shiny. I can almost see my reflection in it! You must have cleaned the hell out of it Rose."

Dr. Webber stepped closer and placed a large round magnifying glass close to the young mans flesh. "It seems to have the skin pulled as tight as it can possibly go. I'd have to say that this is a full erection of some sort." The doctor continued examining both sides of the member. "Hmmm, yes, looks like we have massive swelling here. Have you ever seen one of these Nurse Randall?"

"Sure, just last Saturday. My husband had gone out drinking and...."

"No, Nurse Randall, I mean an erection of this intensity on a coma patient?"

"Oh, uh no, no I haven't. I've seen them get partially erect but no serious boners like this one. I mean....what I mean is...no...uh...none filled to capacity like this one. I must say doctor, it's rather impressive."

"Nurse Randall, get a hold of yourself, please!" Dr. Webber insisted. Both Dr. Webber and Rose looked on as Nurse Randall continued stuttering through her words in an attempt to correct her initial reply. "How about you Nurse Sterling, can you tell me what you witnessed?"

Nurse Randall looked over at Rose who was now trying to conceal her embarrassment even more now. Rose cleared her throat then calmly answered. "I turned him and then bathed him but it must have occurred minutes after his bath."

"Ah, I see," said the doctor. "Perhaps the bath stimulated some of his neuro membranes. Let's set him up for another scan," Dr. Webber stated as he clicked the small device in his hand and pointed the small beam of light into his patient's eyes. "His facial expression, was it like this when you came in?"

"No sir," Rose quickly answered. "It wasn't until we became aware of his…well his other change that I noticed the change in his expression."

Young Ralph continued to lie still in his bed. His eyes were no longer closed shut. They stared upward toward the ceiling and both corners of his mouth were turned up slightly, as if he were smiling. Dr. Webber then focused on the young man's crotch. He placed his hand on the young man's penis then turned to Nurse Randall. "It's hot, there's definitely some blood circulation here."

"Doctor…" The nurse mumbled as she nodded her head drawing his attention to the young man's face. What they saw then was even more inconceivable to their intellect. Young Ralph's smiling expression had returned to his original blank stare and his stiff flesh was now deflating slowly to its original flaccid state. "What's going on here? Why is he not responsive now?"

"May I have a try?" Nurse Randall asked.

"Yes, maybe the temperature of my hand or even my voice could be causing his brain to react differently. Yes, yes please by all means see if you can re-stimulate his brain."

Nurse Randall grabbed onto the young man's member as tight as she could. She squeezed and pulled. She jerked up and down, up and down stretching the tight swollen skin just a little farther. She massaged the shaft roughly and then tried bending it but its stiffness would not allow any bow. She then placed the palm of her hand flat upon the head of the young man's penis and stared at it. It was as if she marveled at it. Just as she began to lower her head, Rose realized that Nurse Randall was about to place the man's penis in her mouth. Rose yelled out, "Water! I think he might respond to water."

"Water? Nurse Randall wait!" Dr. Webber asked.

"Yes, I did bathe him just before we noticed the change."

"How did you bathe him?"

"Just a few wipes with soap and warm water."

"Well let's give it a try," replied the doctor.

Nurse Randall still leaning over Ralph's penis with her mouth open, blurted out, "Water, saliva, what's the difference? Maybe he'll respond to saliva just as well."

"Nurse Randall, no. You can't place your mouth on that young man's penis," said Dr. Webber.

"Well why not? It's in the interest of science. I'll be glad to do it, for science of course."

"No Nurse Randall. Rose please proceed."

Rose quickly rushed over to the sink with the bowl in hand. She filled the bowl with the exact mixture as she had before then quickly walked back over to young Ralph's side. Nurse Randall stepped up and picked up the sponge.

"No, I'll do it. Maybe there was something with the way I washed him that stimulated him, stimulated his brain that is. Maybe it was my voice or my touch or something."

"Yes, she has a good point," added Dr. Webber.

Rose reached for the sponge and pulled gently. Nurse Randall's grip was so tight that the sponge was beginning to rip in two. Rose released the sponge and held out her hand. "Nurse Randall, the sponge please." Nurse Randall looked at the young man and then over to Dr. Webber before placing the damp sponge into Rose's hand. Rose dunked the sponge then drained the excess liquid from it just as she had before. She placed the damp, soft sponge against young Ralph's penis.

"Sir!" Nurse Randall whispered.

Dr. Webber looked over at Nurse Randall who was pointing at young Ralph's face. That's right, his smile had returned and seconds later so did his full erection. His smile was even bigger than before and not only was his penis pointing toward the ceiling but it was shaking from throbbing. Nurse Randall quickly grabbed hold of the throbbing flesh but no one in the room could understand why. Both Dr. Webber and Rose looked on strangely as the woman held onto the young man's hot meat. "Nurse Randall, please, back away from the erection. I am ordering you to let the dick go."

Panting heavily and flustered, Nurse Randall finally let go of the young man's member and staggered out of the room. She disappeared for most of her shift and was found later sitting on the loading dock of the hospital smoking a cigarette and yelling seductive statements to the ambulance staff. Dr. Webber prohibited her from entering young Ralph's room.

By morning the young man's erection had dissipated once again. Several tests were run, but were unsuccessful in accomplishing the same result. Needless to say, none of the tests could get a rise out of young Ralph. His smile was no longer visible but his eyes still remained opened. He was eventually wheeled back to his room.

When Rose returned to work later that afternoon, she was approached by Dr. Webber and Dr. Nichols. She was once again asked to perform the sponge procedure on the young man by witness of the other doctor. Rose's attention to young Ralph's penis and testicles produced the same result once again. Rose was later asked to perform the same task on several other male coma patients. None of the other patients responded as Ralph did.

Rose repeated the bathing on Ralph daily. Four days after his first comatose erection, Ralph ejaculated during his bathing and immediately awoke from his darkness. When questioned about his memory during that time, Ralph could only remember dreaming of climbing up a ladder and clawing his way upward through the core of the earth before breaking his way through the soil and pulling himself out of a world of nothingness.

The next day Ralph was moved from the coma ward to another ward where he was kept for observation and physical therapy. This was standard hospital policy. Rose continued working her same shift in the coma ward. One evening, just stepping into the hall from a patient's room, Rose was met by Tammy, Ralph's sister.

"I just wanted to stop by and thank you for all you've done for my brother," she said smiling an angelic smile.

"Oh, no problem at all, I'm just glad he's alright. Up and about is he? We've got people here that have been here for quite sometime. I wish they all were as lucky as your brother. God was surely looking after him Miss Tammy."

"Yes he was. I guess that's why he sent you to him," Tammy said smiling. "I understand you were there when he woke?"

"Uh…yes…yes, I was," Rose mumbled.

"He wants to meet you. Can you come down later and meet him?"

"Uh, sure."

"He's in room B310."

Rose left the young woman and continued with her rounds. The entire time she wondered if he actually would remember what she had done to him. She was afraid that if he saw her face or heard her voice, he could possibly remember what she did and perhaps report her for improper behavior toward a patient. He might even pursue legal actions against her and the hospital. Her career would be over before it had really started.

Rose completed her rounds and it was now her favorite time of her shift, lunch. Although she was worried about meeting young Ralph, she still hadn't lost her appetite. She went to her locker and pulled out her large brown paper bag and headed for the nurse's lounge. Just as she reached the door, "There you are! We've been looking all over for you." It was Tammy. She was pushing her brother in a wheel chair. "This is the nurse. This is Nurse Rose!"

Ralph looked at the large woman strangely. He looked her up and down for a second or two before speaking. "Thank you Nurse Rose," he said with very little emotion displayed on his face.

"So how are you feeling?" Rose asked while trying to disguise her voice.

"The doctors say that I'm fine. Doesn't appear that I have any brain damage at all and everything seems to be functioning normally."

"I'll say! I mean…uh, that's great. Hey, I'm glad everything worked out for you."

"Yeah, me too."

"You two take care; I've got to get to my lunch. As you can see I don't miss many of those," Rose said chuckling. She realized that he remembered nothing of the days of his coma. Rose opened the door to the lounge. Just as she turned away, Ralph spoke loudly.

"That means it's just more of you to love, that's all. Mind if I give you a hug? I would like to thank you properly."

Rose froze. She turned and faced the young, attractive man. She paused for a moment before speaking. "Uh sure, uh, I guess that'll be alright." The young man rose up from the chair with the assistance of his sister. He stepped towards Rose and wrapped his arms around as much of her as he could. He held her close and tight. "I don't know what it is but there's something about you. I just can't…" At that second, the young man froze. He became speechless and his body became weak and his legs trembled. Rose and Tammy helped him back into the wheelchair.

"Are you alright?" Tammy asked her bother.

Looking rather embarrassed, he answered. "I'm not sure. I guess so. I just got a little dizzy, that's all."

Ralph placed his hands in his lap and Tammy got behind the chair. "We'd better get you back so you can rest. I think you've had enough excitement for the day," Tammy said. Tammy looked back at Rose and smiled. "Thanks again Rose. Thank you for looking after my brother like you said you would, you're an angel."

"It was my pleasure."

Rose extended her hand out to Ralph to shake his hand. "You take care of yourself and no more of that crazy driving, Ok? Promise me." Hesitantly, Ralph raised his hand and extended it to Rose. As she followed his hand to hers, she noticed the damp spot on his pants. She could tell by his embarrassment what had happened. Seems as they embraced, Ralph for some unknown reason to himself, had ejaculated without warning. Rose looked at the wet stain then at Ralph. "I feel the same way," she said then smiled.

He lowered his head then glanced up at her. "Like I said, there's something about you." Tammy, unaware as to what the two were talking about, stepped away and gave Ralph and Rose a moment to talk.

After Ralph was released from the hospital, he continued to call on Rose. She continued to hug him and he would continue to saturate his pants. He could never figure out how Rose had this type of affect on him. They were married four weeks after his release from the hospital.

Rose continued working at the hospital for several years and Ralph worked for an accounting firm in Montgomery. Before they both realized, eighteen years had passed. Although without any of the six children that they always wanted, Rose and Ralph were happy. Rose was content with her life. She lived in her dream house, had a great husband and she loved her job. She continued to check on Aunt Becky but still made no attempt to contact her father or Sarah-Ann. Ralph had never met Rose's father and couldn't imagine how anyone would not want to remain close to her.

Another year had passed and Ralph had finally talked Rose into contacting her father. Over eighteen years had passed and it was beyond time to bury the hatchet. Rose telephoned. After several attempts of receiving a "non working number" recording, Rose decided to contact the operator. After being connected and given the new numbe, Rose sat nervously with the phone handset to her ear.

"Hello," said the voice on the other end of the phone. It was Sarah-Ann. Her voice, still sounding exactly as it did years ago. Rose couldn't speak. For some reason she didn't expect Sarah-Ann to answer the phone. After all these years her voice still ran a chill up Rose's spine. "Hello" the voice repeated.

Finally Rose mustered up enough courage to answer. "Um…yes hello. Is this Sarah-Ann?"

"Yes, speaking."

"Hi Sarah-Ann, this is Rose. Is my father there?" There was a long pause. Rose pulled the handset from her ear and looked at the hard plastic phone receiver then quickly returned the device to her ear. "Hello, Sarah-Ann, are you there?" Still there was no answer.

Ralph folded his arms and hunched his shoulders. "Well, what did she say?"

"I think she hung up on me," Rose replied as she tapped on the receiver with her finger before returning it to her ear again.

"Rose? Rose is that really you?" the voice said calmly.

"Yes Sarah-Ann, it's me."

"It's been a very long time since we've heard from you."

"Yes, I know."

"How have you been? We've always wondered about how you were doing, wondering if you were alright."

Rose lowered the phone and looked over at her husband. She turned up her lips in an attempt to display her disbelief then returned the phone. "I'm fine. I'm married to a good man and I am doing well. Is my father there?"

"Well, no Rose. I'm sorry but your father hasn't been around for the past three years."

"Where did he go?"

Once again there was a long, dead silence. Rose could hear Sarah-Ann breathing deeply. With her voice shaky she answered, "Heaven, he's in heaven, Dear. He passed on, Rose. We tried to contact you but nobody knew how."

"Aunt Becky has always known how to contact me, why didn't you have her call me?"

"Rebecca hasn't spoken to your father or me since you left for college. She was very upset with us and wouldn't accept our visits or phone calls. We knew no other way to get a hold of you."

"I bet you didn't!"

"Rose please, I feel bad enough. He was all I had and I feel responsible for his death as it is."

"Why, why do you feel responsible?"

"Because...well, because I crushed his heart, that's how."

"With the tractor?"

"No, not like that. I took away the only thing that your father ever really loved, you Rose. I'm so sorry. I am truly sorry.

There's one other thing Rose, seems like we have ourselves a little mix up here.

"Yeah, what kind of mix up would that be?"

Sarah-Ann let out a phony giggle "Ha ha, ahhh Rose, it's quite silly actually."

"What is quite silly Sarah-Ann?"

"Well somehow your father added your name to the deed to the farm, isn't that silly?"

"What do you mean my name's on the deed?"

"That means technically, the farm is yours," Ralph interrupted.

"Mine?"

"Well no, not really. It was a mistake, that's all. I've been paying the taxes and all. I just need for you to come home and have this small little detail fixed, that's all," Sarah-Ann continued.

"I'm not coming there, do what you want with it. I have nothing but bad memories of that place. No, I won't come."

"Well Rose that's not helping any. I can't even sell it until my name is on the deed."

"Sell it? My father put everything into that farm, everything! Now you want to sell it? No, I'm not coming."

"Rose, this was your father's dream not mine. He said for me to move on if I wanted to; if anything ever happened to him. I'm an old woman now Rose, I can't keep this place up."

"Then move on but you're not selling my daddy's farm."

"Rose…I can't. I've got nowhere to go. I've got no money…I've got no family. I can't."

"That's probably because you have a way of pushing people away from you Sarah-Ann. You are an evil woman who deserves exactly that, no one who cares about you." Rose sat and thought for a moment. Sarah-Ann remained on the phone but was silent. As much as Rose despised Sarah-Ann, she still could not be that cruel to another human being. "Ok Sarah-Ann, I'll tell you what, you stay there as long as you want but you can't sell my daddy's farm."

"But Rose I told you, I can't keep this place up alone, besides I don't want to be here without Sam. Please Rose, please reconsider. Don't make me stay here. I'm sorry for everything I have done to you."

Rose said nothing. She sat quietly with the phone receiver to her ear before slowly returning it to its cradle. Ralph walked over to his wife and placed his hand on her shoulder.

"You Ok?" Rose looked up at Ralph; her eyes filled with tears and her face filled with anger.

"That witch! She finally drove him to his grave." Rose pulled herself up from the chair and walked into the bedroom and closed the door. Ralph did not follow. After that moment, neither Rose nor Ralph had ever made mention of Rose's father or Sarah-Ann.

Two weeks later there was a loud knock at the door. It was early, just after 7:00 a.m. She walked slowly to the door as she tied the cotton belt to her robe together. She opened the door and shielded her eyes from the bright sunlight. After opening the screen door, the man handed her two envelopes.

"Sarah-Ann Sterling, you have been ordered and served," said the officer.

"Huh?"

The man turned away, trotted down the stairs and climbed into his car. He drove off as quickly as he had arrived. Sarah-Ann looked down at the envelope. It read: "*Circuit Court of Calhoun County*". It was a court order stating that she vacate the property. The other envelope was addressed to her as well. Sarah-Ann lowered herself down into the chair in her kitchen and opened the envelope. She pulled out the plain white piece of paper and began to read its contents. It read:

Sarah-Ann, as I stated during our phone conversation, you can stay as long as you want. However, after I hung the phone up, I realized that you said you didn't want to stay at the house without my father. He's gone because of you. I left because of you and now it's your turn.

Rose

Yes, Rose forced Sarah-Ann off of what was now her farm. Rose never heard from Sarah-Ann again but heard that she had remarried and was strangled to death a year after her marriage by her step-daughter. Rose sold the farm and never returned.

Rose and Ralph continued to live a happy life. Ralph retired from the accounting agency where he had worked for over thirty six years and after Rose's retirement from the nursing field, they moved to Fayetteville, North Carolina to live out their days together. Together didn't last long. Shortly after their move to Fayetteville, Ralph departed this earth, leaving his wife of many years. Rose found Ralph sitting peacefully in front of the television. She found him with his pants and underwear pulled down to his knees. The Playboy channel was still running and he was cold as ice. His penis was stiff and still pointing toward the ceiling. This seemed so familiar to Rose. She realized then that she had lost her husband in the same manner as she had found him in that coma ward all those years ago. She wiped away her tears, smiled at her husband then walked into the bathroom and returned with a sponge and a bowl of soapy water.

After Ralph's passing, Rose remained lonely. She had a cousin that lived over in Hopewell but didn't see him much. Rose did volunteer work at the hospital over the years until the aches and pains of growing older prevented her from making that long bus trip everyday. After staying home alone for awhile and experiencing a few falls and spills, Rose decided to check out a few retirement homes where she could be cared for.

That's how Rose ended up as a resident of the Hayfield Streams Retirement Facility.

Chapter 3 - Marva

The choir sang their first selection. As the spirit filled voices echoed throughout the church, the congregation jumped and shouted, giving praises to their Creator. She stood in the front row of the large group of ladies, smiling and watching her father smile back at her. Marva Thomas was a bright, young girl. She sang in the women's chorus at the Mount Calvary Baptist Church of Chicago. It was a small church and like most of the other young women in the congregation, she adored her minister. He was an attractive man. His dark, chocolate colored skin, coal black wavy hair and muscular physique demanded stares from most of the women surrounding him. Marva too, would constantly stare at this strong God filled image of a man as he slammed his hand down on the podium while standing in the pulpit delivering the morning message.

At the end of the service, all the women would paste on their best smiles for their pastor. As they exited the church, the pastor would greet each member. Taking him by the hand and smiling, each interested woman would gaze deep into his eyes and leave him with some type of suggestive message of their own. They would take his hand and caress it then whisper things such as, "You really moved me today Pastor, I mean, you really moved me in a special way," which really meant "Damn you made me hot and moist as hell while sitting in the Lord's house. This ass is yours for the taking, call me."

Though the female parishioners would pass out these compliments freely, Marva would always just smile at him and speak the same words to him each Sunday as she left the church. "See you at home Daddy." She would then give him a big hug then head home with her mother.

Marva was a quiet girl. She was shy and stayed to herself most of the time. Singing was the only time she wasn't quiet or shy. She loved to sing and her voice was beautiful. She would sing all day. She sang when she woke up in the morning. She sang in the shower. She sang after breakfast, lunch and dinner and they couldn't keep her quiet at choir rehearsal. Singing made her feel alive. Her favorite song was "Amazing Grace".

Marva would use each solo opportunity she had with the church choir as her own personal weapon. She would step forward and sing as loud as she could. The congregation would always scream and clap. When finished, Marva would roll her eyes and turn up her nose at all the fashionably dressed women sitting in the front row gawking at her father and seeking his attention. She would return to her place with the group then take her seat and stare at the women for the remainder of the service.

Marva loved her father dearly. Her mother did as most mothers did. She worked hard to bring her daughter up to become a respectable young lady. This wasn't difficult because Marva had always been a sweet girl and her mother was very proud of her.

Just arriving home from church the two young ladies entered their home. Marva's mom quickly kicked off her high heeled shoes and sat her bible on the dining room table. She placed her hands firmly against her lower back just before reaching up and began massaging the back of her neck. She looked over at Marva sternly, "I saw the way you were looking at Miss

Brown and the other ladies in the front row today. What did I tell you about that? I told you, God don't like ugly! And here you are up there carrying on like you're some kind of church bouncer! That is no way for a young lady to act, girl. Now I'm gonna tell you once more, I don't want to see you up there showing off and acting ugly anymore! Some of those other fools may think that it's cute and get a kick out of watching you act like some type of protective watchdog, but not me, so cut it!"

"But Ma, they're always looking at Daddy like…like they're gonna just run up on the pulpit and just eat him up. It's disgusting the way they look at him."

"Girl, your Daddy aint thinking about none of those old, crazy women so why should you? Besides, aint nobody runnin' up on nobody's pulpit eatin' up nobody."

"It doesn't upset you, not in the least little bit?"

"Nope."

"Well, they just make me angry. They really make me mad with all of that 'Oh Pastor, that's a really nice suit you're wearin' and it fits so nice and oh Pastor, your sermon sent chills up my spine today!' They just make me sick!"

"Girl, that's just those demons running up their backs, that's all. It's either demons or gas, take your pick. Either way, you shouldn't worry about it. You're too young for all that stress."

Marva's mother flopped down onto the couch and extended her legs out. She rested them on top of the coffee table before continuing, "Besides, I don't hear you complaining about the young men gawking at you. Now bring me something cold to drink and come massage my feet for me, Child. This bunion is killing me."

"I told you about wearing those too small shoes, tryin' to look cute," Marva yelled to her mother while chuckling.

"Girl, just bring me my drink!" her mother replied while laughing.

Marva stepped into the kitchen and opened the small ice box. She pulled out the glass pitcher of lemonade and filled the glass she had retrieved from the shelf. After placing the glass in her mother's hand, she dropped down on one knee and began massaging her mother's feet.

"Oh yeah, that's it, rub that bunion down," her mother moaned while sipping the glass of lemonade with her eyes closed.

Marva and her mother sat and talked for over an hour before they both stood up and headed for the kitchen. They knew that after all the visits, the pastor would soon be arriving tired and hungry. Each and every Sunday after service, Marva's father would take communion to the sick and elderly of his congregation before his return home.

Shortly after the ladies had set the table for dinner, the doorknob turned slowly and in walked the pastor. Marva put the last glass down on the table and walked into the living room to greet her dad.

"Hey Daddy, you're right on time."

"Hey Precious. Something smells good."

"We made your favorite today, fried chicken, green beans and mashed potatoes."

"Where's your mother?"

"In the dining room sitting down, she had another bunion flare up today," Marva said laughing.

"I told her about trying to squeeze her size nines into a size seven."

"I HEARD THAT!" Her mother yelled.

"Uh oh, I think we're in trouble," Marva said while smiling, "She's just trying to look good for you Daddy, that's all."

"Baby, your mama knows that she'll look good to me no matter what she wears, even shoes that fit!" The pastor said still chuckling.

"Well Daddy, she got to do something to keep up with all those jezebels who are always lookin' at you like they're in heat or something."

"I HEARD THAT, TOO!" her mother yelled from the dining room once again.

"Girl, your mother's not worried about those ladies. They're just lost, that's all.
You shouldn't worry about them, either. You should be praying for them, that's what you should be doing."

Marva helped her father remove his jacket and took his hat. She placed them on the coat rack. Marva headed for the dining room to join her mother while her dad entered the bathroom to prepare himself for dinner. He soon entered the dining room and walked over to his wife who was sitting in her usual place at the table. He leaned over and kissed her before making his way to his seat. He extended his arms out to each of the ladies who sat opposite of each other and they all joined hands as he blessed the food.

The next day was like most days for Marva. She went to school and was treated like she always was, like one of the teachers. All of the students knew that she was a straight laced Christian girl. They would call her names like "Church Girl" and "Reverend Marva" but she didn't care. She would always hold her head up high and keep her bible resting on top of her stack of books. None of the boys ever asked her out or even tried to make much conversation with Marva. She liked boys but just couldn't stop herself from preaching to them whenever she saw them doing something wrong.

This was Marva's senior year in high school. It was nearing graduation and prom and none of the boys had asked her to accompany them. This troubled Marva but she never let it show. Her mother knew that Marva had looked forward to going to the prom since she had started high school and now it wasn't looking promising for her little girl at all. She spoke to her husband about Marva's dilemma. "We'll just have to pray on it dear. If it is His will, Marva will attend the prom," he would say.

Days passed and now only two weeks remained before prom. Marva was barely able to conceal her disappointment. Her father, too, could see her disguised pain. He looked over at his precious daughter to offer some words of encouragement.

"Stand strong before the Lord, Baby, and hold on tight to His unchanging hand. Don't you worry, things WILL work out. The Lord answers prayers, you know that don't you?"

Marva nodded her head and embraced her father's words. She then pushed up both corners of her mouth and mustered up the best smile that she could for him.

The following Friday was the senior class talent show. Of course, Marva was too shy to enter.

Her mother saw the flyer on the dining room table and immediately asked, "So Marva, what are you going to sing in the talent show?"

Marva looked at her mother then shook her head. "Nothing, I'm not singing or anything else in that stupid worthless contest."

"Well aren't your friends going to be there and some of your classmates who have never heard you sing?"

"Sure they will but it doesn't matter and besides, they'll only make fun of me."

"Marva Leeann, why should you care if they laugh? You'll be singing to and for the Lord. You don't know who the Lord might touch through song that night. You're just His instrument child, let Him use you."

"Mom, they don't want to hear me sing!"

"Maybe not, but I'm sure God would. After all, He's the one who gave you that wonderful voice so don't you think that He'd want you to share it with everybody?"

Marva stood there looking as if she had been lectured by God Himself. She said nothing; there was nothing she could say. She smiled at her mother then headed for her room.

The next day, Marva signed up for the talent contest. As she scribbled down her name and talent, the young lady at the table watched closely. She was curious to see what talent "Reverend Marva" would perform. It was no surprise that Marva entered the contest as a singer. The song that she was to perform was none other than "Amazing Grace".

"Well thank you Marva, we look so forward to you singing in the talent show. Good luck to you, I'm sure you'll be a hit," said the young lady sitting behind the table. Marva knew that the young lady was being sarcastic but ignored her and hurried off. Marva knew that if she was planning on winning the contest she would surely need Reginald.

Reginald was the pianist for her church choir. He could play any song you could name and was one of the finest piano players in the city. He played at the church on Sundays, and also played at one of the downtown establishments during the week. He was a very busy man and Marva wasn't sure if he'd be able to help her. She decided to wait until Saturday, after choir rehearsal, to ask him.

Saturday came quickly and Marva rushed out the door to get down to the church. She was a bit nervous but at the same time very excited about choir rehearsal. As each member filed through the door of the church, they would greet the other choir members then quickly climb the stairs which led to the choir stand.

The song for the Sunday choir selection would be decided by the choir director, Mrs. Ashby, and the hymn books would be turned to the proper page. Reginald would strike up the tune and the choir would join in, only to be interrupted several times by Mrs. Ashby to adjust and designate harmony parts. Once everyone knew their parts and pitch, the choir would sing the song several times. Usually the choir sang three songs during the Sunday service. They would sing one new song and two older songs that most of the congregation knew to allow them to join in with the choir. Mrs. Ashby would also select the two other songs and the choir would rehearse them as if they were newly learned too.

After the choir had finished rehearsing, Marva rushed down to the piano where Reginald was still tinkering on the keys.

"Is that a new song you're working on Reggie?" Marva asked.

"Yeah, it's something I've been working on for the choir. I'm still working on the words though," Reginald replied.

"Oh, it sounds nice but then everything you play sounds nice."

"Why, thank you, Marva."

"You're probably the best piano player in the city."

"Well I don't know about all that, but thanks anyway."

"Hey, you know I just had an idea, you know the high school that I go to is having a talent contest. It's for the seniors. I was thinking about entering but I'd probably need a piano player if I did, you know, somebody that I was used to singing with."

"Is that so? Well, I know you'll do just fine Marva, you have a great voice."

"I'd have to have a piano player that was really good if I…"

"Had a piano player like me, huh? Is that where you're going with this?"

"Yeah, I never thought of that. Yeah, with a piano player like you, I would surely be able to sing my best."

"When is this talent contest Marva?"

"It's next Friday."

"Next Friday, girl you know I play down at the 'Boom Boom Room' on Fridays."

"Yeah but you don't play down there until what, ten o'clock? The talent contest starts at six o'clock. You'll be gone by seven."

"Well...well I guess I could do that but we'll have to practice."

"Yes, yes we can practice whenever you want to."

"And what might I ask are you singing?"

"Amazing Grace."

"Amazing Grace? You gonna sing that at a talent contest? Oh you're definitely not planning on winning are you? Why don't you let me get something together for you? Something more suitable for a contest. In the meantime, you go ahead and sign up."

"Oh, uh, about that... Uh, I wasn't quite truthful with you when I said that I was thinking about signing up, I kinda already did."

"Miss Marva, I can't believe it, you played me like a fiddle. I'm telling your father."

"No, please Reggie, I'm sorry. I just didn't know how to ask you."

"Gotcha! You know I wouldn't do that. Hey ladies, Miss Marva here has signed up to sing in her high school talent contest next Friday. Looks like Miss Shy Thang is finally breaking out of her shell!" Reginald said laughing loudly.

"Go on Marva, you let them know how much voice is hidden under that shy exterior and if you need a background singer I'd be more than happy to sing for you," said one of the choir members.

"Yeah me too Marva, I'll sing for you if you need me," said another lady of the choir.

Soon, most of the ladies all had heeded to the call as background singers and Marva was truly amazed and grateful.

"Ok Marva, looks like you have a piano player and background singers. Now all we have to do is set up some rehearsal time. The only day I can rehearse in the evening is on Tuesday," Reginald said.

"In that case, Tuesday it is. I guess we can practice here right after bible study. I'll check with my dad."

"I'll have a song ready by then. Ok ladies, everybody who's interested in helping Marva with her talent contest be here on Tuesday at eight o'clock."

Everyone nodded and agreed. The choir members all had ideas of which song Marva should sing and Reginald skimmed through the hymn book to see if he could find a song that would blow the roof off the auditorium.

Marva ran all the way home filled with excitement. She immediately rushed into the living room where her father sat quietly reading the newspaper. She asked him about Tuesday rehearsals and without hesitation, he gave her his permission. "Only for one hour Marva. I will be back to pick you up from the church at nine o'clock sharp." Marva agreed and called each choir member to let them know that Tuesday was rehearsal day.

Tuesday couldn't get there fast enough for Marva. When it finally arrived, Marva even showed up for bible study. She was so excited. After bible study, she walked up and sat in the choir stand and waited for her group. She started singing softly to warm up her vocal chords. As she sang, she could hear the echoing deep voice call out, "Nine o'clock Marva. I'll be back at nine." Marva sat waiting patiently. It was now eight fifteen and still no sign of Reginald or any of the choir members.

Suddenly the door opened and in walked Mrs. Boxley. She hurried in and rushed up to the choir stand. "Sorry I'm late, where's everybody?" she asked.

"Nobody's gotten here yet, you're the first. Actually, I don't think that anyone else is com…" Just as Marva had given up, in walked Reginald, followed by three of the other choir members.

"I'M LATE, YES I'M LATE SO LET'S GET STARTED LADIES. HURRY, HURRY! Marva get down here, I want to go over the lead of this song with you. Well don't just sit there, COME ON!" He shouted.

Marva couldn't believe her eyes. She rushed down and sat next to Reginald and they went over the song for about twenty minutes before showing the choir their part. The entire choir had still not yet sang the song together. Marva took her place in front and Reginald started playing. His hands made the piano sound like beautiful thunder as he rocked back and forth and shaking his head.

Marva stepped forward and began singing. She sounded like an angel and the choir was singing in perfect harmony behind her.

The piano stopped. "Ok you two ladies singing soprano, hold the 'Yes Lord' a little longer before you go into the main chorus, ok?" The two ladies nodded. "Ok ladies let's take it from there," Reginald continued.

Just as he started playing, he was quickly interrupted.

"Marva, it's time to go, it's nine o'clock." It was her father. They had started so late that time had passed rather quickly.

"Ten more minutes Daddy?"

Everyone stood quiet and still, awaiting the pastor's answer. He walked over to the long bench and sat down comfortably. He removed his hat and smiled. "I could hear the sound of heaven as I walked up to the door of this church. Who am I to interfere with that? You all sound wonderful. You go on and sing. I guess I could wait, oh let's say another thirty minutes." Everyone smiled. "I do have one question though. How come you don't sing like that on Sundays? You do sound good and all but not like this, you all sound like angels tonight."

The pastor smiled and sat back on the bench and Reginald laughed as he started playing again. The ladies and Marva sang their hearts out. They sang until Reginald was satisfied. Thirty minutes passed and the ladies began gathering their things while the pastor locked up. Marva once again thanked everyone before climbing in the car with her father.

On the way home, her father listened to her excitement. She was no longer afraid to sing nor did she care what her classmates thought of the song that she would sing. "You sounded really good in there tonight," her father said.

"Thanks Daddy, but I wouldn't have sounded like that without Reggie and the ladies."

"Oh, I don't know about that. They make you sound… I guess you would say 'professional' but you still have a great voice that sounds beautiful alone, too."

"Well thank you, Daddy."

"No need to thank me, you're the one with the angelic voice that made me feel so warm inside tonight, so I thank you."

"Oh Daddy, you're so silly."

"Your mother's going to be so proud when she hears you sing at the talent contest."

Marva and the group had one more rehearsal before the contest and just as before, they sounded sensational. The time had come for Marva to show the other kids at her school her hidden talent and she was more than ready. She put on her best dress and shoes and styled her hair to perfection. After she was dressed and ready to go, she rushed her parents by reminding them that she had to be at the school gymnasium by 5:30 pm.

Marva and her parents arrived at 5:30 pm sharp. She rushed into the gym while her parents headed for the auditorium to pick out the best seats. They sat center stage, five rows from the front. Marva looked around the gym. There were boys with guitars and drums, girls with majorette costumes and batons. There were other singing groups there, too. They stood in different corners of the gym practicing. They were going to sing some of the popular songs of the 1940's. Marva looked around and saw none one from her group but didn't worry because she knew that none of them were very prompt.

All of the contestants were called over to the bleachers. Mrs. Holloway, the vice principal, read the line up and directed everyone backstage. There, Marva watched and waited for her group members. Still not very concerned, she watched on as the parents and friends were greeted by Mrs. Holloway.

It was now 6:10 pm and the first act was called out to perform and Marva still had no one with her. She was to be sixth in the line up. At 6:15 pm, Mrs. Boxley and Mrs. McCray rushed in, followed shortly by Miss Everheart. Marva still had no worries. She knew the women that were there were capable of handling the background vocals. Soon, the last three ladies walked in, offering their apologies. Jean, one of the sopranos told Marva that Reginald had called and said he wasn't sure if he was going to make it because of some personal problem he was experiencing. Marva's heart dropped. She hung her head down and the other ladies consoled her.

"What do you want us to do, Marva? We'll still sing with you or if you want to sing it alone, we'll understand. I know that you were depending on Reggie but you can do this. You have a wonderful voice and they will still love to hear you sing."

"But we've worked so hard!"

"That's right, and that's why you should still go out there."

"No, I'm not going out there, they'll only laugh. I'm sorry you ladies came all the way here and wasted time practicing and all."

"Marva, we are your friends, your choir family. We will…" Before the young lady could finish, the announcement was made.

"Next ladies and gentlemen, we have a selection from Marva and the Spirit of Peace Singers. They will be singing 'Amazing Grace'."

Marva could hear her parents in front clapping loudly. The choir ladies looked at Marva in anticipation. Marva looked down at the floor then at the ladies. "Well, aint no need of wastin' all those nice outfits, what the heck let's do it."

Marva and the ladies stepped out onto the stage. She could still hear her parents clapping and a few of her classmates in the back of the auditorium yelling remarks. "Reverend Marva" was shouted by several of the boys in the back. Marva stepped up to the microphone and announced that she would be singing a different song with the group and that it would be sung without piano accompaniment. She then looked down at her father and smiled. He nodded and she stepped back.

The background singers began singing the introduction of the song just as they had rehearsed. It sounded beautiful. Marva stepped up and began singing the first verse of the song. The auditorium became dead silent. Her voice floated through the auditorium piercing each person's soul one by one. Marva could hear faint whispers behind her but paid them no mind as she was deep into song.

"Woman please, get out of my way," the voice whispered.

By the time the background singers began singing the first note of the chorus of the song, they were joined by beautiful piano playing. Marva looked behind her and there, sitting behind the piano, was Reginald rocking and shaking his head. It was a different kind of rocking than she was used to. He was perspiring heavily and gritting his teeth tightly together but he continued to play beautifully. The sound that the group emitted was unbelievable.

After the song ended, the audience stood and applauded. Marva and the group walked off the stage but the audience remained standing and clapping loudly. It was like the roar of thunder and it was truly incredible. Once backstage, Marva walked over to Reginald who was still pretty twitchy and unsettled.

"I thought that you weren't going to make it," Marva said.

Reginald looked at her and forced out a smile as his perspiration flowed heavily. "I didn't think that I was going to make it either."

"Are you alright? You don't look so good."

"No, I feel awful. I ate a fish sandwich from Miss Dee's Fish Shack this morning and it's been swimmin' through me all day. I'm clenching as we speak. I was prayin' that I didn't lose myself while playin'. Where's the bathroom around here anyway? I think the remainder of that catfish is trying to swim downstream."

Marva pointed in the direction of the bathroom. Reginald nodded and turned to rush off but not before the high pitched squeaking sound carried through the air from his bottom. Reginald rushed toward the boy's bathroom but the catfish, butter bean, and old potato salad smell remained behind for all to smell. This was just a prelude to what the boy's bathroom was about to endure. Everyone quickly grabbed their things, wiped their watering eyes as they evacuated from the flatulence to the opposite side of the stage. There they watched the remaining acts who were gagging and covering their faces.

The other acts that followed were no match for Marva and the group. The stand up comedian wasn't very funny, the majorette dropped her baton and three of the other groups all sang the same song and sang it poorly at best. Needless to say, Marva and her group were the winners of the contest. Marva was presented with a shiny trophy which she held high and proud, for all to see.

For the remaining of the school year, Marva was treated as a celebrity, but still no one asked her to prom.

The following Sunday during the morning service, Marva's father acknowledged Marva and the group and announced their victory at the talent contest. Marva presented the trophy to the church and explained that it was God's victory and how she couldn't have done it without the assistance of the choir and Reginald. As she spoke to the congregation, Marva noticed that several of her classmates were sitting throughout the church and she acknowledged them. It seems they were so moved by the group's singing, that they wanted more and decided to visit Marva's church.

She was so proud to have been used as an instrument of God's and to have touched people with her singing. Deacon Burgess's son, who had just returned home for school break from Wilberforce University, stepped up to congratulate Marva and the group.

"I heard you guys lit that auditorium up!" he said as he shook her hand. Marva just smiled. The deacon's son then leaned in closer and whispered in Marva's ear. "Do you have a second after the service? I need to talk to you about something, if you don't mind."

Marva revved back, "Well, I guess so."

"Ok, I'll meet you out front after the service."

The congregation continued carrying on about the talent contest for a while longer. After Mrs. Florence read the announcements, the pastor gave the benediction and made his way down to the door. Marva did as she did every Sunday, stopped and spoke with her father briefly and then headed down the steps and waited for her mother. As she lowered herself from the last tread of the stairs, she was met by the awaiting young man.

"Hey Marva."

"Hello Richard, you wanted to see me?"

"Yes, I wanted to congratulate you on the talent contest."

"Well, I believe you already did that inside, Richard."

"Well yes, I guess I did. I, uh… also wanted to see how you've been. I mean, I haven't seen you since I left for school and here you are getting ready to graduate. You had the talent contest and now your prom's coming up."

"Well, that's another story."

"You are going to prom aren't you?"

"I don't know."

"You have been asked haven't you?"

"Well no, no I haven't."

"How could anybody not want to take someone as pretty as you to prom? Well since no one has asked you, how would you like to go with me?"

"With you?"

"Yes, with me. I always thought you were attractive, Marva. I was just afraid to say anything because of your father but you're all grown up now and it's time I let you know how I feel about you. I'm hopin' that the prom will be just the beginning."

"Why Richard Burgess, are you asking me to go steady with you?"

"That's exactly what I'm asking you, Marva. I've waited to ask you that for a long time, so how about it?"

"Well you know my daddy won't approve but I won't tell if you don't," Marva said laughing.

"Marva, come on girl it's time to go," her mother yelled.

On the way home, Marva told her mother that Richard had asked her to the prom. Her mother immediately started discussions on her dress and shoes and how to conduct herself. Her father was happy to hear that it was Richard who had asked Marva, one of his own deacon's sons in the church. Richard was trustworthy and knew how to conduct himself; he would know how to treat his little girl.

After graduation, Marva took a job as a switchboard operator for the phone company while Richard continued school. Upon Richard's return from school for summer break, he and Marva married. Richard then showed Marva's father just how well he could treat his daughter. Marva had produced two children and Marva was again with child by the time Richard had graduated from school. Shortly after graduation, Richard took a job as a draftsman for a large architect firm which paid him a decent salary and soon after, moved his family just three blocks away from Marva's parents. Their new home was still close enough to Marva's father's church where they still attended. Richard, like his father, also became a deacon of the church.

Richard and Marva raised their children in a Christian home and always showed them and each other so much love. Marva did most of the raising while Richard spent most of his time at the office. The children grew up and each of them graduated from college. It was not long before Richard and Marva were empty nesters. Richard still worked late most nights on his job and even worked some Sundays. Marva was alone most of the time now and spent most of her time at the church and at choir rehearsal. She still loved to sing.

One evening after choir rehearsal, Reginald asked Marva to stay to work on a solo for a song that he had written. Marva agreed and the two practiced together for over an hour.

"Wow, where did the time go?" Marva asked.

"I know… time moves so fast when you're doing something that you love," Reginald responded.

"This is a fine song Reggie and I'm glad you trust me to sing the lead on it."

"Marva, we've been singing and playing together for over twenty five years and you've always had the prettiest voice in the choir."

"Twenty five years, that's a long time. We've been through a lot together Reggie."

"Yep, your marriage and kids, my marriages and divorces, yep a lot has happened over those years. I remember the time when I almost lost my bowels at the talent contest and you never mentioned a word of it to anybody," Reginald chuckled.

"You've always been a true friend Reggie."

"Up until now, Marva."

"What do you mean up until now?"

"Marva, I would feel less of a friend if I didn't tell you this. It's something that has been weighing on my heart for a while now and I've got to get it off my chest before I bust."

"What Reggie? What is it?"

"Marva, it's Richard. I'm not sure what he tells you or where he says he's been going or doing but I got a new gig down at Ray's Esquire Club. I play down there most nights. Well…uh, I don't really know how to tell you this Marva, but most nights…most nights I see Richard in there."

"Well that's explainable. You see, Richard works late most nights trying to make as much overtime as he can. He probably just goes in there to get his supper that's all. I know it's not the best place for a deacon to the church to be in, but he's a strong man."

"Why would he go there for supper?"

"It's probably close to his job."

"No, it's all the way across town."

"He probably just likes the food there. I'm sure it's nothing."

"Marva, you don't understand, when he comes there…he doesn't come alone."

"See, there you have it. One of his coworkers probably likes the food there or knows the owner."

"Well if she's a coworker, they work really close together because you can hardly see a crease between the two while they're in there. And I don't think I've ever kissed any of my band members on the lips."

Marva froze. She looked down at the floor then back over at Reginald, "She?"

"That's what I've been trying to tell you, Honey. I play down there tonight and if he comes in, I'll make sure that he sees me this time. He's been so into his friend that he hasn't even noticed that I'm the piano player up there watching his every move."

"No, you don't have to do that. I'll deal with this tomorrow night. Thanks for telling me this Reggie. It hurts but I'm glad you told me this. Twenty four years of marriage I've given this man. Twenty four years and three children and this is what I get in return. God don't like ugly, Reggie. He doesn't like it one bit. I'm gonna go home and pray for my husband and pray for myself, too. I'm gonna pray that I don't kill him!"

That night, Reginald played at the Esquire Club and as always, Richard walked in escorted by the same young lady. After the band's first set was done, Reginald stepped to the front of the stage and spoke into the microphone.

"Alright ladies and gentlemen, we're gonna take a short break so in the meantime enjoy your food. Is everybody having a good time?" he yelled into the microphone.

The ladies waved their napkins and the men held up their drinks and yelled in acknowledgment. Just then, Reginald saw Marva walk up the stairs and out of the door. She looked back at him and then lowered her head before rushing out. As Marva exited, Reginald focused on the table where Richard and his date sat. He made direct eye contact with Richard which caused Richard's smile to drop to the floor. His eyes grew larger as he recognized the pianist from his church. Reginald quickly walked off the stage and walked over and took his seat at the band table.

Richard rushed right over. "A ha-ha Reginald, it's funny to see you here, no wonder the music sounds extra good tonight."

"It's even funnier to see you here Deacon Burgess!"

"Oh, well, I just came down with a couple of my coworkers to get some supper. I was just leaving."

"Oh you're not going to hang around for the next set like you normally do?"

"Huh? How long have you been playing here anyway?"

"Long enough I guess. About two months."

"Does Marva know that you've seen me down here?"

"Well I didn't think that you were sneaking down here, so I might have mentioned seeing you here in passing. I'm not sure."

"Oh my God, she's gonna kill me."

"For what…coming all the way across town to get some supper with a coworker? Why would she kill you for that?"

Richard rushed off. He yanked the young lady by the arm, dropped some money on the table and they both hurried out of the club.

Later that night, Richard slowly opened the door to his home. Marva was not in the living room waiting up as she normally was. He looked all over the house for her until he finally stepped into the bedroom where he found his wife sound asleep. She had cried herself to sleep. Richard carefully slid off his shoes and then the remaining pieces of clothing. He slipped into his pajamas and eased into bed next to his wife. He couldn't sleep. The fact that Marva might know what he's been doing left him wide awake and staring at the ceiling. Marva lay breathing deeply as she slept in an unconscious state. After hours of staring, Richard finally fell into a deep sleep.

The next morning, Richard was awakened by the bright sunlight peering through the sheer curtains of the bedroom window. He shielded his eyes as he reached for Marva. She was not there next to him. He felt around for the sheet which covered him during the night which somehow had been removed. He could smell the eye opening aroma of bacon, eggs, and coffee and he began to smile, realizing that Marva had not known about his secret night life. Just as he was about to climb out of bed, he realized that there was something wrong. Not only was the sheet missing, but his pajama top was unbuttoned and pushed wide open and his pajamas bottoms had been removed. He then saw the dark shadow hovering over him.

"Good morning Marva, what are you doing Dear?"

"I just wanted to know if you were ready for your breakfast."

"Uh sure, what are we having? Whatever it is sure smells good."

"Well I'm having eggs, bacon, grits, toast and coffee and you're just having grits!"

Just as Richard began to sit up, Marva dumped an entire pot of grits all over his body. The neighbors could hear him screaming for blocks. Richard jumped up and ran into the front yard where there he passed out. One of the neighbors called the ambulance. He was taken to the hospital and Marva did not go with him.

Richard never returned home. He and Marva divorced shortly after and only saw each other during special occasions with their children. Richard eventually married the young lady that he had cheated on Marva with. Soon after their marriage, she left him for another man. Marva forgave Richard but could never forget how selfish he had become. She knew in her heart that she could never trust him again.

The following years weren't kind to Marva. Both of her parents were called home to glory and Richard soon followed. He had drank himself to death. Richard Junior now living in Fayetteville, North Carolina, asked Marva to join him and his family. Marva accepted. She sold her home and took the long train ride from Chicago to Fayetteville. She stayed with her son for only a few months before moving out on her own. She joined the church near her new home and enjoyed the services. She became very active in her new church home and enjoyed the company of her new friends.

Years passed and Marva was climbing the age ladder much faster than she wanted. It was getting harder to get around and she was becoming more forgetful. She required more frequent visits from her son. Still feeling pretty independent, Marva continued cooking her own meals, catching the bus and walking to church. One morning while getting ready for church, Marva took a bad spill in the kitchen. She was unable to get up and had bacon cooking on the stove.

The bacon burned and soon smoke filled the entire kitchen. She tried crawling but her shaking arms could not endure the task. Marva began coughing then gagging from the smoke. She knew that this would be the end for her. The smoke detector screamed but there was no one in the house to help her. Suddenly, the back door of her home was forced open. It was the young man from next door. He lifted Marva from the floor and placed her outside on the front porch. He rushed back inside and removed the frying pan from the flame and turned off the stove. The ambulance quickly arrived and Marva was rushed to the hospital.

After spending weeks in the hospital for a broken hip, Marva was transferred to the Hayfield Streams Retirement and Rehabilitation Facility to complete her recovery. There, she made new friends and enjoyed the company of the staff. Her ordeal had frightened her so much that she decided to sell her house and become a permanent resident at Hayfield.

Chapter 4 - The Gathering

"Now what in the hell is this supposed to be?" Viola asked Betty, the aide, as she put the steaming plate before her.

This was a daily ritual before each meal. Betty would place each lady's tray in front of them and they would sniff and examine each item on the tray before questioning their meal.

"I'm talkin' to you woman, what in the hell is this green crap layin' up against these things that look like eggs?" Viola asked again angrily.

Betty looked at the small, elderly woman and smiled, "Miss Viola, we go through this everyday and my answer is always the same. If you have any questions about your meal, you have to take them up with Al. You know that."

"Well, get fat boy out here 'cause this looks like something that'll make you lose your hair and I can't afford to lose no more hair!"

"Ok Miss Viola, I'll send him out, but in the meantime, why don't you eat some of your toast and maybe have some coffee."

"What's he done to that? I can only imagine. Now this is just bread that you stick in a metal box and push down a handle so why in the hell is one side black and hard and the other side soft and mushy? How in the world can you screw up toast? I tell you, the man can't boil water."

Betty walked away chuckling with the ladies' empty trays. Viola started mixing her coffee with the contents of the little pink packets lying next to her cup. Marva finished blessing the food then started in on her eggs. Rose sat chewing and staring at Viola.

"Well, what is your problem this morning?" Viola asked.

Rose continued chewing until she was able to swallow the contents in her mouth. "That's fried potatoes next to your eggs; they're good, too. I'll eat yours if you don't want them," Rose said while scooping up another fork full of food.

"I bet you would, Woman. You're probably the only person in this building who actually likes this fool's cooking and speaking of fools…"

Al the cook, as always, jiggled through the rows of tables with a bright smile on his face. This heavyset man was always seen with his black, wooly hair covered with a thin hairnet, a toothpick between the wide gap between his front teeth, and was always jolly. He was a fellow who seemed to never be in a bad mood, although criticized and questioned about his cooking ability daily. He bounced up to the small square table where the three ladies sat. "Ok Miss Viola, what is the problem today?" Al asked while smiling.

"Well big boy, it looks like to me and it could just be me, I don't know, but I've been tryin' to figure out what this is right here smellin' like old dog ass." Viola began picking at the green and brown pile lying next to her eggs.

"Why Miss Viola, I'm surprised you don't know what that is. You know, you ask me that every time I prepare them for you. That there is fried potatoes with onions and green peppers blended in. Taste 'em, go on, taste 'em. I bet you'll like 'em. I added in a little secret ingredient of my own to give 'em a little pow!"

"Well, it don't look much like potatoes, looks more like you pulled out some of the shit from that shit eatin' grin you've got there and plopped it on my plate. Is that your secret ingredient? Uh uh, not me, I aint eatin' this mess."

"I'll eat it if you don't want it," Rose said excitedly.

"You would," said Viola.

Viola pushed her plate over to Rose who quickly scooped the clump of potatoes onto her plate. She started devouring the starchy substance and Viola looked on, shaking her head.

"See Miss Viola, you're missing a treat. The potatoes are very good. You should taste 'em next time," Al said.

"They sure are Vy. They are wonderful. I don't know what your secret ingredient is Al, but I like it!" Rose joined in.

Viola looked at Al, "Get away from me," then over at Rose, "Rose, please! You'd eat the crack out of a pig's ass, so I can't trust what you have to say about anything that this fool cooks. Just don't come cryin' to me when he poisons you. And hell no, I won't give you 'CPR' 'cause I don't know what's been in your mouth! I declare, woman, you'll eat anything!"

Marva looked up at Viola, "Vy, come on now you're just being mean. You know God don't like ugly."

"So you're sayin' God don't like Al?"

"No, you know that's not what I'm saying. You see? That's what I'm talkin' about, that's just ugly," Marva replied.

"Look at this crap he calls breakfast. Somebody told that boy that he could cook. That proves it!"

"That proves what?" Marva asked.

"That proves what I've been sayin' all along."

"What?"

"For Al, cookin' is like masturbation…it's somethin' that he enjoys doing alone and the only person that gets any satisfaction or enjoyment out of it is his sorry ass!"

"Keep on here; you'd better watch who you talk about, especially if it's somebody who prepares your food. Go on, keep it up and you might be the one poisoned…on purpose!"

"But what I'm sayin' is true. Look at him walkin' around here like he just emptied himself into one of those big pots back there and now's ready for a cigarette. He probably did, back there in that kitchen where nobody else can see. That's what's probably in those potatoes tastin' so good to Rose, ha! Hey Rose, I think I just figured out Al's secret ingredient. You might want to go get some mouthwash and a pregnancy test."

Marva dropped her fork on her plate. "Viola, now that's disgusting even for you. You're in need of some serious prayer."

Viola broke out into laughter while pointing at Rose.

It had been over a year since the three ladies met. They had become very good friends. Viola, same as always, never let any words rest on her tongue. Rose still loved her food but could be rather intense herself and Marva, dear sweet Marva, kept the two of them out of trouble most of the time. She was Viola's conscience for sure.

This was part of their every day routine. They would meet in the morning for breakfast where Viola would question her meal. Al would have to stop by the table almost daily to have it out with Viola, just prior to her passing her food over to the awaiting Rose who would always be more than receptive. After breakfast, they would head over to the dayroom where they spent the majority of their day.

They would play cards, talk, enjoy arts and crafts, and even watch television, but most of all, they would amuse themselves just being together. Some days they would spend time in the garden or just lounge on the porch soaking in some sun, but most days were spent in that dayroom laughing, talking, and discussing all types of topics of interest. They really enjoyed each other's company and the time they spent together. Of course, they would have visitors and would return to the dining room for their meals, but they would always manage to end up in the dayroom. It was their meeting place.

The year was 2009. Viola, now eighty six years of age, Rose, a hefty eighty five, and Marva, being the baby of the group, was eighty years young. Although being from very different backgrounds, they had so much in common. For the most part, the ladies were happy, enjoying and living out their golden years amongst new friends. Yes, they had the health issues and handicaps that came with aging, but they hardly ever complained. Marva, dealing with high blood pressure and diabetes, seemed to take it all in stride and never showed any inkling of worry about her health. Rose, who had a hip replacement and being overweight, was often seen rolling and cruising around Hayfield in her motorized wheelchair. Marva was accompanied by a walker since she had severe leg pain and weakness due to her diabetes. Though Viola was the oldest, she was also the most vibrant of the three and watched over her friends as if she were their bodyguard.

This morning was no different than any other morning. Viola was having it out with Al about her runny eggs, Marva was trying to calm her down, and Rose was scooping the eggs from Viola's plate onto hers. After things had calmed down, Rose watched as Betty, their aide, escorted the little lady into the dining room.

She was a small, quiet looking lady and she was wearing some of the most unusual clothing Rose had ever seen. Her feet were covered with flat heeled, red shoes coated with glitter and black fishnet stockings gripped tightly to her thin, little legs. Her skirt hovered about three inches above her knees and her printed blouse was tied together just under her breasts. She wore a bright red wig, which everyone immediately could tell was definitely not her hair, which was tilted over to the right side of her head. Her face had been consumed with a multitude of eye shadow, foundation, lipstick, blush, false eyelashes and in addition, there was an enormous beauty mole penciled onto the side of her cheek. She was truly a sight.

Betty stood in the aisle with the aged Madonna look-alike and scanned the room, searching for a suitable table where the new arrival could be seated.

"Ooh wee, what have we got here?" Rose asked chuckling.

Viola turned and looked over the rim of her glasses. "What in Sam Hill is that? Looks like Dorothy finally found her way back from Oz, huh? My goodness, what was she thinking when she got dressed this morning? Maybe she thought it was Halloween! What a mess!" Viola added.

"What's that the kids say today, she's lookin' a hot mess is more like it," Rose joined in.

"Come on ladies, maybe she just doesn't know any better. It's not like we just stepped out of Vanity Fair magazine ourselves. She's still one of God's children and should be treated as such," Marva said.

"Maybe, but that is just disgustin'. At least she could have ironed the bottom half of her blouse. Look at how wrinkled it is," said Viola.

Rose picked up her eyeglasses and stared at the woman for a few seconds then turned to Viola, "There is no bottom half of her blouse. That's her stomach."

"Then she should have ironed that, too or at least pulled all of that loose skin together and tied that into a knot, too! Who in the hell does she think wants to see that mess this early in the morning? Yuk!" Viola yelled.

The ladies halted with their comments as they noticed Betty pointing to their table. Viola quickly turned and faced her plate mumbling, "I know Betty's not planning on bringing 'Miss Showgirl' over here."

"It looks that way," Rose replied.

Betty took the little lady by the arm and they slowly walked over to the table where the 'Vanity Fair' group sat. "Good morning ladies, I'd like to introduce Miss Lacey. She will be staying with us for a while and I'd like for you all to make her feel comfortable and at home. You can introduce yourselves and get acquainted while I get Miss Lacey's breakfast."

Betty helped the lady into the seat adjacent to Marva and without any hesitation, Marva introduces herself to the new addition to their home. "Hello Miss Lacey and welcome. My name is Marva Thomas and it is very nice to meet you. I hope God blesses your stay here."

The woman smiled meekly and nodded.

Rose soon joined in, "Hi, I'm Rose, welcome."

The woman once again smiled and nodded her head in acceptance of her greeting.

Viola just sat and continued inspecting the lady from head to toe. With a stern look on her face, she took a sip from her cup all the while never taking her eyes off the woman's face.

"Why don't you take a damn picture? It'll last longer!" the woman said.

Viola's mouth flung wide open, "Oh no you didn't! I know you didn't just get smart mouthed with me, Miss Old Hooker!"

"Is that supposed to offend me? Woman, you're so stupid, you don't even know when you're insulting somebody. Spoke the truth is all you've done. I've been around plenty of bitches like you on the block. I'll cut your ass just like I cut theirs so you just keep on talkin' and see what happens."

"Oh, you just turned to the chapter that describes my foot in your raggedy ass. You're not too old to have your ass whipped and I'm just the one to do it. Don't let this gray hair fool you. I'll rip off all that loose skin hanging over the top of your skirt and beat you to death with it!"

"Well bring it on, Hussy! He was wearing a three piece suit and we rode all the way to Atlantic City in that car. Which do you like better, the blue or the red?"

Viola was still trying to push herself away from the table when she realized the words that had just come out of the little woman's mouth made absolutely no sense at all and her facial expression had quickly changed from that of an angry woman, to a cheerful and pleasant one in just a matter of seconds. Viola looked around at the other ladies seated at the table. They, too, were also looking on with expressions of confusion plastered across their faces.

Betty had just returned with Miss Lacey's tray and found each of the three ladies sitting and looking dumbfounded, while Miss Lacey sat smiling and balling up small pieces of napkin.

"I can't believe you sat this cuckoo bird over here with us!?" Viola stated angrily.

"Who you calling a cuckoo bird you Slut? Rainbows are all over the world," Miss Lacey shouted.

"Cuckoo or not, I'm gonna break my foot off in her ass if she keeps runnin' her mouth," Viola grunted.

Betty removed the items off the tray and placed them neatly in front of the woman. "She's not crazy Miss Vy, she's got Dementia and hasn't had her medication yet. Her mind wanders from time to time but she's alright. She'll be better after she's had her meds."

"Well you'd better get 'em to her quick or she'll be needin' an ice pack to bring down the swelling of her eye along with those meds."

"Now Miss Vy, come on, she means no harm. She's really a sweet lady, so don't you be swelling up anything on nobody over here. You're gonna get yourself in trouble."

Betty walked back up to the front of the dining room and the woman began to eat her food.

"Tastes like shit!" she said just after sliding the first forkful into her mouth.

"Well, at least that's one thing we both agree on," Viola chuckled.

The ladies laughed and continued their conversation. The little lady just smiled and ate. She occasionally would join in the conversation but would eventually get off topic, which would cause the other ladies to stare at her and become silent.

"So, Miss Lacey..." Viola started.

"Lizzy, my name is Elizabeth Lacey, but everybody calls me Lizzy."

"INCOMING, GET DOWN! EVERYBODY DOWN!" the man shouted loudly.

Startled, the small woman's head whipped around. She watched as the one legged man in the wheelchair twitched and grimaced.

"Oh, shut the hell up, Arthur! Don't mind him, he always nods off and then wakes up screaming from one of his bad nightmares. He's always having nightmares about planes dropping bombs or grenades going off near him. You know, that war flashback kinda mess," Viola said.

"Oh, did he lose his leg in the war?" Lizzy asked.

"Hell no, he's never been to war or in the service. He's just crazy, that's all, so back to you Lizzy huh? Ok, if that's what you prefer then that's what I'll call you. So Lizzy, what's with the outfit?"

"Oh, these old things? I just like to look nice, you know? Just because we're getting up in age doesn't mean that we have to dress like old biddies! I believe if you still got it then flaunt it."

"MY LEG, WHERE'S MY LEG? JOHNSON, DON'T LEAVE ME HERE TO DIE IN THIS FOX HOLE!"

"ARTHUR!" Viola yelled. "WAKE UP AND SHUT UP! Sorry about that. Now, what were you saying? Oh yeah, flaunting it. Girl, I agree with that to some degree but that outfit that you have on…well, it just reminds me of one of those young girls in one of those rap videos or something. You know, like one of those 'Pop that Coochie' songs. As far as flaunting goes, well, maybe that should be left to the younger generation."

"Girl, I've got to do me. I can't get caught up in this old thing. I don't know if I'll even be alive tomorrow, so I just want to do what I want to do while I still can and if that includes dressing the way other people don't like, then so be it. I haven't said a word about that picnic tablecloth you're wearing. I just figure that's your thing. Some people like converting old drapes or tablecloths into wearing apparel. It looks nice on you, though."

"Wha…tablecloth? Girl, I paid good money for this robe. It keeps me warm and it looks nice and that's all that really matters."

"It's not sexy. It just says· 'Hi, I'm old. I'm old and warm'."

"Well, everybody doesn't think they're seventeen when they're really eighty."

"Yeah, I know I could never wear anything like that," Rose joined in.

Without skipping a beat, Lizzy quickly responded, "No, of course not, your ass is too big. Now, you really do need an old tablecloth or blanket to cover all that flesh."

"Now Lizzy, that's not nice. Rose is very sensitive about her weight," Marva said.

"Nah, uh uh, see that there? That's old fat. That's fat that's been around for a while. Now if that was new fat, I could understand her sensitivity but that fat there is matured fat. Look Rose, what I'm saying is, if you like to eat, you will gain weight and if you don't mind the weight and love to eat then do you. Stop worrying about what other folks are saying; this is your life. Everybody wants everybody else to be just like them. If they're miserable, they want everybody to be miserable. If we do that at any age, we would be lost. Right now we'd all be sitting around at this table wearing ugly but warm tablecloth looking bathrobes. You don't want that for yourself, that's Viola's life and hers alone."

"Amen," added Marva.

"You'd better stop talking about my table.... my damn robe, ya hear?" Viola said pointing at Lizzy.

"I don't really know if you have to have a tail on your kite or not but the grapes taste good," Lizzy's mind wandered off.

The ladies paused for a moment and watched as Lizzy mumbled to herself. She eventually stopped, looked up and smiled before continuing her meal. After realizing that she had just returned to them mentally, the conversation resumed.

"You know Lizzy, I like you. After breakfast we usually go back to our rooms to get dressed and then we meet in the day-room. Do you think you would like to join us?" Rose asked.

Lizzy smiled, "Yeah, that would be nice. I just have to go and feed my dog then get those mice out of my shoes. They just keep nibbling on my ankles, nibble... nibble...nibble is all they do."

"Yeah, Lizzy you do that and don't forget to make sure the nurse gives you all your medication before you come down to the dayroom, Ok?" Viola added.

Rose flipped the switches of her motorized wheelchair and slowly rolled herself away from the table. She waved to the ladies and headed for her room which she shared with Viola. Marva soon followed and then Viola told Lizzy that she would see her in a little while and she too, left for her room.

The dayroom was nice and bright this time of day. The large windows, which spanned the east side of the room, provided plenty of light throughout the day. The ladies always sat right next to the window. The room was always filled with visitors and residents. Mr. Dudley would always come in and play the piano when no one was watching the television. Although he could barely hear what he was playing, he could still read the music from the hymn book and tickle those black and white keys pretty good. It was when he decided to accompany his piano playing with vocal lyrics, that the problems would start. Since he was hard of hearing, he would sing as loud as he could in order to hear himself. He would be extremely off key which in turn, would lead to complaints from the other residents who were present in the dayroom with him.

People sat and read, played cards, and worked on their arts and crafts. The ladies would always sit and talk before undertaking any other activitiy. They'd talk about everything and everybody. They would start their conversation with a 'hello' and it would always take off from there.

Marva was the first of the four to enter the dayroom. With the use of her walker, she shuffled over to their table and eased down into her seat. Betty quickly walked over and asked if she needed anything. She asked for a cup of tea then sat comfortably with her hands folded neatly in her lap. About ten minutes later, Rose slowly rolled herself into the room and up to the table where Marva was sitting. Shortly after Rose's arrival, in walked Lizzy. She had gone back to her room to change. This time, she entered the dayroom wearing some tight fitting spandex pants, flip flops, a low cut dashiki, which revealed a laced push-up bra, her 'Cher Bono' wig, which draped down to the center of her back, and some dark shades. Every head turned and followed her as she strutted down the aisle.

The ladies sat and marveled at their new friend and they could not believe their eyes. She walked up to the table and took a seat. Marva and Rose continued staring until they heard the familiar voice in the distance.

"You've got to be kiddin' me!" It was Viola walking in assisted by her cane. "Don't tell me, you're scheduled to be on 'Soul Train' today, right?" Viola asked jokingly. "I thought I clearly stated that you should make sure you took ALL of your medications before coming down here," she continued.

"I've had my medications for today."

"Then why are you sitting there looking like an eighty pound 'Yoko Ono'?"

"Viola, leave Lizzy alone. She can dress and wear however she wants. She's just being herself that's all," Rose interjected.

"See Rose, that's what I was saying earlier, people who are afraid to step outside of the box will always be the biggest critics of everybody else. Now Viola, from where I sit, your outfit sits somewhere inbetween a cross of 'Pollyanna' and 'Liberace' so you really shouldn't talk so much. All you need is Julie Mills standing behind you holding the candelabra."

"Liberace? How dare you speak ill of Liberace, God rest his soul."

"I'm sorry, you're right, he probably wouldn't be caught dead in that outfit you're wearing. Sorry, Liberace."

Rose and Marva started laughing uncontrollably and were quickly joined by Lizzy, but Viola sat there with a stern look for as long as she could before she too, burst into laughter. "Ok, Ok, wear what you want, I don't care, just don't expect me to have a makeover by you. I'd rather just keep on tucking my boobs down into my slacks is all I'm saying," Viola said, still laughing.

"Whew, could you imagine me cramming all of these into that little bit of fabric that Lizzy's wearing?" Rose said while pushing up on one of her extremely large breasts.

"I don't think anything could contain those things. Sometimes after we get dressed and we're getting ready to come to the dayroom, I can hear Rose's bra screaming. You can only imagine what it goes through. Soon Rose, you're gonna need a wagon to tote those things around. As for now, I recommend an 'Ace bandage' and some duct tape. That's about the only thing that'll keep those things from roaming. I have to admit Rose, when I first met you, I thought you were breast feeding two small midgets with crew cuts before I realized that they were your breasts and the hair from your hair.

The ladies continued to laugh and soon set their sights on other prey to start their discussions. As they panned the room, the door slowly opened and in walked Pete, known to the ladies as "Ashy Pete". He slithered in slowly, followed by Betty who was carrying a tray filled with cups of hot tea for the ladies.

"Just once I'd like to see him put some lotion on his ashy ass," Viola started.

"I keep telling you he probably does but his skin is really dry and it just absorbs it, we don't know," said Marva.

"The man is part reptile Marva, that's all that's to it. Look at him, his lips even point at the ends like a crocodile. I tell you, the man is just going to flake away one of these days," Rose said as she frowned up her nose.

"Maybe we should knock him down and just lick him all over. You know, give him a saliva moisturizer," said Viola.

"I'M NOT LICKING THAT MAN!" shouted Rose laughing.

"Girl, it might just save his life. We could be heroes. Oh, so you'll just let the man dry to death, huh?" Viola continued.

"I've always wondered why he always walks on the back of his shoes, exposing those ashy heels. If my heels looked like that, I'd have them gauzed, taped, and covered with socks and a pair of high ankle boots. They look like they could file the rust off metal, as rough as they are. You know, we had this lotion that we used to use at the hospital for eczema patients. That lotion was thick as molasses. I would put that thick gunk on those patients and it would last for days, can't remember the name of that stuff but that's exactly what 'ole Pete there needs on his rusty behind. I wonder if he's always been that ashy."

"Well if he was, I'm sure as a kid, he stunk at playing hide-n-seek. He'd be the easiest one to find. All you'd have to do is follow the trail of dead skin to his hiding spot."

"Girl, that's just terrible, you two ought to stop talking about Mr. Pete like that, isn't that right, Lizzy? One thing I can say for 'ole Pete, he's always at the church service every Sunday and that makes him more than alright with me," Marva said.

Lizzy looked at Marva through her dark shades then over at Pete, who was just sitting down at the table across from the ladies. She looked over the rim of her shades at Pete then snatched the dark eyewear off her face. "I think he's kinda cute. I like the pretty gray pallor of his skin. I'm sure I could get him good and moisturized. If he had a cape, I bet he could fly then."

The ladies looked at each other realizing that Lizzy had another mental slip. They ignored her statement and continued talking.

Betty had just walked back over to the table. "You ladies alright, you need anything?"

"Yes," Viola answered, "I'd like to have a nice cold beer."

"Miss Viola, you know you can't drink beer," Betty responded.

"Beer, now that's something that reminds me of when I was a young girl. I used to be allergic to beer. It used to swell me up, well, at least that's what I used to think," said Lizzy.

"A young girl, how young?" asked Rose.

"I guess I was about twelve when I first started."

"You drank beer when you were twelve years old?"

"Yeah, I used to drink it all the time when I stayed with the Freeman's. It always made me sick at first."

"What's your story anyway Lizzy, I bet it's a doozy?!" asked Viola.

"No, my life was a pretty simple one. I was born in Waveland, Mississippi back in twenty six. I never knew my mother or my father. They said I was left on the steps of the hospital when I was only a few hours old. I spent most of my early years at the orphanage and was sent to several foster homes as I got a little older. I would go to a foster home and then back to the orphanage so many times that I lost count. This happened so often, I just got used to it and it got so that I didn't mind. I got a chance to meet new people, see how other people lived then go back to my friends at the orphanage for a while. I would learn so many things while I was away and then I'd go back and share them with my friends. I learned what my true talent was when I stayed with the Freemans.

Mr. Freeman was a big man with a big, round, white face. His wife Gertrude, was a skinny, snobby woman who only liked having me there as a conversation piece. She didn't like me much but would always act the part of the loving foster parent whenever they had company over. Mr. Freeman was some sort of salesman. He would work all day and come home late in the evenings, sometimes very late. Well, Mrs. Freeman's mother took ill and she had to go tend to her, her mother that is. That left me and Mr. Freeman to tend to ourselves. He didn't have much time to be lookin' after me with him working so hard and all, so I looked after myself and tried to stay out of the way.

Two weeks had passed and Mrs. Freeman still had not returned home. I could tell this was starting to get to Mr. Freeman by the way he would drink so much every evening. He too, soon grew tired of mashed potatoes and meatloaf which was the only thing I knew how to cook. This one night, while he was sitting there listening to the radio and drinking one of his beers, I asked him if I could have a sip. He told me it wasn't a drink for a child my age then said he guess one sip wouldn't hurt. I took the can and placed it to my lips. I turned the can up and the wonderful taste flowed into my mouth. I was in heaven. I loved the taste. Every evening afterwards, I would ask Mr. Freeman for a sip and he would oblige me.

Three weeks had passed and still Mrs. Freeman had not returned home from her mother's. Mr. Freeman said he was going to ride up to Pas Christian to see her over the weekend. This particular day, he seemed more stressed and somewhat depressed. I asked him what was wrong and he said nothing. As he started in on his first beer, I took his meatloaf and potatoes to him which he pushed aside. I asked him for a sip and he reached over and grabbed an unopened can. He placed the metal can opener against the top of the can and punctured it on opposite sides of the top. He handed the can to me and said 'knock yourself out kid'. I downed the cold, foamy liquid so fast that it made my head spin but still I wanted more and he gave it to me. As we drank, Mr. Freeman finally told me what was bothering him. His sales quota was too low for the month and he thought he was going to get fired. He didn't though. We continued to drink until all of the beer was gone. I was drunk. The room spun and spun. I woke up the next morning in my bed. My head was throbbing and my eyes burned but most of all, my 'giney' was sore and swollen and had been bleeding."

"Whoa Lizzy, what in the hell is a 'giney'?" Viola asked.

"That's what I called it back then. Today it's known as the 'Snapper' or the 'Queen Cat', it's my money maker, come on, you know, my vagina. My pussy was hurting and I didn't know beer did that. Every evening, Mr. Freeman would bring beer home and we would drink it and the same thing would happen every morning. I would wake up with my head and giney hurting but at least there was no more blood. This went on until the day before I went back to the orphanage. It was a Tuesday. Mr. Freeman had come home early, so we had started early. We had quickly gone through twelve beers in no time. As always, I passed out. As I slept, I began to dream about a big dragon trying to lift me and carry me off to its nest to feed me to its babies. I awakened terrified, only to find Mr. Freeman on top of me pumping and sweating. I could feel him inside me thrusting but was too numb to realize how it felt. When he realized that I was awake, he quickly jumped off me and ran into his room. As he rose up, I could see his pecker."

"Oh my," Marva groaned as she covered her mouth with her hand but peered on in interest.

Lizzy continued, "Yeah, his pecker and it was huge. Then I figured out why I was so swollen every morning as he had been pushin' all that into me just about every night. My goodness, I'm surprised I was even able to walk the next day. Apparently he knew he was going to have to knock me out in order to keep me from screaming. He probably got his wife drunk too, because I couldn't imagine anybody in their right state of mind wanting to feel that thing forcing its way into you, but today, that would be a different story. Anyway, I like riding with the top down don't you?"

"Lizzy, what happened after you caught Mr. Freeman on top of you?" Rose asked.

"I told you about that?" Lizzy asked.

"You were just telling us about it."

"Oh yeah, after I caught him on top of me, he ran into his room. I got up and sat on the edge of the bed and placed my hand on my giney hoping to stop the throbbing. After the throbbing had calmed down, I walked to his room and found him there weeping. I approached him slowly. I stood beside him as he sat on the bed looking so ashamed. I placed my hand on his head and gently stroked his hair. He looked at me apologetically then lowered his head once again in shame. I sat down next to him and he turned his head away from me. I gently placed my hand on his chin and turned his face back towards me and looked into his eyes. I took his hand and placed it on my breast while keeping my hand on his. He looked into my eyes deeply then shifted his focus on his hand that was now holding my small but soft tit. I smiled at him and he hesitantly smiled back.

Then I stood up and removed my gown and underwear. I climbed in his bed and lay down. As he stood up I closed my eyes. I could hear him pull his pajama pants off just before crawling into the bed next to me. I told him that I wanted him to do it and that I wanted to know what it felt like. He never said a word. He got up on his knees and spread my legs open. Just before he lowered himself on top of me, I opened my eyes in time to see it again. I was afraid at first but suddenly remembered that he had been doing it to me for so long that surely my giney was used to his massive clump of flesh.

He damned near killed me with that monster he had between his legs. Hell, I kept reaching over to the night stand, praying that a beer would somehow appear there. I made him stop because I couldn't take it and the pain was just too unbearable. He was just too big. That night, Mr. Freeman and I ate meatloaf and drank beer. It seemed kind of strange at first but we both knew this was our little secret and that that was the only way he would be able to have me…passed out cold.

Mr. Freeman would constantly give me money after that and I would accept it. For some reason, I felt as if he should give me money for using me to please himself. I would always hide the money he gave me to save for when I would leave to be on my own.

After many nights of beer drinking and mornings of soreness, Mr. Freeman decided that he wanted to do something nice for me. That day he took me to the zoo. I had ice cream and cotton candy. It was one of the best days I had ever had. That night, after another drinking spree, Mr. Freeman took me back to the room and had his way with me.

I was out cold but apparently Mrs. Freeman made her way home and caught him in mid stroke because the next morning, I woke up with Mrs. Freeman sitting on the side of my bed crying. She kept telling me how sorry she was. I didn't understand. My bags were packed and placed neatly by the front door. She helped me up and helped me get dressed then rushed me downstairs. I could hear her screaming at Mr. Freeman from upstairs. I could hear her telling him about how much damage he had done to me mentally and physically. Shortly after, the car pulled up and I was collected and returned to the orphanage with over fifty dollars and a giney big enough to park a small car in.

After my return to the orphanage, I managed to entice one of the counselors who enjoyed inserting his thick fingers between my legs. Old Mr. Brown, I wonder how he's doin'? You know, birds sing but do they have Adam's apples?"

"Lizzy, stay with us honey, focus, you were talking about Mr. Brown from the orphanage. He used to like to…uh…touch you?" Viola enthused, reminded the woman.

"Oh, did I tell you about Mr. Brown? Yes, he used to like to do more than touch and I would charge that old drunk bastard two dollars each time. One of the boys found out and told a bunch of other boys. One day during lunch, six of them took turns on me in the boy's room. Then they told everybody I was a whore. Shortly after, I was sent to another foster home where I ran away and have been on my own ever since."

"My Lord, how did you survive?" Marva asked.

"With the only thing I had, my body. I was on the street until a young lady took me in at her boarding house. I would clean the rooms and bathroom and whatever else she needed me to do. I would sleep with traveling salesmen and split the money with her. She would get seventy percent, of course. She eventually got three more girls and her boarding house over the years turned into a whorehouse. It was crowded every night, too.

I would sometimes sleep with more than twenty men a day. I was so good at what I did, I would satisfy them all pretty quickly. Some just wanted strange things like for me to beat them or just sit on their laps, but most wanted only to be inside me. I stayed there at that house up until I was eighteen years old and then I moved on. I worked as a prostitute after that. I spent seventeen years on my back, well some of that time was spent on my knees, too, so I guess I should say I spent twelve years of my life peddling pleasure to those lonely and perverted men. Yep, had some good times and some that I would like to just forget. It wasn't an easy job at first. It takes some gettin' used to, having some old, fat slob on top of you sweatin' and pumpin' and smelling like sweat, cigarettes, liquor, and ass!

Then there were those times when a father would bring his son up to the strip to get his cherry popped. That was always fun, quick, but fun. Sometimes, you'd see those boys again and again until they finally found a girlfriend who was willing to let him get in his six humps.

I remember walking up and down that strip day and night. Some nights my feet would be hurtin' so bad I couldn't wait until I had a customer just so I could get off of them. I peddled this hot butt of mine until I was in my thirties but then got out of the business because I was beginning to get beaten up more and more. Once the word would get out that I didn't have a pimp, I would have to move on to another location.

That and getting arrested had taken its toll on me. When I was thirty six, I bought a beauty shop and ran that, then a record shop, and later a barber shop. They made money and kept me out of jail. I sold the shops and bought real estate. I sold all my properties and now I'm here. See, I've lived a pretty simple life."

Lizzy looked around the table and smiled at each lady as they sat with their mouths wide open.

"Afternoon, ladies," Mr. Schneider said as he was slowly wheeled past by the nursing aide.

"Uh, oh hello Mr. Schneider," Rose cordially returned. A similar greeting was delivered by Viola but Marva, still with her mouth opened, continued sitting in shock and staring at Lizzy. Lizzy sat sipping the red cup filled with the hot, brown liquid. She slowly turned her head to acknowledge Mr. Schneider then focused her sights directly to the elderly man's display.

He was sitting with his legs resting comfortably on the footrests of his wheelchair. The print of black snowflakes against the baby blue background of his pajamas became blurry and out of focus as Lizzy's eyes rested on the sight at center stage. Mr. Schneider had no idea his pajama bottoms were unsnapped and pulled opened. Lizzy stared for a few seconds before deciding to make it a conversation piece.

"Oh, Mr. Schneider is it? I'm Lizzy and it's nice to meet you. Today is my first day here, I came in last night. I enjoyed my first breakfast with these ladies today. What a warm reception they gave me at breakfast. Uh, speaking of breakfast, you might want to tuck that away before somebody in here mistakes that thing for a sausage and jams a fork in it."

Mr. Schneider's hearing wasn't very good and most of the time he was without his hearing aid. So what was said to him normally in conversation was almost never interpreted correctly. "Who's Sam Tornick?" the elderly man asked loudly.

"No, I said jam a fork in it!" Lizzy shouted.

"Who's going to jam a fork in her?" he replied as he pointed to his nursing aide.

"No, in not her, in your willy."

"Is who silly, me?"

Lizzy began to laugh. Marva kept her head turned away and Rose chuckled with Lizzy. Viola reached up and tugged gently on the young nursing aide's smock.

"Child, the man's dick is out again, please tuck that thing in. Nobody wants to see that," Viola said boldly.

The young aide stepped around in front of the man's wheelchair. "Oh Mr. Schneider, let me fix your bottoms."

She reached down and began snapping the open fabric together. When she finished, Mr. Schneider looked up at the young lady and thanked her. He was not embarrassed one bit.

He looked over at the ladies and spoke in his hard of hearing shouting voice, "Sorry about that ladies, seems like the Colonel wanted to stand and salute as he passed by the parade. Sorry about that," he was then slowly pushed away by the young aide.

After Mr. Schneider was out of hearing distance, the ladies chuckled.

"The Colonel looked more like a disabled veteran to me," said Viola.

"No, that soldier was missing in action, but I'm sure that I could train it to be all it can be!" said Lizzy.

"You wouldn't, Lizzy! That is just too unbearable to think about. I couldn't bear to look," Marva said blushing.

"Well, I did and all I saw were two flat duffle bags and if there was a soldier in there, he was wounded," Rose grunted out while laughing. "You know, that reminded me of a time when I was working in the doctor's office. I was in the examination room when a man walked in. I took his blood pressure and checked his pulse, that sort of thing. He looked at me strangely the entire time.

When the doctor came in, he pulled the partition over and I stepped around to the other side. I opened the door to leave but realized that I had not taken his temperature which was standard procedure. I walked back over to the table, still outside of the partition, and sat down as I began to jot the information down. The man must have thought I had left out when he heard the door close.

I heard the doctor say 'Well, what seems to be the problem?'. The man hesitantly answered and when he spoke, his voice was shaky and low. He told the doctor that he didn't want to say because he felt a little embarrassed and he knew the doctor would laugh at him. The doctor explained to him that he was a professional and that there was nothing he probably hadn't seen before. The man still was afraid to show or tell the doctor his problem.

Finally, the doctor convinced the man that the only way that he could help him was to show him his ailment. I could hear the man unbuckle his pants and slide them down. The doctor took a deep breath and then another. He then began to snicker and then the snicker became a giggle. 'Wait, I'll have to get my tweezers for this' the doctor said then he burst into laughter. The man said 'See I told you that you would laugh. What happened to all of your professionalism and how you've probably seen everything?'. The doctor stopped laughing. He sat quietly for a moment trying to collect himself. 'I'm sorry' said the doctor, 'but I thought that I had seen everything.

I must admit, that is the smallest penis that I have ever seen but that's Ok we'll fix whatever's wrong here. Ok, what seems to be the problem, what's wrong with your penis?' the doctor asked. I sat quietly waiting to hear what was causing it to rot away or what ridiculous thing that he had done to cause it to shrink. The man remained silent for only a moment then whispered, 'It's swollen.' There was a big commotion and before I knew it, the partition I was sitting behind was knocked over. It seems the doctor was laughing so hard he fell off his stool and onto the floor and his head rammed into the partition, knocking it over. There I was, sitting in the chair with a shocked look on my face. I looked at the patient, he looked at me and I couldn't help myself, I had to. I looked down at his thimble like pecker and couldn't believe my eyes. The doctor was still laughing so loud that the man could do nothing but snatch up his trousers and storm out the door."

"That's terrible Rose," said Marva.

"I know but I couldn't help it."

"I used to love riding in that wagon. We would go so fast. That was a woodpecker feather in that hat, too."

"Lizzy! Lizzy!" Viola yelled.

"Huh?"

"Did you take ALL of your medication?"

"I sure did. Hey, what happened to the old stripper guy? Is the show over? If he had ditched his nurse, I could have massaged his little pecker for him for ten bucks," Lizzy said.

"Lizzy, you really shouldn't talk like that, God IS listening, let's not forget," Marva stated.

"Ok, then $7.50 but that's as low as I'll go. So where did he go, him and his little pecker?" Lizzy whispered, looking up at the ceiling.

"He was wheeled over for his daily Viagra injection," Viola said laughing.

"Viagra, what's that?" Marva asked.

"Girl, haven't you seen those commercials about four hour erections and such?"

"FOUR HOUR ERECTIONS!?" Marva yelled.

"Yes indeed, these men are really trying to kill themselves. My husband only needed a good forty five minutes or so and he would sleep like a baby. Hell, me too, 'cause the man sure knew how to please me."

"Wait," Marva said as she leaned closer to the table, "Your husband would…well you know…he would give it to you for forty five minutes?"

"Oh yeaaaaaaaah, sometimes even longer and if he had been drinkin'…you'd better pack a lunch 'cause he was going to be awhile," Viola said laughing.

"My word."

"Your Richard was quick, was he?"

"Quick isn't the word for it," Marva grunted while frowning. "Huh, all I ever got was three pumps and an apology! It took me longer to toast bread. He would start his pumping and would always ask me if I liked it, by the time I said ye...he was done. He would roll over afterwards talking about give him fifteen minutes to collect himself. His watch must have stopped every time he relieved himself because his fifteen minutes sometimes lasted for days. If I added together the times we had sex in three years, it might come up to forty five minutes. No, make that five years."

"My Ralph would sometimes lose his self if I hugged him too long," Rose joined in, "but if we didn't hug, that man could go all night if I let him. I used to call him 'Choo-Choo-Charlie'."

"But I thought his name was Ralph," Marva said.

"Not in the bedroom it wasn't, it was Charlie. Every time I thought that train had come to its final destination, he'd throw some more coals on that fire and off he went Choo! Choo!" Rose yelled while pumping her hand in the air as if she were pulling the cord to the whistle of a locomotive.

"Well, not that poor excuse of a man that I had," said Marva. "One time, he wanted to do it and at the time I had a bad cold. He just had to have it. He entered me, I sneezed, he started shaking and jerking. I reached over and grabbed my hankie. By the time I turned back over, he was sound asleep. I can't believe that somebody else had the nerve to marry him."

"See Marva, you should have worked some roots on that man of yours," Viola said.

"No Viola, I don't work roots, I pray, and God answered my prayers by getting that two timing dog of a man out of my life."

"Well, I say a strand of his hair along with a little of your pee in his cup would have kept him home."

"That man was not worth any of my pee and if that would have kept him home with me, then no thanks! Is that how you kept your man home all those years?"

"Hell no! I just pumped him every time he thought about it and when we got older, it got easier. Once I was so tired that I went to bed with my pantyhose on. I had been working in the garden all day and then got dressed and went to our neighbor's home for their anniversary party that evening. By the time we had gotten home, I was exhausted.

My husband came in the room and climbed in bed. He was on me so fast and I was so tired that I didn't get a chance to tell him I was still wearing my pantyhose. He started pumping and grinding and before I could say 'Pollyanna' he had blown a gasket. Just after, he rolled over and fell asleep. I reached down and squirmed out of those ripped opened nylons and tossed them in the trash. I looked over at him and he lay there sleeping and smiling. I went into the bathroom and patted my kitty cat down then returned to bed.

The next morning, all he talked about was how tight I was after all those years. After that, I went to bed with pantyhose on every night! Sometimes when I pulled those just sexed pantyhose off my thighs, my kitty would look like uncooked Belgian waffles but that was a small price to pay for tightness!"

All the women chuckled and the chatter went on.

Hours had passed and it was time for lunch. All the ladies, with the exception of Viola, headed for the dining room. She headed back to her room. Shortly after the ladies were seated and settled at their usual table, their trays were brought over to them. Each lady began transferring the plates and eating utensils from their flat, hard, brown plastic trays to the table, making each item more easily accessible. They began making all the necessary adjustments and preparation to their meal. Rose quickly began seasoning and tasting every item on her plate while Lizzy sat quietly, tearing small pieces of her bread from one of the slices and rolling them into tiny little balls and then placing them in straight neat rows in front of her.

Viola entered the dining room minutes later. She walked up to the table, smiled then took her usual seat amongst her friends. Her tray was promptly brought over to her by the aide. As the young lady began removing the items from the tray to place them in front of Viola, she was met with the tiny elderly woman's hand raised in the air shielding her area from the aide's delivery.

She angrily gestured with her hand, sweeping it through the air then grunted, "I don't want that crap, take it back to the garbage pail that it came from!"

The young lady looked at Viola then at the other ladies around the table. Lizzy continued playing with her food, Marva looked at Viola shaking her head but continued eating while Rose was already preparing additional room in front of her to accommodate Viola's food that she knew was soon to be in her posession. The aide remained standing next to Viola, not sure of what to do. Viola turned and looked at the young lady directly in the eye. She clenched her teeth together then continued in her harsh tone.

"You heard me right, take that mess away from me!"

The young aide only smiled and spoke to Viola as calmly as she could, "Now Miss Viola, you know you need to eat something. Come on, just try the soup then."

"I'm not eating that garbage and what is that mess Rose is enjoying so much? It looks like dog shit!"

"Viola! Now that's enough of that language. Some of us ARE trying to eat here. We don't need to be reminded how bad it is. We get it, Ok?" Marva interjected.

Rose lifted her head for only a brief second to comment. "I don't know what she's complaining about, this is good," then quickly dove back into her lasagna.

"Woman, you'd chew off the side of a monkey's ass if you thought it was tender enough!" Viola said while directing her attention back to the aide.

"Viola!" Marva shouted.

"Ok, Ok."

The aide lifted the soup bowl from the tray in another attempt to get Viola to eat. "Miss Viola, this is good for you, come on, just try a little."

Viola grabbed the large spoon from the tray and placed it close to her mouth. She spoke into the spoon as if it were a microphone. She tapped on the top of the metal spoon then placed her mouth as close to it as she could without the cold metal touching her lips.

"I do not want the soup… I repeat… I do not want the soup or anything else on that tray…thank you…over and out!"

The aide chuckled for a second then placed the bowl in front of Viola. "Ok Miss Vy, just eat the soup and I'll leave the crackers, too. You're so crazy."

"Helloooooo, did you not hear me? Is this thing not working?" Viola began tapping the spoon on the table again then placed it back in front of her mouth with the back of the spoon facing her then began to speak into the spoon. "Testing… testing….1...2...3. Is this thing on?"

Viola looked over at Lizzy who was looking back at her smiling. Viola passed the large soup spoon over to Lizzy, "Lizzy, do you know how to work this thing? Maybe I'm doing something wrong because apparently she's not hearing me. Can you please check that microphone out? Maybe you can get it to work."

Lizzy looked at Viola strangely at first then began smiling again. She accepted the spoon from her friend then slowly placed the spoon up to her mouth and began speaking into it, "Testicles, testicles 1...2..3… testicles, testicles, 1..2..3..4.."

"THAT'S TESTING!" Marva yelled out. "It's testing 1…2…3. That's disgusting!" she continued.

Lizzy looked at her new friend and smiled. She nodded in compromise then calmly spoke into the spoon, "Testing testicles 1...2...3, testing testicles 1...2…3...4."

"I'm going to pray for you woman, and I am going to pray hard. I'm going to ask the Lord to send you some sense."

"While you're at it, can you ask Him to send me a pony, too? No, can you ask Him for a pony with a saddle? No, wait… make that a pony with a saddle with his own groomer. Okay, I know what I want. Can you make that a pony with a saddle with his own groomer who has some nice testicles and maybe a nice pecker to boot? Wheeeeew, all this talk about testicles and peckers has made me hungry! Let's see, what kind of meat are we having today?" Finally, Lizzy stopped playing with her food and started eating it.

"Disgusting, that's what you are, just disgusting. You shouldn't play with the Lord like that,Woman. Don't you have any religion at all?" Marva asked.

"Why yes I do. I read the bible."

"Well, it would seem you would have gotten something out of it."

"I did. I use to get all of my numbers from the bible. I use to open it up and place my finger on a page and play the chapter and verse, Girl. I used to hit quite often, too. Oh yeah, made me a believer! I hit with John 3:16 I don't know how many times."

"Blasphemy! Just blasphemy! Never mind, Lizzy, just let me bless the food, somebody has to," Marva said shaking her head.

"I'll say grace. I'll say it for all of us."

"You're gonna say grace?" Marva asked.

"If you don't mind?"

"Please, by all means."

Lizzy lowered her head, followed by Marva and Rose. Viola kept her focus on the aide whom she was ready to tear into but paused momentarily for Lizzy's prayer. Lizzy started with her prayer;

"*Dear Lord, please bless this food which we are about to eat. We are lucky to have this food 'cause old man Jed, he barely kept his family fed and then one day he was shootin' for some food and to the republic for which it stands, one nation under God…AND THE ROCKETS RED GLARE…*"

"Lizzy, enough! Thank you, that was a wonderful prayer!" Marva shouted

"Amen," Lizzy mumbled.

"Yes, Amen," Marva said while looking down and shaking her head.

"I'm gonna beat your ass if you don't get this soup from out of my face!" Viola groaned at the still persistent aide.

"Ladies please, Miss Marva, can't you help me talk some sense into your friend over here?" the young aide interrupted.

Marva looked at the young lady with her eyebrows wrinkled up and frowning, "What could I say to Vy to change her mind? That's like asking a mountain to move. Baby, you're on your own. All I can do is continue to pray for her."

"That's right," Rose added, "that would be like asking a dog to stop licking himself."

"I know you didn't just call me a dog, Rose, and Miss, you really need to get out of my face with that tray!" Viola started again.

As Viola continued to argue with the aide, the large, glass filled, double doors leading into the dining room were forcefully pushed open. Everyone's attention now focused in the direction of the large woman storming into the room.

"Miss Viola!"

Viola looked over her left shoulder. Standing behind her was the administrator, Miss Hamilton. She stood there clutching a small, brown paper bag.

"Viola, how many times do I have to tell you, NO FOOD DELIVERIES?"

"Oh, is that my sandwich? It took them long enough. See young lady? I have my food so take that tray out of my face, please."

"Viola, you know the rules. All your meals are provided here. For the last time, do not place any more food orders and have them delivered here. They will no longer be accepted or paid for by the front desk. The money that was paid for this WILL be deducted from your account, so when you're finished here, please come sign for the deduction."

Viola shrugged her shoulders, "I don't care what you deduct. It's not like I'm saving up for a cruise around the world or anything. Let me ask you this, since you're so quick to judge, do you eat the food here?"

"What's that got to do with anything, Viola?"

"It has everything to do with it, so just answer the question. Do you or do you not eat the food here?"

"Well no, no I don't. The food prepared here is for the residents only, not the staff and besides, I bring my lunch everyday."

"So you have no idea what this slop tastes like, huh? You see that stuff there on Lizzy's plate and around Rose's mouth? They're calling that lasagna. Now, look at it and think about what that must taste like. It looks like mashed spam and armpit hair jammed between two pieces of construction paper, now doesn't it?"

Miss Hamilton said nothing. She looked strangely at Viola, then at the steaming glob of meat and noodles on the tray. She frowned up her face before a slight shiver had taken over her body then handed the brown sack to Viola's eagerly awaiting hands. As Viola began ripping open the bag, Rose reached over and accepted Viola's tray from the young aide.

"I'll just hold on to that; just in case she's still hungry. That sandwich might not be enough for her, you know. Don't worry I … I mean she won't let it go to waste."

The aide removed each item from the tray and placed them on the table. Rose reached over and slid each plate, bowl, and saucer closer to her reach. Meanwhile, Viola had just begun to bite into her specially prepared deli sandwich. At that moment, everyone at the table was satisfied. Viola was enjoying her sandwich, Rose was enjoying both her and Viola's lunch, Marva was enjoying her meal along with reading her bible, and Lizzy was enjoying the lasagna while she continued to ball up the small pieces of bread. Yes, each lady was in her own world.

"Helloooo ladies, I'm baaaaack," said the thick, feminine voice entering the room. The ladies looked over in the direction from which the voice came, with the exception of Lizzy, of course. She was now sliding her finger through the meat sauce on her plate, pretending that her hand was an ice skater. The ladies knew exactly who it was before they even looked. That voice was unmistakable.

"Oh, you're back. Welcome back, it's nice to see you and I'm glad you're feeling better," said Marva.

It was Simone. He wheeled himself up to the table and as always, he began talking about everybody in the building. He was the chatter box of Hayfield and the president of the gossip committee. Anything you ever wanted to know about anybody in Hayfield, Simone knew even if it were true or not. He rolled up and looked around the entire table at the ladies before continuing.

"Girlfriend, you know there hasn't been a hospital built that can hold me. I told those people 'LET ME OUT OF HERE!'" he said as he giggled.

Simone would usually stop by and chat with the ladies on occasion. He'd talk to them about everybody else, and of course, about himself. He'd always tell the same stories about when he was a fashion model and how he used to dance in the theater. He was very different and very flamboyant. From his clothing ensembles up to his wet long lisp, he was just one of the girls. Occasionally providing the ladies with fashion tips and advice on men Simone was a friend to the ladies, except when he was talking to someone else then all of their business would be distributed like an old news flyer.

"What were you in for this time, a hair caught in your throat?" Viola asked jokingly.

"Girl, I should be so lucky. No child, these hemorrhoids again. They flared up and I felt like I was about to explode back there. Girl, this ass was smoking like you wouldn't believe!"

"Hmm, I thought you would like that. You're not use to it being hot and steaming back there?"

"Viola, I don't have time for your smart mouth today, I'm hungry, Girl. What's that you're eating? I need to be eating one of those with a nice merlot."

"Sorry, but you're having nasty lasagna with a nice hot tea, so be gone. You're beginning to breathe a little too hard on my sandwich here. You might spread some of that hemorrhoid disease over here and believe me, if my butt starts hurting I'm coming to see you, so if I were you, I'd be on my way about now."

"Woman, you aint nothin' but the devil! That's Ok, Missy. You keep your little sandwich over there and I'll go see if I can get that hunk of a man, Al, to make me something special," Simone said laughing. "Oh, I see we have a new addition to the little group. Hi honey, I'm Simone, Simone Deveraux and you are?"

"Don't let that puppy lick you in the mouth 'cause the wheels on the bus go round and round," Lizzy mumbled.

Simone gently placed his hand against the soft, silk fabric which covered his chest and gasped. He lowered his head then carefully began tucking his ascot neatly into the collar of the colorful shirt.

"Oh my word, Honey, somebody done drained the milk from her frosted flakes, haven't they? And what's with that ensemble she's wearing? Who gave her permission to dress herself? I guess she doesn't think anyone here believes that's she's a true red head. Who in the hell is she trying to be, Lucille Ball?"

"Stop it Simone, that's not nice. She just goes in and out sometimes, that's all. Lizzy!" Marva yelled.

"Goes in and out of what…'The Twilight Zone'?" said Simone.

"Is this fake Liberace talking about me?" Lizzy asked calmly.

"Didn't I tell you to stop bad mouthing Liberace?!" Viola interjected.

"Well, Honey you seemed to be talking out of your head for a moment there, Girlfriend," Simone answered defensively.

"So, tell me what's better, to talk out of your head or your ass!? You don't know me so don't act like you do…and I'm not your girlfriend. Mess around and find yourself being choked with that damned ascot!"

"Oh no you didn't! You bring it if you think you can! You'll wake up with your makeup on the way it should be! If you're feeling froggy, Girlfriend, you come on and leap right on over here, come on, bust a move!"

"Calm down, calm down you two…" said Marva.

"Yeah, calm down ladies," Viola said laughing hysterically.

Marva pointed over at Simone. "Simone, now you started this mess saying all those ugly things about Lizzy. Now don't you think you owe her an apology? Sure you do, now go on."

Simone looked Lizzy up and down then apologized to her, although he really didn't mean it. Lizzy looked at him apologetically, too, then started singing the lyrics to 'The Beverly Hillbillies'." with that, Simone just shook his head and wheeled himself to his table mumbling, "The bitch is craaaaaaazy."

After lunch, the ladies returned to the dayroom, all but Lizzy. She had gone back to her room to change and freshen up her makeup. Viola's son, Cecil, stopped by and chatted with the ladies as he usually did at least twice a week. They would sit around the table and he would tell the other ladies a different story about his mother's escapades during her younger days. The stories were always so entertaining and funny. Viola would always sit solemnly, listening and barking at her son to be quiet. He would only stop momentarily then rub her arm gently before he continued. Sometimes, even the aides would come over and listen to some of Viola's old antics and insert their comments between episodes. They'd yell out "She hasn't changed a bit has she", or "She still does that today." Cecil would only smile at his mother while she waved her fist at the aides.

Forty five minutes had passed before Lizzy made her way back to the dayroom. She walked through the door and as usual, every head turned. Lizzy strutted into the dayroom dressed in some tight, cut-off denim shorts, this time adorned with red fishnet stockings. The stockings were worn in reverse as she had the thick seam running up the front of her legs. The sweater she had on was also very tight and the top three buttons were undone to expose her two huge balloons resembling breasts. Some of the men stared while most of the women just shook their heads as she strode by, stuffing dollar bills deep into her pushup brassier.

"Oh my goodness, I guess I'm still not quite used to Lizzy's outfits yet," said Rose.

Cecil looked over and said, "Is that a friend of yours, Mom?"

"No comment," replied Viola.

"Ah come on ladies, remember the woman that Jesus saved from being stoned? Jesus didn't turn his back on her and we're definitely not any better than he. He simply told her to go on and sin no more," Marva joined in.

Viola looked over at Marva with her lips tightly pressed together and twisted to one side of her face. "Child, if Jesus had walked up on that woman and she was dressed like that, he probably would have hit her with a few rocks himself! That woman's walking around here dressed like she's still looking for her lost mind!"

Lizzy bounced up to the table and stopped after seeing Cecil sitting next to his mother. She smiled at him then looked over at Viola. "He's cute, Viola. Is this your husband?"

"What, my husband? Pump your brakes Lizzy Lou, this is my son, Cecil," Viola replied.

"He's very handsome. Hi, I'm Lizzy, and just in case you're interested, I'm available."

"Woman, you'd better get out of here with that mess. Right now the only thing you should be available for is shock treatment! My son is not thinking about some old, crazy woman tryin' to give him the cooties, so don't even think about it!"

Lizzy smiled and responded just as expected, "You know, the rooster crows seven days a week, that's every day!"

"I rest my case," said Viola.

The ladies sat, talked and listened to Cecil's stories about his mom before he left. The rest of the day was pretty much the same. The ladies continued talking and playing cards until it was time for dinner. They all went back to the dining room to eat where once again, Viola argued with Al about the food he had prepared. She had managed to make it through dinner but asked one of the aides to send him over after she had taken one glance at her dessert. Al approached the ladies' table, smiling as he always did. The other ladies looked at him apologetically and Viola started in on him.

"What is this brick with this white goop on it, Al?"

Al looked down at the small cube on Viola's plate. "Miss Vy, that there is my special butter cake with vanilla icing. Try it, you'll love it."

"Like most things you cook around here, this looks like crap."

"Miss Vy, I made that cake from scratch," Al said chuckling.

"From scratch? I bet you did just that, Al. I bet you used that nasty looking little fingernail right there to scratch the top open off the cake mix box, you lyin' sack of shit! This is box cake if I ever seen one. It even smells like box cake."

Rose scraped the edges of her teeth as she withdrew the metal fork from her mouth, "No Viola, this cake tastes…"

"I know…I know, it tastes great. Everything you slide into that pie hole of yours tastes great," Viola interrupted.

"Oh leave him alone Vy, if he says it's homemade, it's homemade. Why would he lie to you?" Marva joined in.

"Because he wants to poison us!"

"Miss Vy, I'm telling you the truth, it's homemade. If you don't want it then you don't have to eat it but I'm telling you, you're missing out on some good cake," Al said before heading back to the kitchen.

"IT PROBABLY HAS YOUR PUBIC HAIR IN IT!" Viola shouted to the exiting young man.

"Viola, how could you say such a vile and disgusting thing? Actually, why do I even ask why you say these things? I'll just keep on praying for you girl, that's all I can do," Marva said.

The ladies ate their desserts with the exception of Viola, of course, and talked for a while before returning to their rooms where they all received their medications and prepared for bed.

Chapter 5 - The Secret

Several weeks had passed and most days were just like the ones before; breakfast, lunch, and dinner, with the dayroom in between. And this morning was no different than the morning before. The ladies were brought into the dining room and their trays were rushed over as always. Lizzy would walk into the room wearing one of her crazy outfits, and displaying one part of her body or another. There was conversation and threats of reporting her to the fashion police, whom she thought was an actual law enforcement agency. Lizzy would always shout, "They can come and get me if they want to. I've been arrested plenty of times but they won't take me without a fight! Now, who's behind me?"

"Satan's behind you, 'cause woman, you are definitely crazy!" Viola always responded.

This morning as the ladies sat and chatted, an amazing sight made them all freeze. They all stared, and one at a time with the exception of Lizzy, who was scraping the lipstick off her lips and drawing cartoon characters on a napkin, each woman's mouth flung wide open.

He was escorted past the ladies' table. He smiled and waved as he maneuvered himself past the other residents blocking his way.

"Is that?" Viola asked.

"I can't believe it," said Rose.

"You see, miracles happen everyday," Marva added.

It was "Ashy Pete". He walked in fully moisturized. His skin looked silky smooth. There was even a certain glow to him along with the fresh clean scent of cocoa butter. After Pete was seated, Viola waved Betty over to the table. She rushed right over. "Yes Miss Vy, what do you need?" asked the aide.

"I need to know how in the hell y'all got dusty over there to oil up? What did you do? Did you toss him in a bathtub of 'Skin-so-Soft' or something?"

Betty chuckled for a second before answering, "No, we didn't do anything like that. He decided for some reason that he wanted to put on lotion. He even started wearing a little cologne, too but that's a good thing I guess. He's changed quite a bit."

"Maybe he's stressed or tired and possibly began the first phase of N.W.T.T.?"

"N.W.T.T.? I'm not sure I'm familiar with that medical term, Miss Viola. What exactly is N.W.T.T.?"

"Not Wrapped Too Tight! I've been expecting that for quite sometime."

"No, actually he's been sleeping more than usual. For the past few days, he's been taking long naps shortly after lunch. It's a bit different than his usual routine but just the same, it's normal."

"Well, I don't care what it is as long as it keeps his ass moist. I thought the poor man was going to just crackle to pieces at one point. Hopefully, he'll keep this up and you won't have to worry about him slitting his throat by accident with one of those dry-ass arms in his sleep."

"Miss Vy, woman, you are something else!"

Betty returned to one of the residents and the ladies began to eat. "Ummmm, these grits sure are good," Rose said.

Viola peered at her heavyset friend from over the top of her eyeglasses, "Rose, you are the ONLY person I know who can eat grits with some green indescribable nastiness in them and still say that they're good. Do you really have taste buds or are you just fooling us all? You just eat for recreation, don't you?" Viola asked laughing.

"Oh Vy, leave Rose alone. Even Jesus ate as He traveled, spreading the gospel," Marva added.

"Child please, if Jesus ate like Rose, the only thing He would have been spreading was some butter over every loaf of bread He could find! The shortest scripture would have been in the book of Grub, chapter 4, verse 13. It would have read, 'Ate'. Now go on 'cause I aint tryin' to hear no word today."

"The word is something that you can always use. The word says that man can't live by bread alone. Rose gets her daily word every morning."

"LOOK AT HER MARVA! Surely you don't think the word has done all that to that woman sitting there. Oh no, that was assisted by pork chops, green grits, and some more stuff. I'm not sure how much 'word' was in the mix but I'll bet you a dollar to a donut that it wasn't much. That's ribs plus the word plus two more steaks and potatoes. Oh no, aint no word done that to that woman. Rose only needs one word and one word only and that's 'DIET'!"

Rose waved her hand at Viola in a gesture to let her know she wasn't paying her any mind.

The ladies completed their meals then returned to their rooms to freshen up and receive their medications before meeting in the dayroom, all with the exception of Marva. Today was Tuesday, one of the days where Marva spent almost all day away from Hayfield. Marva was a renal patient. She had to receive dialysis treatments three times a week. She normally left shortly after breakfast and then would return about four hours later. The treatments would often cause her to feel tired and weak. After her return, if she stopped by the dayroom, she never had much to say. Most days she would just return to her room and sleep.

During Marva's absence, the remaining ladies would continue meeting together and did what they always did, play cards, and talk. The absence of Marva's sermons was always missed by the ladies. They would all stop by and check on their friend upon her return and sit and chat with her until she would doze off before they would return to the dayroom. Whenever any of the ladies had guests, they would always bring them to the dayroom to chat with the other ladies and if Marva was in her room feeling weak and run down, they would insist that their visitor stop in to say hello to her before leaving.

Guests were always a treat and the ladies tried to share them with one another, especially with Lizzy, who never seemed to have anyone drop by to see her. No one ever called; not even a letter was ever delivered for this woman who seemed to have dropped from the sky.

Rose and Viola were sitting at the table when they noticed her. Lizzy walked in wearing her bright yellow jumpsuit with her collar pulled up and a short haired wig. With her lipstick smeared, cramming dollar bills into her brassiere, she rushed over and sat down quickly.

"Oh no you don't, Miss Lizzy. Come on, get up. You're going with me to see the administrator," said the nurse.

"I'm not going anywhere with you," Lizzy replied.

"I can't believe what you've done."

"What, jealous?"

"No, but that is not acceptable behavior here at Hayfield."

"Wait, wait, what's going on here?" Viola asked the nurse.

"It's a matter that Miss Lizzy has to take up with Miss Hamilton. This explains quite a bit, Miss Lizzy."

Lizzy looked over at Viola, "She came in and caught me satisfying Pete."

"What do you mean satisfying him?"

"You know, saaaaatisfying him."

"No, I don't know what you mean by saaaaatisfying him."

"I guess you could say that I was taking care of his manly needs."

"Girl, you mean you've been sleeping with Pete? Wha…Child that's just nasty."

"No, not sleeping with him, he's got a bad back! I would just kiss him in certain places until he was happy. Hell, he'd give me twenty dollars everytime I did it, so what's a girl to do? And twenty bucks just to lap a little saliva on his willy for a few seconds; that's my kind of hustle. Shucks, a girl could make a killing around here."

"No, a girl could DO some killing around here. You know these men's hearts can't take all of that excitement. You been done sucked the life right out of 'em with your nasty ass. Betty, can I get a different colored cup? I don't want ours to get mixed up. You ought to be ashamed of yourself."

"What do you mean by that?"

"Woman, you're not gonna have my lips itchin'. Oh no, you're not gonna have me over here scratchin' my lips all day. Nah, you keep your little, nasty lips right over there. Lordy, I'm glad Marva's not here to hear this; she'd probably drop dead on the floor after hearing this. Why, just the visual alone is enough to stir your bowels in an uproar!"

"Viola, it's a normal need. Pete's not complaining."

"He will when they start shoveling dirt over him. You've been puttin' the man to sleep for half a day, for twenty bucks."

"Come on Miss Lizzy, you need to come with me. I had an idea something like this would happen when Miss Martha told me about the moaning and strange buzzing noises coming from your bed late at night," said the nurse.

Lizzy looked up at the lady once again folded her arms and grunted, "No, and what I do in my bed at night is my business. I have to keep my skin clear somehow."

"Lizzy, get your crazy ass up and go explain yourself. You did the crime and now it's time to pay the fine. And go wake nasty Pete's ass up too 'cause he's just as guilty!"

Lizzy looked at Viola then slowly rose to her feet. She looked at the nurse and said, "Timmy, where's Lassie? The gingerbread is cooking slowly in the oven, watch it while I'm gone."

"Just take her," Viola mumbled to the nurse.

Rose put her cards down on the table and looked at Viola. "Wow, that Lizzy is as crazy as they come."

"Well, she wasn't too crazy, she charged Pete's old, crackly ass twenty bucks a visit!" Viola chuckled.

As Lizzy was being escorted out of the room, Simone was being wheeled through the dayroom doors. He was proudly wearing his shiny, silver silk shirt, some bright, gold and black slacks, a bright gold and silver scarf tied neatly around his neck, knee high sheer stockings, and no shoes. As he was being wheeled past the ladies' table, he motioned the aide to stop.

"Hey ladies, where are they taking your girlfriend, to the office to wait for the psycho wagon?"

"Well, before you start being all nosy in somebody else's business, what's with those?" Viola asked while pointing to the man's feet.

"Oh girl, I had to let these bunions breathe today. They have been killing me today some kinda bad."

"Bunions… feet! Is that what those are? Hell, I thought you were wearing a pair of pointed moccasins. I was about to comment on how comfortable they looked. Those are your feet?"

"Yeah girl and they're killing me today."

"Wow, look at these things Rose, they kinda remind you of a cake cutter, all triangular shaped and all."

Rose quickly directed her attention over to Simone, only because she had heard the word 'cake'.

"Will you stop talking about my feet? Do you have some type of foot fetish or something Viola?" Simone said.

"No I don't, what I have is a foot fear and those feet scare me! If they look that crazy wrapped up, Honey, promise me that you'll never unleash those things!"

"I beg your pardon Miss 'V', I'd like you to know that I get a pedicure once a week; my feet are scrumptious and beautiful."

"With those bunions lookin' up hear screaming at us, you're going to tell me that those feet are beautiful? You need to stop."

"Enough about my feet, what happened with Miss Lizzy?"

"Well, if you must know, which I'm sure you must, so you can plaster it deep into everyone's ears you see today and I know your nosy butt will only bug the hell out of all of the staff until somebody tells you like you always do, I'll just tell you now and get it over with. She has been accused of over fraternizing with other residents."

"What do you mean by over fraternizing, Dear?"

"Well, let's just say she was caught moisturizing Ashy Pete in a certain area that some of the aides still aren't quite comfortable moisturizing, if you know what I mean."

"Moisturizing? You mean she was putting lotion on Pete?"

"No, she was putting saliva on Pete's privates. Wow, that kinda sounds like one of those porn movie titles, doesn't it? 'Saliva for Pete's Privates', coming to a theater near you."

"Oh my goodness, I don't believe it. I am shocked! You mean to tell me Pete can still…and he likes…"

"Now, don't you go getting any ideas over there, 'Mr. Brokeback Mountain'. Don't start crucifying her, she just needs help and she's still my friend, not close, but still a friend."

"I won't say anything to anybody about this and no, I'm not interested in Pete's crusty butt, I'm just shocked. My goodness, I guess you just never know people, huh? That Lizzy is something else!"

"You've got that right. That's all she seems to think about, sex, money and maybe going to Disney World."

Simone sat and inhaled as much information as he could before leaving the ladies. As he was wheeled away, he stopped past every table en route to his table, whispering loudly to anyone that would listen. Viola watched on while shaking her head and mumbling.

"Just look at him, the 'Rona Barrett' of Hayfield."

The ladies continued playing cards until it was time for lunch. After lunch Rose and Viola left the dining room and went back to their room. They wanted to rest up for the evening. Today was bingo night. On their way, they were passed by Al who was on his way home.

"And where are you off to in such a rush, killer of appetites?" Viola asked.

"I don't have time to mess around with you right now Miss Vy, I've got to get home and get ready for my date."

"Date? Who in their right mind would go out with you and please don't tell me that you gonna cook for her, it is a woman, right? I mean today you just don't know."

"Of course it's a woman and strangely, she is in her right mind."

"Well, if that were true, I'm sure she could find somebody a little better lookin' than you, porker!"

"Viola, leave Al alone, he's sweet," Rose said.

"Nah, now the man needs to know his offering potential…zero. Look at you, go on take a look at yourself and tell me honestly, if you were her, would you date you?"

Al turned and peered at his reflection in the large glass window of the dining room. After a moment's evaluation he turned to the ladies with a shattered ego.

"Well I don't know, I guess I am a bit overweight and I could stand a shave. I could be a better dresser, too, I guess. And it couldn't hurt to have this ugly chipped tooth fixed and I guess I should cut these long hairs that protrude out of my nostrils. Well Miss Vy, maybe you're right, maybe I wouldn't go out with myself. I never thought of it that way and now standing here looking at myself, I realize… I really am an unattractive man. There's got to be something attractive about me."

"Ah, Al you're a very sweet man, isn't he Vy?" Rose said as she nudged her instigating friend.

"Oh, uh…yeah…that you are," Viola said after being caught off guard by Rose. "Yeah you are sweet Al and there's another thing that I just realized about you, after you described what you saw in your reflection…There aint a damn thing wrong with your vision!"

"Viola!" Rose shouted.

Al turned and hurried down the hall mumbling to himself. Rose and Viola continued their walk back to their room.

Rose rolled over to her side of the room and picked up the remote control and began fumbling with it.

"Girl, you always have the hardest time with that thing. Do you want me to come turn it on for you?" Viola asked.

"No, it's just that the letters are so small and they have the 'power' button somewhere in the middle of this dang thing. It always takes me a minute to figure it out, that's all. I need one of those 'clapper' gadgets so I could just come in and clap on!" Rose replied as she giggled.

"Don't even get me started on those things. Jessie got one of those things when they first came out, ordered it off of the TV. He hooked it up to our bedroom lamp so we could just walk in and clap on the light. Child, we disconnected that thing the same night."

"How come, it didn't work?"

"No, on the contrary, that damn thing worked just fine. Actually it worked too well. Jessie plugged the lamp into it and the Clapper box into the wall next to the nightstand. Later that night, I clapped the lamp on when I went into the bedroom. I walked over and flopped down on the bed. Our headboard on the bed was a little loose so when I sat down, that wobbly thing slammed against the wall and the light went out. I had to clap it back on. Then I kicked off my shoes. The light went off with one and on with the other. After that, I moved around quietly in my room until I was able to get into my bed. Shortly after, Jessie came into the room and experienced the same frustration but did manage to get into bed. We lay there quiet and still for a while until Jessie started in on a little hanky panky. We started up and the light came on. I clapped it back off. I moaned and the light came back on and Jessie clapped it back off. We did it slowly and quietly until Jessie was gettin' close. He started pumpin' me and I exploded and he kept a pumpin'. I thought I was about to pass out because with each pump that 'ole headboard would slam against that wall and all I saw was flashing lights. When Jessie had finally stopped, he got up and pulled out that 'Clapper' from out of the wall and chucked it in the trashcan."

They laughed as Viola walked over to Rose's side of the room and turned on the TV set for her. Rose looked at Viola then clapped her hands together two times and they both broke into laughter once more.

The ladies met in the activity room excited and ready to play. It was BINGO night and there was money to be made; two dollars a game. Marva stayed in her room after she had returned from dialysis and Lizzy had returned after her release. With her short flowered dress and her big hat, she was the hit of the evening. Even the ladies admired her outfit and she was in her glory.

The ladies set up their bingo boards and placed their drinking cups and eyewear nearby. There were small group conversations throughout the room. The activity director continued setting up and assisting others with their boards and chips before returning to the front of the room and picking up the microphone.

"Ok folks, we're about to get started. You all know the rules, if you get a full column or row, yell 'BINGO'."

Everyone continued setting up their boards and talking to their neighbors. As soon as the first combination of letters and numbers was announced over the speaker, the elderly group became very serious and competitive.

"G…14," yelled the voice through the speaker of the small P.A. system, "G…14".

The players scrambled as they slowly placed their chips on the squares of multiple boards for the combination called. The announcer turned the handle of the small, thin, wire basket filled with the little, ivory colored marked cubes. Once the basket was at rest, the announcer would reach into the square opening, retrieve the next cube and would recite its markings.

After several cubes had been pulled and several numbers were announced, the high pitched voice screamed out proudly, "BINGO! BINGO…BINGO…BINGO!"

The entire room turned to view who had achieved such a remarkable feat, especially since only eight numbers had been called. There in the back of the room with both hands raised, stood Lizzy. Not only did she not have BINGO, she didn't even have a board or chips.

"Lizzy, what are you doing?" Rose asked the woman who was now dancing as if she had just won the lottery.

"Girl, you can't be yelling out BINGO! Especially when you're not playing; these old birds will kill you for that! Shoot, there's $2.00 on the line here."

"Yeah…gasp…gasp…sit your ass…gasp…down…before I…gasp…gasp…just sit down," Harvey said as he inhaled from his oxygen tank.

Harvey carried that tank everywhere he went. He had been a life-long smoker. He had his first cigarette at age six and had been smoking ever since. By the time he was fourteen, he was up to four packs a day. And for a man who had such trouble breathing, Harvey was always ready to hang a boot in somebody's bottom.

Just as quickly as she had jumped to her feet, Lizzy flopped down into her seat, folded her arms and stared at the table. The other players quickly returned their focus to the game after mumbling their sarcastic comments and obscenities regarding the premature declaration of BINGO. The ladies continued listening for their lucky numbers over the small speakers. There was a light hum throughout the room as the seniors spoke to themselves while concentrating on their chip placement.

Rose was the only one that remained silent as she was eating a drumstick that she had wrapped up from the dining room earlier. She had missed several numbers as she concentrated on devouring the grease covered fowl.

Viola looked over at her heavy friend and could only shake her head in disbelief. "Didn't you just finish eating?" she asked.

Rose never looked up during her reply. "I'm still hungry. That little bit of food wasn't enough to fill me up."

"Rose, you ate two plates of food and look at your board, it's covered with grease and crumbs. You can't even tell what the numbers are."

Rose looked down at the grease smeared board and quickly licked her index finger. She pressed it firmly against each of the crispy fried chicken crumbs which lay on her BINGO board and transported them to her mouth.

"BINGO!" the voice yelled out. All heads in the room turned in the direction from which the voice sounded. It was Pete. He had just entered the room. After noticing the glare of angry faces looking upon him, he then completed his statement, "BINGO, now that's my game!" he yelled. The obscenities were again repeated by the other players. Pete walked by Viola, Rose and Lizzy. He looked over and smiled, "Hey Lizzy."

Lizzy said nothing. She continued sitting there with her arms folded staring at the table.

"Hey Lizzy? Is that the only person you see sitting over here?" Rose asked.

"Sorry ladies, how are you doing?" Pete asked smiling.

"I'm fine," Viola quickly responded. "I hear you're doing fine yourself there, Pete. You look relaxed. Been getting plenty of sleep, have you?"

Pete ignored Viola. He looked back over at Lizzy and once again acknowledged her. "Hi Lizzy, how are you feeling today?" Again the response from the little lady was absent. Pete's smile soon faded. He slowly turned, never taking his eyes off Lizzy then walked over to the game mediator.

While he waited patiently for his board and chips, Simone rolled over to Viola's seat. "Looks like the new discoverer of moisturizer has fallen for Miss Lizzy over there, huh? She must have blown his mind!"

Viola stared over at the well dressed, nosy man then raised one of her eyebrows, "First off, he hasn't got much mind left and secondly, I'm sure she blew much more than his mind."

As the two began to chuckle, the raining sound of chips carried throughout the room. Pete had dropped his carton of chips all over the floor. The activity counselor slid her seat back from the table and immediately began retrieving the chips from the floor. Pete placed his arm on the back of Miss Evans chair and slowly began to bend over to assist the young lady.

"No, Mr. Pete, I can get them; you go on and have a seat and I'll bring them to you."

Pete, being the stubborn man that he was, continued trying to bend over to help.

"Oh my Lord," Rose mumbled.

Viola and Simone turned to see what had caught Rose's attention. There peeking just over the perimeter of elastic around the waist of Pete's sweatpants, was the seam of skin covered flesh that separated both halves of Pete's buttocks.

"I haven't seen a sight like that since I had the plumber over to fix my kitchen sink," Rose chuckled.

"I haven't seen that much crack since that movie…uh…oh yeah, 'New Jack City'. That's simply disgusting. It even has hair at the top. Looks like an upside down goatee. Pete, get up man you're making us nauseous over here!" Viola yelled while turning away from the grotesque sight. Viola looked over at Simone who was locked in on Pete's exposed flesh. She reached over and tapped Simone on the shoulder, "You alright there fella?"

Simone didn't budge. He continued to stare as he mumbled just loud enough for the ladies to hear. "Oh no, I must be addicted to crack, I can't look away. Somebody help me. Oh my goodness, look how shiny his butt is."

"You'd better calm down man, before your pacemaker explodes," Viola said.

"That's not crack, that's canyon!" Rose chuckled.

Soon after gathering up all the chips, the counselor helped Pete up and escorted him to a seat. She helped him set up his boards and returned to the microphone and basket to continue with the game.

After the game was over, the activity room emptied almost as quickly as it had filled. Most of the residents returned to their rooms with the exception of Miss Evans who sat talking with her daughter. Pete sat on the long plaid sofa and became engrossed in the television while Lizzy sat quietly at the table staring out the window. Pete watched the television for only a few minutes before cautiously pulling himself up from the soft cushions.

He walked over to the table where Lizzy sat quietly and pulled out the chair across the table from her. He sat down and placed his hand on top of the table. He looked into her eyes and smiled as she continued staring out the window past him. He slowly reached across the table and took the inattentive woman by the hand. Her eyes soon shifted to his smiling face. He opened her hand and slid a crisp, folded twenty dollar bill inside it. She looked down at the folded bill then looked up at him and she too, began to smile. He stood up from his seat then left for his room. Lizzy got up from the table moments later and followed.

The next morning was no different than any other at Hayfield. The ladies met in the dining room as they did every morning. Marva, who was feeling much better, accompanied her friends at their table. The trays were delivered as they were every morning and the ladies started in on their breakfast.

Lizzy arrived later than the other ladies once again, as she did every morning. This morning she was extremely bubbly and cheerful. Her ensemble this morning consisted of a blue, red, and green plaid mini skirt, a white, button down collar, oxford blouse with the top three buttons undone so that her breasts could be displayed clearly, a pair of red, six inch heels and white, lace-top nylon ankle high socks. The socks were folded over neatly, displaying the fine lace pattern. Her blouse was tucked neatly inside her skirt and the back of her skirt was tucked neatly inside the back of her panties.

She pranced by Viola who caught a glimpse of the sight. She just looked, shook her head and mumbled, "My Lord". Lizzy took her seat and her tray was placed in front of her. She looked around the table and greeted her friends.

"Good morning, ladies. Fine morning, isn't it?"

"What's making this morning any finer than any other?" Viola asked.

"Oh, I don't know, today just seems special for some reason."

"Maybe today you'll do something special, you know, like finally beat us at cards or perhaps sit for a fraction of the day with your legs closed."

"Maybe you're right! Maybe I'll go on an adventure or something today. It's a nice day today maybe I'll just go for a drive or something."

"A drive, how are you going to do that? You need a car to go for a drive and how would you get out of here if you did?" Rose asked.

"I could get a car. Yeah that's it, I need a car. I need about five thousand dollars and then I can go buy me a new car."

Marva quickly joined in, "Five thousand dollars? You can't buy no car for five thousand dollars, you need more like twenty thousand dollars."

"Twenty thousand! Cars cost that much now? Well in that case…I need a man!"

"Girl, quit with all that fussing over there. You're not getting a car, a man, or out of here to drive across the country so there, end of discussion," Viola said.

"You don't know what I'm gonna do, Viola. You're just jealous of the fact that I can get a ma…" Right at that second, the ladies' argument was interrupted by a bright, repeating, flashing light and the constant beeping from the room just down the hall.

"Code blue 312…code blue 312," was announced over the building intercom.

The ladies watched as the nurses and doctor on duty rushed through the hall toward the room from which the flashing light and bell originated. Everyone in the dining room became silent and attentive to the hallway.

Suddenly, Lizzy slowly rose to her feet. "312, did they say 312? That's Pete's room." She walked from behind the table and started for the door.

As she neared the door she was met by Betty, "Where are you going Miss Lizzy?" she asked.

"That's my friend's room that they called. I just want to go check on him."

"Now you know no one is allowed in the hall during emergencies of this nature. Just give the doctor a moment with him then I'll let you know how he's doing, Ok? Now go on back over to your table and finish your breakfast."

Lizzy stood there for a second before she acknowledge the aide. She nodded then walked back over to the table and sat quietly staring through the window into the hallway with the others.

They walked down the hall eagerly but not rushing. One carried the large black box while the other pushed the expanded bed on wheels. There was no urgency about either man. At the sight of the two men everyone lowered their heads. Everyone knew that whoever they were there for was not alive.

"Lord, have mercy on his soul," Marva whispered.

Viola looked over at Lizzy who was still staring through the glass window. Minutes later, the men rolled the gurney down the hall. Pete lay there with his eyes closed. He looked as if he were only asleep. They all watched as the two paramedics rolled him out through the back of the building to their awaiting vehicle.

Betty returned to the dining room and Rose quickly got her attention. "What happened?" Rose asked.

Lizzy got up from the table and walked out of the dining room toward Pete's vacant room.

Betty looked down at the ladies sitting around the table sadly then spoke to them in a calm, quiet voice. "It's Mr. Riley, he..." Betty let out a long sigh before continuing. "The paramedics are rushing him over to Cape Fear Hospital."

"That man was dead! Girl, we know dead when we see dead and that man was dead! Dead, dead, dead, D.E.A.D. His mouth was all hung open and it didn't seem to us like the paramedics were rushing him out. Did you see any rush about those men Rose?" Viola asked. "Girl, you must think we're stupid, is that what you think? Now, you want to tell us what's really going on?"

Betty looked over at Viola who was looking up at her over the rim of her eyeglasses. Betty kneeled down beside the stern faced woman and began to whisper. "Mr. Pete didn't wake up this morning. They said his heart probably stopped while he was sleeping but just keep it to yourselves, Ok?"

"Uh huh, died in his sleep, huh? Yeah right! I bet you that man died from dehydration. An overdose of 'Headbobbolytus' was probably what took him out. Would that be considered a homicide? That old coot let that woman blow him right on out of here. She sucked the life out of him, that's what she did. I told her that they were too damned old for that mess!"

"Viola, stop it! Have you no respect for the departed? Besides, no matter how he left this earth, he's in a better place now," Marva interjected.

"Let me get this straight, the man was eighty four years old and getting his 'tallywacker' kissed and whacked off anytime he wanted by a professional, senior citizen, retired hooker, and now he's dead probably lying in a cold box in the morgue and you're calling that a better place."

"No, I mean heaven."

"Did you not hear a word I just said? The man was getting oral sex at eighty four; I doubt if he's listed for the express lane through the gates of heaven. If anything, he's probably standing in one of those long lines like you hate at Disney World where you inch up every ten minutes or so."

"Just quit it Vy. You need prayer woman, constant prayer."

Betty stood up shaking her head, "Well, I'm going to leave you ladies on that note. If I hear anything else I'll let you know."

"Thanks Betty," Rose whispered. Betty waved to the ladies as she walked off, heading for the kitchen.

"Marva, I'm just saying what you're thinking. Well, did anybody notice what time 'Miss Hottie' got back to her room last night? I know the two of them were in the activity room when we left," Viola continued.

The ladies remained in deep discussion until they saw Lizzy enter the dining room. She had gone down to Pete's room. She looked very upset and distraught. She took her seat and placed her hands on top of the table. Marva reached over and held one of Lizzy's hands.

"I'm sorry about Pete Lizzy, I know he was special to you. Just remember, God loves him."

"Yes Lizzy, I'm sorry too, he was a very nice man," Rose added. "Are you going to eat your potatoes?"

Lizzy looked over at Rose strangely then slid her plate of food over to Rose's awaiting chubby hands.

Viola continued eating. She never looked up. Suddenly, Marva began clearing her throat to get Viola's attention. Viola looked up at Marva then over at Lizzy's cheerless face then tossed her fork onto her plate.

"Ok, Ok, I'm sorry about Pete, too. Oh yeah, and he's in a better place," Viola said sarcastically.

"Are you Ok, Lizzy?" Marva asked "Would you like to pray with me?"

"Pray, why?"

"For Pete. You seem pretty upset."

"I am upset!"

"Well, I find in sad times like these, prayer always helps."

"Sad time? Oh no, this is not a sad time, this is a mad time and I'm mad as hell!"

"Well that's normal, a lot of people get upset with God when they feel that a loved one has been taken from them before they should."

"Loved one? I didn't love that fool. No, I'm angry because that old bastard took one of those blue pills that he got from his son before he came to BINGO. He asked me to come to his room because he had something to show me that he thought I would like. I went into his room and there it was standing like one of the rockets from the fourth of July, ready to blast off.

I had to do him twice just to calm that thing down. He said he would give me twenty dollars and then another twenty if I did it again. I just searched his room and that old goat didn't have a dime. I woke up this morning with my jaws sore and a damn crick in my neck. If he hadn't died I would have killed him myself."

The ladies all looked at Lizzy. She slammed her fist down on the table igniting a thunderous thud. She reached over and grabbed her plate from in front of Rose and began digging into her food angrily then shoved it into her mouth. No one else uttered a single word, no, not even Viola.

Chapter 6 - The Arrival

The sun peered through the blinds of the ceiling high window and cast its horizontal spotlight on the shiny floor of the dayroom. It was shining brightly this particular morning. Lizzy focused on the beam of light as it shone in the center of one of the linoleum tiles, while the other ladies played a hand of cards.

"What are you staring at Lizzy?" Marva asked.

There was no answer. Lizzy continued staring at the floor.

"Maybe that's the light the aliens sent to beam her back up," Viola said laughing.

"Viola, that's terrible," Marva replied.

"What, I'm just saying…"

"Some people do have feelings, Vy."

"I'm hungry," whined Rose.

"Yes, I know and some people have large appetites. Rose you just ate less than an hour ago. Recognize the difference in hunger and greed, Child," Viola barked.

"See Vy, that's exactly what I'm talking about. People have feelings. Don't you think Rose is offended that you keep calling her greedy? And look at how you treat Lizzy, always calling her crazy and nuts when all she is, is ill. I keep telling you that God doesn't like ugly, but you continue to torment, mock and even threaten the people you call your friends. I will continue to pray for you Vy, but honestly, it doesn't seem to be working."

"Ok Marva, I hear you. I will try to do better I promise, but first can you get that greedy wench over there to throw out a card and get that crazy woman to stop staring at me?"

Marva looked at Viola in true disbelief. She couldn't believe just how insensitive her friend could be. She threw her cards down on the table and turned her head. She placed her hand on Lizzy's shoulder. She had returned to the small beam of light.

"That light sure has you captivated doesn't it?" Marva asked.

Lizzy continued in her fascination and Marva continued trying to converse with her. "Just think, in the beginning of time after God made the heavens and earth, he said 'Let there be light' and there was light and do you know that the light you're looking at right now is the very same light God created on that day? That light provides so much life in so many ways. It helps our gardens grow; it warms our planet and tons of other things you'd never realize. I can see you're really impressed with its beauty."

"Child, the only reason she's been staring at that light for so long is because it's passing through the leg of that table which is casting a shadow that sort of resembles that of a man's privates," Viola said.

Marva looked over at the beam of light then tilted her head slightly to the left and studied the shadow for a brief moment, "Oh my!" she gasped.

Lizzy reached out in an attempt to feel the shadow before she was pulled back by Marva.

Rose marveled at the sight for a moment. "Yep, that looks like one alright, a big one but nevertheless, it does look like one. It reminds me of the first day I met my Ralph. My Ralph, now he was a man. Wheeeeew, he sure knew how to please me if you know what I mean!" Rose said while fanning herself and taking a blast from her inhaler.

"I hear you, Girl," Viola said, stopping briefly to take a sip of water from her red plastic cup. Her throat was still a bit dry from arguing with Al earlier that morning over how hard he had cooked her bacon. "Now my Jessie, now he was still a wild tiger in his fifties! He was a mild buck in his sixties but his seventies were very unkind. That thing would just lie there like the tongue hanging out the side of the mouth of some road kill. I hated to see it go; boy did I hate to see it go."

"Yeah, the years definitely have affected us all differently," Rose said. "I still miss my Ralph, how about you Marva?"

"I don't miss that old dog Richard at all!" Marva grunted.

"No, I mean how much different do you feel since you were in your fifties."

"Well let me think…I've got sugar but I can't have salt. My body holds fluid except when I need it to. I can barely walk but I always have the runs. My feet swell but my boobs have shrunk. Although my food is swallowed in solid form it quickly returns disguised as gas, gas I can't control that is….Oooops, excuse me. The one thing that has remained steady in my life all these years has been my God."

"OH MY GOD!" Lizzy shouted.

"You know him too don't you Lizzy?"

"No but I sure want to. He's so sexy!"

Marva revved back from Lizzy with a kind of confused but yet angry look upon her face, "Sexy?"

"Yes, don't you think he is the sexiest man you've ever seen? Look at him!" Lizzy said with a shaky voice as she looked past Viola with a bright smile on her face.

All of the women turned their attention to the large windows of the dayroom which provided a full view of the hallway. There, walking with his daughter and the administrator, Mrs. Hamilton was the elderly gentleman that had caught Lizzy's attention. He was tall and very well groomed. His gray wavy hair was trimmed to perfection and combed back. His complexion was that of sweet, dark chocolate and his slim physique was that of a fifty year old. His name was Javier Chadwick. He was to become the newest resident of Hayfield.

Like most facilities, Hayfield had notified Dr. Chadwick as soon as a space was available to him. Pete's bed was still warm when the call was made to inform the man of its availability. Javier had been on the waiting list for sometime. He was currently residing with his daughter and her husband after he had moved to the east coast from California. He was originally from Lafayette, a small town in Louisiana. He was Creole and still spoke with an accent. For his age, he was still a very spry and attractive man.

The man soon faded from the women's view. "Oh my Lord, did you see him?" Lizzy asked. "He's mine, he's all mine!" she continued then lifted herself up from the table and walked out of the room singing, "I'm in the moooooood for love…simply because I'm horrrrny!"

"There she goes again. Looks like she's planning another murder, this time it's premeditated!" Viola said.

"Yes but he was very good looking wasn't he?" asked Rose.

"Yeah, I guess if you're in to *those* kind of men," Viola replied.

"*Those* kind of men, what do you mean by that Vy?"

"You know the kind of men that have a certain kind of look about them."

"Oh she means Back men Rose. Looks like Miss Viola hasn't quite stepped out of the 1950's yet. Oh, so a Back man can cook your food, transport you when you're sick, help you in every way as long as you didn't have to be seen with him in public in any other capacity, huh?"

Viola removed her glasses from her face and peered at Marva. "So what are you trying to say over there, that I'm a racist?"

"Well, seems like you're calling yourself one by what you're saying…those kind of men, just what DO you mean by that?"

"Look, I don't bite my tongue and everyone knows that but if its one thing that I'm not and that's a racist. Some of my best friends over the years have been Black, Negro, Colored, African American or whatever you're calling yourselves these days. And if you're calling me a racist you're also calling me a traitor to my country because my President, the President that I voted for too is a Negro, Colored, African American, Black or whatever it is you're calling yourselves. Now the type of man that I was speaking of Miss '*I know everything because I read the bible all the time*' is the type that looks so good that he's either so conceited because he thinks he's prettier than you or he's so boring because all he ever talks about is himself! Oh, and by the way Missy, when

I have my Thanksgiving turkey…I like the dark meat, thank you very much!"

"I like the dark meat, too," said Rose.

"Rose you'd eat whatever piece of the bird that was piled on your plate."

"Yeah I would but I like the dark meat best."

Marva looked over a Viola apologetically, "Sorry Vy, I don't think that you're a racist it's just the way you said it. I…"

"Don't worry about it Marva, you just have to stop being so sensitive about things all the time. Believe me, us White folk are definitely aware of your struggle over the years. Hell, y'all remind us constantly. Y'all have us so confused all the time. We don't know what in the hell to call you from day to day. One day you're black and the next day you're African American then they've got talk of Ebonics and I still don't know what in the hell that is. We have to be so darn careful with what we say. Like what I just said but you heard something totally different, that has happened to so many throughout the years. We say 'nice Black guy', he hears 'spear chucker'. We try to pay for something in the store and say 'here's the money', the Black man behind the counter hears 'you jungle bunny'."

"Alright VIOLA, now you're pushin' it. Please don't make me lose my religion."

"No, I'm just sayin'. I remember when my heater broke on a very cold day and I asked the repairman if he could come soon. He refused to service my unit because he said that I called him a coon. I remember that well because I froze my butt off that day. This has to stop and it has to stop now. We all voted our President in to office, an African American President, not just blacks,

Coloreds, Negroes, African Americans or whatever it is you're calling yourselves…ALL OF US."

"You're right Vy and I'm sorry," Marva said sincerely, "and by the way, you can just call me Marva, your friend."

"Apology accepted Marva, my sweet, Black, African American, Negro friend," Viola said then began laughing.

That evening in the dining room was different from any of the past days at Hayfield. The ladies would usually meet at about 5:15 or so for dinner. Lizzy of course, always arrived later. This particular evening both Viola and Rose had arrived at five o'clock exactly. They had gone back to their rooms to freshen up then returned promptly to make sure they would be one of the first to meet the new resident.

Marva arrived and met up with the two at her usual time. She noticed their stylish outfits and how well groomed their hair was. They were even wearing makeup which was definitely out of the ordinary for both women. A little lipstick was as far as either woman would go normally.

The ladies sat down at their table. Marva looked at both of her friends and only shook her head.

"What?" Rose asked with an innocent but devious look about her.

Marva pointed at the two ladies shaking her head. Just as she was about to comment on their underhandedness and outfits, he walked in, the new 'Cary Grant/Denzel Washington' of Hayfield. He was escorted by his daughter and Betty the aide. Betty had pointed to a vacant table where Mr. Gale was sitting alone.

His daughter held on to the back of his arm as they proceeded toward the table.

"Ahem!" sounded the loud, raspy noise from Viola's throat. Betty looked over at Viola and smiled. Viola continued to clear her throat again, this time even louder than before. Betty knew what Viola was attempting and knew if she didn't stop and address her she'd never hear the end of it. Betty stopped the couple and turned her attention to Viola who now was holding her hand to her throat.

"Are you alright, Miss Viola?" the aide asked.

"Oh yes, Honey I'm Ok, I just had a little something in my throat. It was so sweet of you to check on me," Viola answered in her sweetest sounding voice. "I see you have some guests with you. Don't let me detain you any longer. You just go on ahead and take care of them, I'll be alright."

"Oh I'm sorry, where are my manners? This is our newest resident, Dr. Chadwick and his daughter Lucien. Dr. Chadwick had his own practice right here in Fayetteville."

"Oh, a doctor huh, what an exciting profession. I guess I'll know who to go to when something ails me. Well, welcome to Hayfield Dr. Chadwick, I hope you enjoy your stay here. I'm Viola but most folks around here just call me Vy. You're welcome to sit here at our table if you'd like."

Dr. Chadwick smiled and nodded and Viola's grin expanded as wide as a river. Marva could not believe what she was witnessing.

"Miss Vy, what about Miss Elizabeth?" Betty asked while looking over at Lizzy's vacant chair then back over to Viola with disbelief smeared across her face.

"Oh Lizzy, well...uh...she doesn't eat anymore. She decided to only eat in her room starting today."

"Now Viola, you know Lizzy will be in here as always. It's nice to meet you Dr. Chadwick, I'm Marva and this is Rose."

Rose couldn't speak but she did manage to wave her hand at the gentleman. He nodded his head, smiled and greeted the ladies. Viola was just about to speak when the door opened and every head turned in that direction. Lizzy walked into the room wearing a tight, black and white polka dot, low cut dress which displayed most of her breasts. Her legs were covered with black, sheer nylons and she wore black and white polka dot flat heeled shoes. She was wearing her long, blonde wig with a shiny tiara on top. Javier and his daughter turned to see what had caught everyone's attention. He looked at Lizzy and smiled.

The little woman walked up to the new resident and looked deeply into his eyes then spoke softly, "I've been waiting for you."

Viola leaned over toward Rose and mumbled just loud enough for the man to hear. "Who is she today, Alice from Wonderland?"

"That's nice Miss Elizabeth, but right now Dr. Chadwick is hungry so we need to get him something to eat. We're serving his favorite today too, greens so I'm sure he's ready to eat. You need to get ready to eat too, Miss Lizzy," Betty said.

"I'm Elizabeth but you can call me Lizzy and I want to be yours. I will bear your children and lick you in places that only your mother knew about. I can be your wife or your mistress or just a late night booty call, what do you say?"

The nice gentleman only smiled at the propositioning woman before greeting her. "Nice to meet you Lizzy, I'm Javier Chadwick."

"Javier Chadwick, now that's a beautiful name. Mrs. Javier Chadwick, that sounds even nicer."

"Ok, Ok, Miss Lizzy he's got to go now. He's got to get something to eat. You can talk to him later, Ok?" Betty said while prying Lizzy's hands from the gentleman's arm.

"Ok, we'll talk later on my darling. Yes, I have so much I need to share with you, until we meet again Javier," Lizzy said. She placed her hand to her ruby red lipsticked lips tightly then blew Javier a big kiss. "I'm not wearing any underwear in case you're interested!" she yelled.

The man, his daughter, and aide Betty left Lizzy standing in the middle of the floor. She watched on, smiling at Dr. Chadwick until he was seated. "Will he have to go through that every time he comes in here?" his daughter asked.

"Oh no, Miss Lizzy just gets like that sometimes, that's all. As soon as she gets used to seeing him she'll not bother him at all," Betty replied. She introduced him to Mr. Gale and the two men began conversing. Betty left the woman and her father and shortly returned with his tray. His daughter embraced her father before leaving the dining room with Betty.

As the ladies looked on, they could hear him shouting from the entranceway, "Hello ladies!" It was Simone. He was very cheerful and happy that evening.

"What has your bowels in such an uproar this evening?" Viola asked.

"That's exactly it Vy, my bowels. I just found out that I have been scheduled for a colonoscopy on Friday. Wheeew, I just get all hot and bothered just thinking about it. You know, the last time I had one, they tried to put me to sleep. I told them "Nah uh Honey, I want to be fully awake. I want to feel the power of the 'Man Ram'. Shoot, you know a man my age doesn't get much action so I need all the stimulation I can get. Shoot, the way I see it…stimulation plus pumpafication equals gratification and that's what I'm aiming for. The doctor got so upset with me during my last one because I kept yelling 'deeper…deeper…' so he cut the procedure short, talking about 'He's alright'. Girrrl, I was some kind of mad, Child, and sometimes…"

"Simone, I'm glad you're excited but I'm getting ready to eat so we'll have to talk about your ass and your bowels later, thank you very much, now goodbye," Viola interrupted.

"Well, Ok then…uh, I guess I'll talk to you later about it…see you ladies later." Simone was wheeled to his table where he once again began to share his good news with anyone who would listen.

The ladies' trays were brought over to them and they slowly made their dining preparations. Each lady would periodically glance over at the new guy to try to get his attention but he was in deep conversation with his new friend while eating his meal. As the ladies began their meals the large shadow of a pot bellied stove was cast over their table. Viola looked up and there standing towering over her was none other than Al. He looked down at her as she emptied the small white package of salt over the gravy covered meat which lay in her plate.

"So, Miss Vy, what do you want to complain about today? The meat isn't seasoned enough, or are the greens soggy or too leafy, which is it?" the cook asked. Viola noticed Javier and others were looking over inquisitively. She didn't want him to think she was as disorderly or complaining as she really was so she simply sat back in her chair and smiled at the heavy man.

"No Al, the food tastes wonderful today as it does most days. I only added a little salt because I like my food just a bit saltier than most but it doesn't spoil the wonderful taste of the meat at all and these greens are wonderful. You know that greens are my favorite," she said as she dug into the leafy vegetable and began shoveling them into her mouth.

Al took a step back from the pleasant speaking Viola then looked around the table at the other women who were all smiling. "WHO ARE YOU?!" he shouted. "Where's Miss Viola? Who's taken over her body?" Al continued while laughing. "So I finally got one right, huh? You really like it, huh? I knew I'd get you sooner or later. Wait a sec, I thought that you told me a while ago you didn't eat greens because they didn't agree with your stomach?"

"Who me, no, I love greens and these are the best! The meat is good, too. In fact, it's the best tasting imitation liver I've ever had."

"Huh, what do you mean imitation liver?"

"Not…gasp….real…meat…gasp…gasp…gasp…that's what she means," Harvey said as he and his oxygen tank rolled by.

Viola could only keep up this facade for so long. Her real self was slowly pushing through the wall of pretense that she had constructed. "Surely you're not saying that this is real meat, young man. Now, as an imitation liver, the taste would be considered Ok, but this is real liver? You've got to be kidding me. Is real liver supposed to be this tough and bland?"

At that moment Viola realized that she was talking loud enough for all in her immediate area to hear. She looked over and sure enough Dr. Chadwick was looking in her direction with some of the others. He looked at her and smiled. This only added fuel to the fire. Viola tore into Al like vultures on road kill. After Al headed back to the kitchen with his tail between his legs, Viola looked over at Dr. Chadwick and smiled.

Lizzy saw the two make eye contact and immediately became angry with Viola. She stood up from the table and peered at Viola then slammed her hand down on the table, "I TOLD YOU HE'S MINE!" then stormed out of the dining room.

After dinner most of the residents proceeded to the dayroom. Viola and Rose positioned themselves in the seats at their table as to have a full view of the hallway. Marva headed down to Lizzy's room to see if she could calm her angry friend down. As she approached Lizzy's room, she could hear the sound of the whiney, high pitched voice speaking calmly.

"He doesn't want that old ugly lady anyway. She doesn't even wear her teeth in her mouth half the time. Nope, he wouldn't want to be bothered with that old, poor white trash."

As Marva approached the doorway she glanced into Lizzy's room. There she saw Lizzy holding a stuffed teddy bear up to her face and speaking to it as if it were human. Even with Marva there in the doorway Lizzy continued to hold her conversation with her silent roommate. "I know he loves me, I just know it.

I'm going to make him the happiest man in the world and no one is going to get in the way of us."

With that, Marva backed her wheelchair up and rolled her way back to the dayroom where she found her immature friends gawking and competing for smiles from the new gentleman who had finally made his way into the dayroom. They were acting like two high school girls. Marva rolled up to inform the ladies of Lizzy's actions she had witnessed earlier, but before she was able to get out a single word, Viola stood up and walked over to Javier's table. She sat next to the man and began conversing. Marva positioned herself next to Rose.

"You gals better watch yourselves with Lizzy. She has really gone off the deep end with this man and what, you and Viola plan on sharing this guy or what?"

"No, I'm not thinking about Lizzy, that's number one and number two, Viola and I have already discussed the matter and we've come to the conclusion that he's a 'muchright man'," Rose stated.

"A what, a 'muchright man'? What in God's name is that?"

"I've got as much right to him as anyone else. It's every woman for herself!"

"Well I think you both should back off when Lizzy's around. She's already got it in her head that he's her man."

"Lizzy's got much more than that in her head. Look, she's sweet and all but she doesn't have claims on that muchright man, she's not his wife and yes we know she's a little cuckoo but just look at him Marva. Now that's a man!"

"Lizzy's not the only one that's gone cuckoo. He's just a man, Rose, a man. And besides, the only one he seems to be interested in is Vy."

"Well we'll see about that."

Right at that moment Lizzy walked into the room and as usual all heads turned toward her direction. She walked up to Javier's table, stopped and struck a pose of that of a model. She stood before the entire room with only a pair of white cotton socks, white canvas sneakers, her short blonde wig, and naked as a jay bird from her calves up with the exception of the bathrobe belt she had tied neatly around her waist. Oh yeah, I almost forgot, and her tiara. The aides rushed over from all directions to assist the elderly exhibitionist back to her room. Before getting her to cooperate she merely patted her left breast with her right hand then her opposite breast with the opposite hand. Then moving her hands down to her crotch, she patted her private area and flicked her fingers at Dr. Chadwick as if she were performing some voodoo ritual. She was escorted back to her room.

"Like I said, you gals better watch your backs!" Marva warned.

"That…gasp…gasp…woman's crazy…gasp…" Harvey mumbled as he rolled by.

Viola sat beside Javier and put on her best show. She smiled and batted her eyes almost as much as she had questioned the soft-spoken man. "So, you were a doctor, huh? That sounds like a very interesting job. I know you drove your lady patients crazy didn't you?" Viola asked but Javier would only smile. "You know, I've never really ever been a very attractive woman so I could only imagine the attention that you've gotten over the years from your patients," Viola stated.

"No, you're a very attractive woman, Viola. I don't know what would ever make you think otherwise," Javier replied knowing the response Viola was looking for.

"Oh really, you really think so?"

"Yes, yes indeed, you're a very pretty lady."

"Well thank you. I haven't heard anything that nice since my late husband's passing. I did mention that I am a widow, didn't I?"

"Well, actually you hadn't but I would assume most of the residents here are without their former spouses."

"Have you ever been married Dr. Chadwick?"

"No, I haven't."

"Well, why not? You're such a sweet and adorable man."

"Well I…"

Just as Dr. Chadwick was about to answer, Mr. Gale interjected, "A doctor, I didn't know that you were a doctor. You know I've got this pain right in the middle of my back, perhaps you could…"

"Excuse me! Excuse me, but we are trying to hold a conversation here if you don't mind," Viola interrupted then without warning, her stomach began to churn. She was now feeling the results from the garlic greens she had devoured in this man's honor. She wiggled a little and inhaled deeply as she could feel the small gas bubbles making their way through her intestines.

"I am not going to be able to hold this," she thought to herself but she did not want to give up her position with Javier. As the small bubbles collided together forming now one large bubble, Viola had to make her decision. She would either have to go back over to her table and relieve herself or take the chance that it would release quietly and odorless. Viola opted to go with her instinct and chose option 'B'. She asked the attractive man about medical school and the difficulty he might have had with his studies during those days.

As Javier began describing his experiences, Viola leaned over and rested her elbow gently upon the table. She shifted her weight just enough to provide a clear path for the warm air to escape. She let go and to her surprise it made not a sound. She continued to display her pasted on smile and pretended to show intense interest in his conversation. She slyly inhaled and smelled nothing. Satisfied with herself, Viola rocked herself back into the upright position in her chair. That's when she felt what no man or woman ever wanted to feel.

As soon as her leg made contact with her seat cushion she had realized that her silent and yet odorless passing was neither of gas or solid form. She could feel the steamy wetness squirt down the back of her thigh and within seconds the foul odor was upon them. Javier's life story was brutally interrupted by the smell of vaporized defecation.

His eyes began to water and his face frowned. His face appeared as if he had bitten into the sourest lemon imaginable. He didn't speak. It was as if he was afraid the stench would get inside his mouth and he would be able to taste it. After seeing the look on her 'muchright' man, Viola quickly stood and excused herself.

"I'll be right back. I think I left Marva's scarf that I borrowed in my room. I should get it and return it to her. I've had it for quite sometime." Javier sat silently with the same bitter sour lemon look upon his face and only nodded his head.

As Viola turned to leave, everyone with a rear view of the woman could see the wet flower print dress matted to the back of her thigh and backside. With cane in hand, Viola waved Betty over for assistance. As she shuffled down the aisle toward the door she could hear the snickers from Rose. Betty took Viola by the arm and escorted her to her room.

"I can't believe this would happen today of all days," Viola said while inching into the bathroom.

"Don't you worry about a thing Miss Vy, we'll have you cleaned up in no time," Betty encouraged the woman.

"You know, that's the story of my life. When I was home and cooked the best meal ever, there was no one around to taste it. When I was in the shower and hit all the right notes to my favorite song, there was no one around to hear it. When I picked the freshest flowers from my garden there was no one there to smell them. But crap your pants just one time," Viola said shaking her head, "I'm sure everyone smelled it, could hear me squishing by, saw my wet dress matted to my ass and probably tasted it, too! I still don't know how that happened."

After watching one of her closest friends exit the dayroom in humiliation Rose knew that there was only one thing for her to do. She quickly rolled over to Dr. Chadwick's table and took Viola's place. While waving her hand briskly in front of her nose, for the very first time Rose addressed the gentleman directly. "Pew, I guess those greens really didn't agree with my friend, huh? I've never had that problem but I guess you can see that I'm no stranger to food. So are you finding everything Ok here?"

Javier looked at Rose with his nose still twisted and frowning, "I guess so. It sure has been interesting to say the least. That Viola sure knows how to make an impression."

"Oh yeah, well Viola is something else. Did she talk you to death, too?"

"No, not really."

"Well she likes to talk though, too much if you ask me and that woman is as mean as a snake. You know, I just don't understand her. I mean, most times she's just mean for no reason at all. I feel for any man that deals with her. You two seem to be hitting it off quite nicely. I guess you prefer smaller women as opposed to a woman of my size, huh? You know, a woman with some meat on her bones. A woman that's just a little more filled out. You know, fuller."

"I know what you're saying there Rose," the polite soft spoken gentleman replied. "I think you're just fine the size you are and no I don't prefer any particular size or type of woman. I've noticed that you're the quiet one out of the group, huh?"

"Well, I guess you could say that. You know, when that Viola talks, you pretty much have to give her your undivided attention because she's so forceful and Lizzy's just plain crazy at times. Marva only speaks religion most times but me, I mostly just like to listen."

"I see. Most people don't realize you learn more just by simply listening sometimes."

"Yep, and you know there's nothing worse than a bunch of old women sitting around cackling all the time. Don't you just hate that? Most days I can't even get a word in between Viola's complaining and Marva's sermons. So you were a doctor, huh? I was a nurse before I came here, well I retired but I was a nurse for a long while. Yep, I was an R.N. I learned a lot of things working at those hospitals, too. You know, I give a hell of a sponge bath, I sure do. That's how I got my first husband. I really enjoyed being a nurse except for the shift work though. I guess I never thought about that. What was I saying? Oh yeah, Marva and her sermons, you gotta be careful what you say around her or you'll get slapped with a scripture."

"So how long have you…"

"And then there's Lizzy, it's like playing that children's game you know the one when you have to freeze until…oh yeah 'red light green light' you know that game? Well ,that's what it's like when you're talking to Lizzy. The conversation stops and goes then goes on for a while then stops again then the next thing you know you're talking about something totally different."

"So were you a residen…"

"And you know, I get so sick and tired of that darn Viola. She is such a pain in the ass sometimes. You don't work on those do you? I mean pains in the ass?"

Rose continued to talk nonstop. It was as if she had been uncorked and every thought she had ever conceived during her stay at Hayfield had been poured out of her. Javier sat patiently smiling. His appearance was of a man paying attention to a dear friend when in reality he was contemplating a polite way to say "WILL YOU SHUT THE HELL UP!"

As he solemnly sat, he could see her movement in the distance. Rose had been talking so long that it sounded as if she was now speaking a foreign language to her listener. He refocused his attention to her and realized it was, in fact, still English and she spoke a lot of it.

The little figure approached the table slowly then cleared her throat before speaking. "Sorry for leaving so abruptly, I thought I had left my heating pad on in my room. Now where were we?"

"Well, he was here talking to me and I believe you were somewhere else," Rose answered callously.

"Well, I'm back now and you're in my place so if you don't mind I'd like to get back to my seat," Viola replied just as cruelly, but still with her forged smile plastered to her face.

Rose looked at Javier then at Viola in disbelief. "Go on, move over Rose. These legs are getting a bit wobbly," Viola said loudly. Realizing that Viola was only trying to get her to relinquish her position, Rose gave her friend the dirtiest look that she could muster up then inched herself back toward the end of the table. Just as Viola reached for the chair between the two, Rose rolled herself forward to block the chair that Viola was so anxious to occupy.

"It'll be easier for you to get the chair behind me," she said smirking. The hot air passed through Viola's nostrils like that of a raging bull. She reluctantly pulled out the chair on the opposite of Rose and flopped herself down into it. Angry as hell, Viola immediately started in on Rose.

"So Rose, how many horsepower does that chair of yours have anyway?"

Rose looked back at Viola inquisitively then slowly answered. "Four, it's a four horsepower chair, why?"

"Oh I was just wondering. Wait, you mean to tell me that it takes the power of four strong horses to drag your big butt around? Wow, you must be pretty heavy."

"Well yeah, I guess it does if you want to look at it that way but I'm sure that would be an easy task for them. I like horses; they are beautiful animals. I remember the horses we had on the farm. I used to brush their soft hair everyday. I loved the feel of their hair. It was so soft, may I Vy?" Rose extended her hand toward Viola's wig.

"You'll pull back a nub if you touch my hair," Viola grunted through her teeth.

"Oh, that's right, that is your hair and after all you did pay for it but I'm sure there's at least seven freezing, bald horses somewhere that are so pissed off at you. You ever have the urge to gallop?"

"I'm going to gallop right up the back of your head if you don't take that back you wheelchair riding warthog!"

"Who are calling warthog you broom riding witch? I can't help it if you're wearing a horse hair helmet!"

With that Viola rose to her feet with her little hands balled into tight fists. She inched herself forward and cocked her arm back. She swung as hard as she could aiming for the back of Rose's head. Her punch was knocked off course by the slapping of her son's hand.

"Mom, what are you doing? You could have hurt Miss Rose," Cecil said.

"That was my intention Son. She needs some shuttin' up that's what she needs."

"Come on here. Come on, let's go talk for a while."

"I don't want to go talk, Son. I want to stay here and punch Rose."

"No Mom, you can't do that. That is not nice."

"Son you don't understand, I don't want to be nice right now, just one little punch?"

Cecil helped his mother up from between the chairs then escorted her out of the room.

"There she goes again," Marva said while waving to Viola.

Meanwhile, Rose was back at it. She began to talk poor Javier's ear off. "See, that's exactly what I'm talking about. She is always so violent. A snake, that's what she is, a gold digging snake. Oh yeeeeeaaaaah, don't think that she hasn't check out your financials. She's hoping to get you to marry her and then she'll work your nerves so bad until you'll have one foot in the grave and one on a bar of soap and she'll be standing behind you with a cup of water. She's the kind of woman who'll line the stairs with banana peels, too! I tell you, you'd better be careful around that woman. You can tell by that look of hers and know she's nothing but trouble. She looks like a nasty infection is what she looks like yep, a nasty little infection."

About thirty minutes had passed and Rose's mouth now had small white dried up saliva resting in the corners. Javier was talked out of his mind and could only stare at the gummy, spackle like substance which stretched as Rose spoke.

"Yeah, yeah Son, you came, you saw me now get the hell out. What are you coming around here worrying me for? Don't you have a family you have to go home to? Go worry them." Viola was so afraid Rose was gaining the attention of Javier that she was running her own son off just to be able to perch herself between the couple.

Cecil would not leave. He had traveled too far to see his mother and wasn't about to visit for a mere thirty minutes then take that long drive home. Cecil sat with his mother and attempted to hold a conversation with her but Viola wasn't having any part of it. She sat silently for the most part as she was trying to keep her eye on her prize, Javier. Cecil continued talking only to receive an occasional "uh huh" or "you don't say" from his mother. Finally he gave in to his mother and decided it would be best if he left so that she could be with her friends.

"Do you need anything Mom?" Cecil asked.

Viola, never taking her eyes off Rose and Javier began nodding her head and mumbling unclearly, "Uh huh…uh yeah…you're right, the roads are probably clear this time of day…uh yeah, probably. I'm sure there's hardly any traffic. Uh…I love you, too Son. Bye." Viola then stood and walked over to where her prize was sitting, leaving Cecil sitting at the table looking dumbfounded. He had not a clue of what his mother was speaking of. He only knew she was not in need of his company that day. After ensuring that his mother was fine, Cecil left for home.

The conversation was flowing, one-sided of course. Rose was talking a mile a minute and Dr. Chadwick was sitting, looking numb, staring at the hole in the back of Miss Swazi's favorite sweater and constantly rubbing his right ear with his index finger checking for blood.

Viola walked over to the table once again. "SHUT UP ROSE, I NEVER KNEW YOU COULD TALK SO MUCH!"

Dr. Chadwick looked up at Viola with his face filled with an abundance of gratitude. Viola then pulled the chair from under the table where it rested and lowered herself down comfortably next to the man.

"Now where were we?" she asked.

"I beg your pardon, we were talking," Rose interrupted.

"No, YOU were talking, HE was suffering."

"Well excuse me!"

"No Rose, there's no excuse for you. Now if you don't mind…"

Rose sat there boiling as Viola and Javier began discussing arts and crafts night at the facility. She shifted her motorized wheelchair into "reverse" then turned sharply to make her exit. She shifted her small vehicle back into the "drive" position and began to make a "U" turn back towards the table where Marva was now sitting alone. As she swept past Viola who was now engrossed in conversation, Rose held out her hand and with one yank, snatched Viola's wig off her head and quickly sped away.

"Oh hell no she didn't!" Viola said in a calm but scary tone. "I'll be right back, Javier. I just need to go slaughter the cow that those four horses are carting about." And in a flash (that would be a senior citizen flash, that is) Viola stormed off for retribution.

After catching up to Rose, Viola clenched up her fist and grunted angrily at the petrified heavyset woman. "GET READY TO MEET YOUR MAKER, CHUBBY!" Viola yelled.

"NO, YOU GET READY TO MEET YOUR'S, BOTH OF YOU!!!" yelled the voice from the hallway. It was Lizzy, slowly charging (if there is such a thing) into the dayroom. "I told you both to stay away from him because he's mine but I see you both have to learn the hard way!"

"Oh my Lord," said Marva. "You ladies have just gone plum crazy."

All three ladies looked on in awe as they bore witness to their friend standing before them in gym shorts, knee high stockings, sneakers and an old basketball jersey. She had white gym socks wrapped around each of her balled up hands and Vaseline smeared over her face as she rocked back and forth ready to fight.

"Now…now…Miss Lizzy, come on now. You don't want to fight anybody here. We're all friends in here, right?" said Betty.

Lizzy stopped her rocking motion and looked up at the aide. "Wel,l I…I guess not. I just want them to stop being whores that's all. See…" the little lady pointed over at Rose. "See…her right there? Now she's a whore." Then Lizzy pointed over at Viola. "And that one right there is what you call an aggressive whore and that one…" she said while pointing over at Marva, "That one…well that one's alright. She's nice to me and doesn't try to get my man. I think she's a lesbo. I think she wants me but that's alright because I've been with women before, not for free though."

"Come on Miss Lizzy, let's go get you cleaned up. There's nobody to fight right now."

The tiny, little lady began removing the wrapped gym socks from her hands. She looked up at her aide and mumbled, "I could have been a contender you know," then with her head hung low she was escorted back to her room. No one uttered a word after Lizzy's departure from the dayroom. Viola looked at Rose then at Marva as if she wanted to apologize but suddenly turned and left.

During dinner for the first time since they had become friends the ladies did not dine together. Lizzy sat and ate with Marva while Viola sat at the table with Miss Swazi and Rose sat alone. As soon as Javier entered the dining room, each lady's focus and attention was on him. He walked in slowly and as he passed each lady's table he would smile and speak to them. He made his way to his usual table with Mr. Gale.

"Are you by yourself today?" Mr. Gale asked.

"Yes, I believe so," Javier replied.

"Good because those old, cackling hens can make a man lose his appetite! That big one with her constant farting, I guess she doesn't think we hear or smell them, huh? And Viola, she'll probably kill you in your sleep if you say the wrong thing to her and that little one there, man, she's just plain crazy. Man you sure attract some doozies!" The men laughed then started in on their meals.

The next morning wasn't much different for the ladies. Lizzy had gotten up and put on one of her best outfits. She hadn't yet taken her medication and her mind hadn't quite gotten on track. She saw Rose as she was on her way to the dining room to get the first glimpse of the doctor as he entered the room. Lizzy walked up to Rose but this morning her outfit was very attractive on her. Her make up was on correctly and her hair looked wonderful.

"Good morning…I…I know you, right?" Lizzy asked confusedly.

"Yes, Lizzy it's me Rose."

"I'm sorry, sometimes I just forget things. I was wondering if you could point me in the direction of the dining room, I'm meeting my husband there."

Knowing that Lizzy was referring to Dr. Chadwick, Rose immediately felt threatened by the petite woman's attractiveness this morning. She wanted to choke her for looking so good and she knew that Javier would think the same.

Rose thought that maybe today Javier would look at Lizzy in a different light. That he would actually see that the small and still shapely woman was the most attractive of the three, hands down. As much as she hated to she directed her new friend.

"Yes, I'll show you where it is, just follow me I'm heading there now." Rose slowly rolled her wheelchair down the hall and down the corridor. She stopped at the large door and pushed it open. The room was empty. "Well, I guess we're the first one's here. Why don't you take a seat and I'll see if I can find your husband."

Lizzy smiled, walked over and sat down at the long wooden table. Rose switched her chair into "reverse" and backed out of the doorway. She headed back up the hall and through the double doors which led into the dining room and settled at their usual table.

Marva entered the dining room and joined Rose. Viola followed shortly but found sanctuary at another table only to avoid Rose. The ladies' trays were brought over and they began to prepare their breakfast. "I wonder where Lizzy is this morning?" Marva asked.

"Hmmm, I don't know. I haven't seen her this morning," Rose replied.

Just after Rose had made that statement, in through the doors came Lizzy escorted by one of the aides. "She got a little turned around. I found her in the employee lounge, she thought she was in here," said the aide as she helped the well dressed woman down into her seat.

"You look real nice today, Lizzy," Marva complimented.

Lizzy looked over at Rose, "Thanks for helping me this morning but the lady said that was the lounge for the employees only and that I was supposed to be in here. I'm glad you found the right place."

Marva looked over at Rose strangely.

"I don't know what she's talking about," Rose said smiling sheepishly.

"Sure you don't," Marva said. "Are you alright, Lizzy?"

"Oh yes, I feel fine. I'm meeting someone here this morning."

"Who, who are you meeting, Honey?"

"Uh…I think…um…I can't remember their name."

"I see, well you just go on and eat and I'll let you know when they get here, Ok?"

"Ok, thank you. You are a nice lady."

Shortly after breakfast, Marva left for her dialysis. The other women stayed clear of each other and would fill the seat next to the doctor whenever the opportunity presented itself.

That night while lying in their beds Rose realized that the two of them had not spoken to each other all day. She decided to be the bigger person and break the silence. "He doesn't want you, Viola," she whispered.

"I suppose you think he wants you, huh? I can just see it now, a handsome doctor walking down the street with a bear on wheels," Viola grunted.

"Well, he told me my size didn't matter and that I was attractive regardless."

"He said I was very pretty and was very good company."

"He said we could sit together during BINGO," Rose said proudly.

"We're meeting in the garden after breakfast tomorrow so stuff that in your pie hole!"

Rose became furious. The two ladies spoke not another word to each other that night. Viola, satisfied with herself, looked up at the ceiling smiling before drifting off to sleep. Rose lay there for most of the night with her blood boiling from Viola's arrogant attitude and sharp tongue.

Day broke just as quickly as night had fallen and Rose was still upset. She felt somewhat better as the short slumber had taken her mind off Viola and her morning garden courtship. Rose reached over and slid her hand down the left side of her bed feeling around for the long cord. She pulled the cord that had somehow found its way under her left thigh and gripped the oblong button which was attached at its end. She pressed the red button then placed the cord back beside her. Only a few minutes had passed before Betty entered the room.

"We're an early riser this morning, huh Miss Rose?"

"Girl, I've got to get out of this bed this morning. I've got to get out of this room. Come on, help me up please."

Betty stood next to the huge woman's bed and continued stretching the tight latex plastic over each hand. Once her gloves were snug against her hands she reached over and helped Rose up. She helped her into her chair and into the washroom they went. Betty assisted Rose in getting cleaned up and dressed before checking on Viola who was still in a sound sleep.

Before Rose wheeled out of the room she pulled along side of her bed. "Betty, can you please pass me my knitting bag over at the head of the bed?"

"Sure Miss Rose, couldn't sleep last night?"

"I had the hardest time trying to get these eyes to close last night so I did a little knitting. That usually wears me out. I thought I'd do a little more knitting this morning while I wait for breakfast."

"Well, that sounds relaxing Miss Rose. You go on ahead and I'll check on your buddy here in a few minutes and when she wakes I'll let her know you're already down there."

Rose smiled at the aide then quietly rolled down the brightly lit hallway towards the dining room.

Betty did just as she promised. After about fifteen minutes or so, she walked down to the where Viola was just pulling herself up. Propped up against her pillows she stretched out her arms slightly and yawned. "Good morning Miss Vy and how are we feeling this morning?"

"I don't know yet, I haven't tried to move anything. We'll both know in a second, huh." she replied.

"Well come on, let's get your day started."

"Yeah, this should be a good day, too."

"What's making your day so good today, Miss Vy?"

"Girl, got me a date with the sweet doctor today."

"A date, what kind of a date is this? What are you two planning on doing?"

"We're going on a sit down in the garden kind of date. I've haven't been courted in so long. It's going to be wonderful and I want to look nice, too. Look in my closet and pull out my black slacks, you know the ones that you always say make me look like I've got a little butt back there. I think I'll wear those and my sexy black and purple blouse."

Betty began pulling out each garment that Viola requested. She assisted her in getting bathed and dressed then stood back and looked the elderly fashion model over from head to toe. "Miss Vy, you look like a million bucks. 'Ole Dr. Chadwick is in for the shock of his life."

"I don't want to shock him too much Dear I'm not sure how strong his heart is. Now pass me that perfume over there. I think this should take him over the edge."

"He doesn't stand a chance Miss Vy, not a chance."

"I know that Rose is hot, too," Viola said giggling. "She actually thought she had a chance with him."

"Now I know you two weren't competing over the doctor?"

"Competing? There was no contest. Like I said, she didn't have a chance."

"Is that why she left out of here so early?"

"She probably just wanted to go down to the dining room and smell the food as it was being cooked. She's probably trying to guess what Al is cooking her to eat. Speaking of eating, pass me my teeth from off the nightstand please."

Betty walked over to the small wooden table which sat between both ladies' beds. She picked up the small blue plastic container which was filled with the 'Efferdent' and water solution and passed it to Viola. She sat on the side of her bed and adjusted her clothing and checked her hair once more before adding the last and finishing touch. She opened the container. Just as she reached in she realized that there was nothing but the water and chemical mix present.

"Did I leave my teeth in the bathroom, Betty?"

"I didn't see them in there a moment ago. Hold on, I'll check."

Betty walked back into the bathroom and searched for Viola's dentures. She walked back into the room and over to the nightstand from where the empty container was. She looked under the beds, in the drawers, and even in the closet. Betty looked over at Viola hunching her shoulders. "I don't see them anywhere, Miss Vy. Where could you have put them, any ideas?"

"Rose!" Viola groaned.

"Rose? Why would Miss Rose take your teeth?"

"Because she's mad about Javier. I can't see him like dis."

"Well, I'm sure he probably knows that you wear dentures, so does he, I think."

"I DON'T CARE! HE CAN'T SHEE ME WIP OUT MY PEETH!"

"Ok, Ok, I'll go up to the dining room and ask Miss Rose if she's seen them, maybe she picked them up by mistake thinking that they were hers."

"Rose doesn't wear dentures. If there's anything that that woman has probably exercised, it's her teeth. They can probably rip through steel! Ever seen how she gnaws through dose rib bones? Oh no, you don't want to get in the way of those things, not ever!"

"Ok Miss Vy, I'll be right back."

"Can you please hurry; Javier could be on his way there already."

Betty walked quickly to the dining room and rushed over to the table where Rose sat alone, knitting and sniffing the aroma filled air. "Miss Rose…"

"Yes, Honey?"

"Miss Vy has gone and misplaced her teeth. Do you have any idea what she could have done with them?"

"Her teeth! Wait…can you smell that hickory in that bacon? Al has really outdone his self this morning. I think he's making French toast, too."

"Miss Rose…Miss Vy's teeth, have you seen them?"

"Oh no Child, I haven't seen that woman's teeth. She probably chewed somebody's butt off and they're probably still embedded on the remaining butt cheek. Who knows what that crazy woman has done with those things."

"Ok, you're sure you haven't seen them? This isn't your way of keeping her away from Dr. Chadwick, is it? I know you both have an interest in him so I hope you wouldn't do something like that."

"Oh no, I don't need to take that woman's teeth to make her look ugly, she can do that just by waking up in the morning. Besides, he's not thinking about Viola."

"Ok, I'll go back and check the room again," Betty rushed out of the dining room back to the impatiently awaiting Viola.

"Well, did she have them? Did she know where they are?"

"No, but I'm sure they're around here somewhere."

Betty searched the entire room. She checked everywhere. Viola's disappointment was etched across her face. "What am I going to do?"

"I'll tell you what you're going to do, you're going to walk into that dining room and you're going sit with your new man and eat your breakfast. After that, you're going to sit out in the garden with him and enjoy the fresh air, that's what you're going to do."

Viola's head remained hanging. Betty walked over and lifted the woman's head up by her small pointed chin.

"Come on Miss Vy let's go get your man," Viola raised her head upward until eye contact with the aide was established.

She smiled at Betty then whispered, "You're right, I'm going do get my man…as soon as you get your nasty hands out my face."

"Girl, you're a mess! Let's get you down to the dining room and I'll ask around for your dentures."

Betty escorted Viola to the dining room where upon entering, they saw Dr. Chadwick just lowering himself down into his seat. Viola approached his table and greeted him. While placing her hand over her mouth she spoke. "Goot morning Jabier, you're looking pine piss morning."

"Good morning Viola, I was just speaking to Rose. She said you might not make it in here today. She said you were thinking about eating in you room today."

"Oh, I washent peeling well," the woman slurred through her gums.

"Oh, that's odd, she said something about you not being able to find your dentures this morning."

Viola quickly cut her eyes over to Rose who was sitting at the table smiling and pouring syrup over her steaming French toast. Viola slowly and silently mouthed the words, "I AM GOING TO KILL YOU."

Rose waved to her angry friend with a slice of bacon in her hand then continued to eat. Viola turned back around and forgetting to place her hand back in front of her mouth, smiled. With her mouth sunken deep into her face and her lips pushed out resembling the beak of a duck, she bared it all. In that second she could see that Javier was not receptive at all to her new but old look. Their trays were brought out and the two remained silent through breakfast. Javier would only glance over occasionally to get a glimpse of Viola gumming her food.

After Dr. Chadwick had left the dining room, Viola stopped by the table to speak to Marva. The ladies greeted each other and enlightened one another with small talk.

Later that morning, Dr. Chadwick cancelled their garden sitting. He said that he wasn't feeling well but could not be found in his room during that time.

"How was the garden?" Rose asked smugly. Viola looked at her with one of her famous nasty looks. "I bet you're hungry being that you really couldn't eat without your teeth," Rose continued. Viola remained quiet. She stood there rubbing her gums together and peering at Rose.

"I'm sorry your little doctor decided that he didn't want to sit out there amongst those beautiful flowers today and I knitted you a special blanket just for the occasion. Although you're not going now, I still want you to have it."

Rose pulled the nicely knitted blanket from the bag that she had been carrying and Viola's evil look dissipated. She realized that Rose, although angry with her, was still such a good friend to have done that. As Rose pulled out the last remaining section of the blanket, Viola's dentures fell onto the table. Viola's face turned beet red.

"I think you'd better head for the hills!" Lizzy warned the heavy woman.

"Are those Viola's?" Marva asked. "Now Viola, I'm sure there's a very good explanation for this. Isn't that right, Rose?"

Viola began inching her way around the table.

"Betty! Betty, you'd better get over here," Marva shouted. Betty rushed over to the ladies just in time. Viola's fist was revved back and ready to fly.

"What is going on over here?" Betty asked.

"Look down on the pable," Viola grunted. "Do dose dentures look pamiliar?"

"Oh you found them?"

"No, dey were in Rose's bag, she hid them prom me. She pook dem and put dem in her bag so I couldn't go poo the garden with Jabier. She was jealous, dat's what she was."

"Is that what happened Miss Rose?"

"No, that's not what happened. It was an accident," Rose said as she backed her wheelchair up.

"It was no accident," Viola said now lowering herself down into her chair.

As Rose rode by Viola she looked back and smirked. It was the same smirk Miss Thelma had given her on that bus some fifty years ago. Rose smirked at the angry woman and mumbled, "It was an accident! I meant to flush them down the toilet!"

Viola struggled to get out of her seat but it was too late, the kitchen crew in the back of the dining room could hear Rose's tires squeal from there. Viola was given a mild sedative to calm her down for the rest of the day.

Weeks had passed and Viola and Rose still had not spoken one word to each other. Viola was still flirting with the doctor but he seemed uninterested in anything but a mere friendship with her. She could tell that his interest lay elsewhere. Viola watched as he and Rose seem to talk more often, now with her doing more listening than talking. They sat together during BINGO and arts and crafts. "What could he possibly see in that tub of lard?" she would ask herself. Still angry at Rose for possibly ruining any chances she could have had with the doctor, Viola was determined to get even.

Later that day, Viola watched as Rose went through her usual routine. She would come back from lunch and watch "Texas Ranger" before dozing off for her afternoon nap. This particular evening Viola, still determined to get her man, didn't nap. She sat, watched and waited as the unsuspecting Rose drifted off. As she sat comfortably in her wheelchair with her head tilted over toward her right shoulder, Viola went to work.

It was 4:45 pm and time for BINGO. Viola used the remote control and increased the volume of the television set. Rose woke up abruptly. She looked at her watch then reached for the ice pitcher next to her and poured herself a cup of cold water. After drinking her water she put the cup back onto the small table. "Why is the TV up so loud?" she asked.

Viola just looked at her for a second before replying. "I couldn't hear it besides it'll keep you company while I keep the good doctor company at BINGO. I'll tell him you said hello."

"Sorry Vy, your chances with Javier are gone. He's not thinking about you. Who does he sit with now?"

"Well, he'll be sitting with me today because you won't be there."

Rose looked at Viola strangely then switched her wheelchair on. After moving only about six inches the chair made a loud clanging sound followed by a muffled crunch. The chair would not move. Rose looked down at the chair and saw her roommate's cane jammed between the spokes of both wheels. Viola stood in the doorway for a brief second only to ensure that Rose was immobilized before disappearing into the light. "VIOLA! VIOLA YOU EVIL WITCH GET BACK HERE!

SOMEBODY, ANYBODY, HELP ME!" she called out but no one could hear her.

Rose tried backing up and even tried to pull the wicked woman's cane from her transport but was unsuccessful at each attempt.

"Two can play that game, see ya when I get back and try not to burn your motor out," Viola chuckled and headed down the hall.

She used the wall as a crutch and finally made it up to the activities room where everyone had gathered for the game. She looked around for Dr. Chadwick. When spotted, Viola soon saw the familiar face sitting next to him. Lizzy was perched in the seat next to the man. Viola knew that there was only one way Lizzy would give up that seat. She thought for a second before sashaying over to the table unassisted by her cane. She walked up to Lizzy who was smiling and stamping her BINGO board even with the absence of a letter being called. Viola placed her hand down onto the table then leaned over and placed her mouth near Lizzy's ear.

"Hey Lizzy, the Easter Bunny is in the lobby and he's not going to be here long."

"You're kidding. Excuse me, I'll be right back. I've been dying to meet him. Do you think he'll give me his autograph?"

"I'm sure he will."

Lizzy got up from the table and headed for the lobby singing "Here comes Peter Cotton Tail…hopping down the bunny trail…"

Meanwhile, Viola had managed to position herself back by the doctor and remained by his side throughout the entire game.

She helped him with his BINGO boards and indulged in great conversation. Viola was feeling back in control. She thought about Rose stuck back in the room bound to her wheelchair and she chuckled to herself. She sat back in her chair to savor that moment. She leaned her head back and inhaled deeply.

"MEDIC! MEDIC, I NEED A MEDIC OVER HERE!"

"ARTHUR, SHUT THE HELL UP AND GO BACK TO SLEEP!" Viola shouted.

"Viola, he doesn't mean it, he's just having a dream. Where's your compassion?"

"I know and you're right, he just startled me is all," she said smiling, "I'm sorry Arthur, go on, go back to sleep. I didn't mean to yell at you."

Javier smiled at Viola and she returned her best compassionate facial expression to him before sliding her chair closer to her BINGO partner. She had once again returned to heaven.

Chapter 7 - Friendship

Days passed and the feuding among the ladies had worsened. Marva perched herself on the side of the table nearest the dining room door in hopes of luring each of her friends back to their table where they belonged. Viola was the first to enter. Walking slowly without the assistance of her cane the fragile woman shuffled slowly down the aisle. Marva waved her over to "their" table and Viola obliged. She walked over to the table and pulled out the chair that she usually sat in. She was dressed smartly and her hair, her own hair, was looking fabulous.

Marva followed her and took her usual seat. "Good morning Viola, don't you look beautiful this morning," she said.

"Why thank you Marva, I had Colleen, you know the aide that works the evening shift? I had her do just a little something to my hair last night."

"Well she did a wonderful job, I must say. Where's Rose?"

"Oh, she's still in the room. I heard her over there mumbling something about not being able to find her inhaler. You know how she is if she can't eat it she'll lose it. Have you seen Javier this morning?"

"Nope, can't say that I have. What's with you all anyway?"

"Well outside of him being interesting and handsome and…"

"No, not him, I'm talking about you, Rose, and Lizzy. Don't you think that it's pretty silly, and not to mention unchristian-like to be competing for some man?"

"Girl, he's not just some man. Have you taken a good look at him or talked with him, and if you have, I want to know when and why?"

"No, I haven't."

"Oh good, but Girl, he is everything!"

"No, Jesus is the only man who has walked this earth that is everything. Dr. Chadwick is just a man."

"Just a man…gasp…gasp…just a…gasp…just a man…gasp…there's only one…gasp…gasp…God," Harvey said passing by and inhaling.

"Well, he's just going to be my man once I get those other two out of the way and get them to realize that he is MY man. Can I get an AMEN?" Viola said grinning from ear to ear.

"Uh, no you can't. See, that's exactly what I want to talk to you all about. You are letting a man interfere with your friendship; all of you."

"Girl, friendship can't keep you warm at night."

"And neither will he. He has his own room and so do you and you share yours with Rose, your friend."

"Well, you know what I mean, it's the companionship."

"You have companionship now with us, all of us."

"Well, I just want him. Now leave it and me alone."

"Look Vy, I just want to…," before Marva could complete her statement, in walked Lizzy smiling and waving. She greeted everyone as she passed by their table. She walked over and sat down in her usual seat.

"Good morning, Ladies!"

"Good morning, Lizzy," said Marva, "What makes you so happy this morning?"

"I saw a butterfly this morning while I was getting dressed."

"A butterfly?"

"Yes a tiny black one."

"Where did you see a butterfly?"

"It was in my room."

"There was a butterfly in your room this morning?"

"Yes, it was so lovely. It could fly so fast, too. First it flew to my window then it flew over and landed on my denture cup. It sat there smiling at me and rubbing it's legs together. Its eyes were huge. It sat there for a while then flew back over to the window. It buzzed loudly. I guess that was it's way of singing a beautiful song."

"Where did it go?"

"As it sang its beautiful song and then Betty came into my room. It flew by her head then around the room quickly. She left out and came back with a magic newspaper because when it flew back over to the window, Betty swung the paper and hit the window. That made it disappear through the glass. When she left, it flew back into my room from the bathroom."

Realizing that Lizzy had been mesmerized by a fly and not a butterfly, both Marva and Viola looked on strangely as Lizzy finished describing her glorious morning adventure. As they continued to listen to Lizzy's story, in rolled Rose barking at the top of her lungs.

"I KNOW YOU HAVE IT, WHERE IS IT VIOLA? I SAID, WHERE IS IT?"

"What is she talking about, Vy?" Marva asked.

Viola shrugged her shoulders then returned her attention to the angry woman rolling toward her.

"Where is it, Vy?" Rose repeated.

"Where's what?"

"You know exactly what I'm talking about, my inhaler! It was on my nightstand last night and now it's missing. So is that what's going on now? You're stooping to these low down dirty tactics just so you can get to him first? That's low, that's lower than low and you ought to be ashamed of yourself. Well don't get happy too fast, the nurse is getting me another one so you didn't slow me down too much."

"Rose, I have no idea what you're talking about. Why would I do such a thing? Maybe you ate it or maybe it's down in your…"

"Here it is Rose," Betty cheerfully said. "Somehow it got stuck underneath Miss Viola's mattress. I don't know how you managed that and on the opposite side away from your bed, too. You really ought to try to keep up with this thing. It can be pretty dangerous if it got lost."

Rose looked at Viola but Viola would not look over in her direction. Rose leaned over toward Viola, "You don't know what happened to it, huh?" Rose asked angrily.

"Look Woman, I think you should be getting out of my face. Now, I told you that I didn't know where it was, I don't know how it got there. Maybe you were sleepwalking."

"Sleepwalking, you're kidding right?"

"Do you see me laughing?"

"Heeeeey, that's right, I don't like you do I?" Lizzy asked while pointing to Viola.

"Ladies! Ladies! Look, you have to stop this right now. Viola, this is exactly what I was just talking about. Now all of you just stop it. Some man walks in the door and you all just lose it. Ok, he might be handsome and charming and all of that other stuff, but he's just a man. He's not someone worth losing yourself or your friendships over. Now come on, please, won't you all do what God Himself would want you to do? Please, make up and forgive each other. Y'all know that God don…"

"DON'T LIKE UGLY! We know, we know. How many times do we have to hear that from you?" Viola blurted out.

Viola looked over at Rose apologetically and in a low monotone mumble, "I'm sorry for hiding your inhaler, I don't know what got into me. You are my friend, Rose and I know that sometimes I can be a real pain but you've always accepted me for that and put up with me and my mouth. Marva's right, we shouldn't let a man destroy our friendship." She then looked over to Lizzy, "Lizzy, you're as nutty as they come but you are my friend, too. If you want him then go get him, Girl."

Lizzy looked up at Viola with nothing but forgiveness in her eyes and spoke to her friend with such gentleness, "Choo-choo trains blow out the most beautiful smoke that you'll ever see."

"We'll take that as an 'apology accepted' from you Liz," said Marva.

Rose continued to pout for a few more minutes before she too, gave in to her companions. "Apology accepted, Vy. I too, am so sorry for snatching off your wig and putting the red pepper in your coffee and for sealing up the holes of your hearing aids with 'clear coat' nail polish. I'm glad that it scraped right off. Oh yeah, and I'm sorry for dropping your wig in the toilet last night. I tried running over it several times but my wheel marks wouldn't show up, so I dipped it instead."

Viola first glared and then smiled at her friend. "I hated that wig anyway but my hearing aids? Girl! I couldn't hear a thing for three days and that red pepper gave me the runs something awful. I apologize for jamming my cane in your wheels and leaving you stranded in the room for two hours."

"Girl, I was so mad I couldn't see straight. Oh and by the way, your cane is in Miss Swazi's bathroom, sorry."

"And I'm sorry for being a bird!" Lizzy shouted.

"That's Ok Lizzy you be a bird if you want to. It's Ok with us," Marva said smiling.

Then out of nowhere, Lizzy shouted at the top of her voice as she pumped her fist high in the air, "HOS BEFORE BROS! That's right ladies, we're not going to let some man come between us. I mean…you know…of course if we were having a threesome but that's the only time or if…"

"Lizzy, that's enough!" Marva snapped. "First of all, I'm not a whore or ho or whatever you want to call it. None of us are. We are all children of God, so don't belittle me, not today, not any day."

"That's right and I'm no whore either!" said Viola.

"Uh…me either," Rose added.

"Rose, you sound a little unsure, are you certain about that? You did look a little familiar to me when I first arrived here. Anyway, I was one and a damn good ho, too. Hoing paid my bills and bought me whatever I wanted," Lizzy said proudly.

"The key word here is WAS. You were a whore, as you put it, back then. You are no longer a woman of that profession and God has forgiven you for all your transgressions. This is a new life for you, now live it and enjoy your peace," Marva preached.

Lizzy smiled and nodded. The ladies were just as they had always been before their small feud. They laughed talked and ate as they used to do.

"Rose, do you want my toast?" Viola asked.

"No, actually I don't think that I'm going to eat my own. I'm not really that hungry this morning," Rose replied.

"Huh? What do you mean? You, not hungry, what is this?"

"Well, one thing I did learn through all of this is that I am a bit over weight. I guess I could stand to lose a few pounds."

"But you said 'I like to eat, that's what I do'."

"Yeah but people change, I've changed."

"Wow! I'm in shock over here."

"Leave her alone Vy, if she wants to lose some weight then I think that we should encourage her. I hear that the 'Atkins' diet is pretty good, Rose. You can eat all the meat you want, just lay off the carbs. You should probably check with your doctor first because you know, these new fangled diets are made for the young folks." Marva added.

"I was thinking about that new 'Lettuce Diet'."

"What new Lettuce Diet?" Viola blurted.

"Yeah, they say if you eat a plate full of lettuce three times a day you'll lose weight fast."

"Yeah, it's called ashes and dust. It'll be what's laying in the bottom of your casket. Are you crazy, there's no way anybody can survive on just lettuce, I mean unless you're a damn rabbit. I think they meant as long as you have lettuce with your meals," Viola stated. "How about a lettuce and steak diet instead?"

"Well yeah, I mean…I do like steak or I could do lettuce and chicken or lettuce and pork chops."

"Yeah, that'll get the weight off."

"See ladies? I'm so glad you've cleared everything up and are back together as friends. Everything's back to normal," said Marva.

Just as those words passed through Marva's lips, the doors to the dining room opened and the man of their dreams entered through them.

"Wow, look at him!" Lizzy screamed. Each woman stared and smiled as Dr. Chadwick glided by. "Who is that guy?" Lizzy asked.

"He's just a guy that's visiting, Liz pay him no mind," Marva said.

The ladies said not a word. Viola began primping and adjusting her hair. Rose slid all of her food to one side and only picked at her eggs. Lizzy sat watching him while sliding her middle finger deep into her mouth and slowly pulling it out.

"Ladies! What about our bond and promise to each other?" Marva questioned.

"Oh yeah, uh…yeah…uh…I'm still with you on that," Viola mumbled.

"Uh yeah…me too," said Rose.

"I'm all over that thing!" said Lizzy, panting and playing with her right breast.

"Ladies, all eyes on me, he's just a man!" Marva shouted while pointing at her face. "Come on now, you can do this. Don't let him get into your heads."

Each woman, with the exception of Lizzy, turned her attention to Marva. She reached across the table and took both ladies by the hand.

"Lizzy, look at me."

Lizzy just couldn't do it. She was dialed in on the doctor. Finally Marva let go of Rose's hand and grabbed Lizzy by hers.

"Lizzy, I said look at me," Marva repeated. Lizzy slowly turned her head in Marva's direction. She looked over at Viola then at Rose. They both smiled.

Lizzy turned and peered deeply into Marva's eyes and calmly said, "Are you sure you're not gay? I mean, all of that hunk-a-chunk-a-man over there and you want me to stare into YOUR eyes? Noooooooo way!"

"Lizzy, stay focused here, Ok? Now, we're trying to prevent any unnecessary anger from entering our group, right? So that man is now officially off limits, Ok?"

Marva dug in preparing herself for the long debate that was about to occur between her and Lizzy because she knew that Lizzy was the weakest of the three when it came to men.

"Ok," Lizzy answered without giving it a second thought.

Marva revved back then nodded her head, "Uh…well then…Ok then, agreed."

The ladies remained together for the entire day. Toward the end of the evening after retiring into the dayroom Marva had noticed that each lady was leaving the room a little more often than usual. They had taken several restroom visits or required something from their rooms on different instances. While heavily engrossed in a game of cards, Viola interrupted the game stating that she had forgotten her hearing aids in her room and needed to go to retrieve them. This was very interesting to Marva, especially when she could see her more than deceitful friend's hearing devices protruding ever so slightly just above her earlobes.

"I'll be right back, Ladies," Viola said. She lifted herself up from her seat and slowly proceeded toward the exit.

"I'll be right back too, Ladies," Marva said and she wheeled herself over to the door. She slowly opened the door and inched her way out into the hall. She rolled herself past her room then past Viola and Rose's room.

It was just as she had suspected, Viola was nowhere to be found. She continued around the hall toward Javier's room.

"Oh, you say the nicest things Dr. Chadwick."

Marva could hear Viola's chatting and giggling coming from Javier's room. She rolled herself back to the dayroom and waited patiently for Viola's return with the other ladies.

Upon her return, Viola was smiling sheepishly. The other ladies didn't notice the guilt written across her face, no one did, no one with the exception of Marva. The card game resumed. Marva had now realized that Viola wasn't the only snake at the table.

Between each hand of cards each lady would come up with an excuse to leave the room and Marva would follow each lady to

Javier's room. Marva said nothing. She didn't want them to know that they had all lied to one another. She didn't want the bickering to start all over again. The ladies continued their disappearing acts throughout the entire day. Finally, there was no need to sneak from the room. Dr. Chadwick entered and had taken a seat near the front of the room. He appeared to be preparing a postcard of some sort to be mailed. Mr. Little had sat down at the piano and was playing of the old standard jazz and piano songs that he could still remember. For an elderly man who had lost some of his hearing, he still played beautifully.

Each woman periodically shifted their attention to lone Dr. Chadwick while trying to maintain their composure. Marva watched on and knew it was just a matter of time before one of them would walk over to him and break the truce and start the battle for his attention all over again. She knew that if she hadn't done something to prevent this catastrophe that her friends and their friendship was truly doomed.

Marva slowly backed her wheelchair from the table. "Wait, where are you going Marva, the game's not over?" Viola asked while primping her hair.

"I'll be right back," Marva replied and off she rolled toward the front of the room. She pulled up next to the old cherry wood piano and mumbled only a few words to pianist. She positioned herself facing the others then pushed the chrome clamps on both sides of her chair to lock her wheels in place. She shyly looked over at Mr. Little and with only a quick nod began to transpose herself back into the gospel diva from Chicago. As Mr. Little began to play softly, Marva started. She began to sing her favorite song "Amazing Grace". Everyone in the room sat quietly and in awe as she sang beautifully. No one there had ever heard her sing before not even her dearest friends.

After the completion of the song the entire room remained silent with the exception of one person sitting at the front table, Dr. Chadwick. He rose to his feet and clapped his hands together loudly until others joined him in his display of appreciation of her talent. He walked up to Marva and leaned over to hug her. "That was beautiful," he whispered. Marva smiled and nodded as the other residents cheered and praised her talent. This didn't sit well with Viola at all. Not to be outdone in front of Dr. Chadwick, Viola rose from her seat and marched down to the piano.

"Do you know 'Order My Steps'?" Viola asked.

"No, I'm afraid I don't know that one," Mr. Little responded.

Viola looked down at the frail man then tapped him on the shoulder. "That's alright I don't need no dang piano anyway."

Viola clasped her hands together in front of her like an opera singer would and sucked in a lung full of air. She lifted her head and closed her eyes just before she began to blast out some of the most unusual squeals, screams and sounds that you could ever imagine. To say the least, it was awful. Marva quickly unlatched her wheelchair and rolled back to the table. Mr. Little placed his hands over his ears and Dr. Chadwick walked out followed by others.

After Viola had completed her assault on both her vocal chords and everyone else's ears she opened her eyes to an almost emptied room. She looked over at the empty seat that was once occupied by her dear Dr. Chadwick. Her heart and mouth dropped. She had realized that she had just humiliated herself in front of all of her friends only to outdo Marva. She quickly turned her attention to the table where Marva sat. Remembering the praise and congratulatory smile from Dr. Chadwick to Marva made her blood boil. Marva too, had just become one of Viola's competitors and Marva had realized by that one look from Viola that her plan to keep them together had failed.

Sunday morning was always an exciting day. After breakfast, all of the ladies would gather in the activities room for a not too lengthy church service. Baptists would meet at ninc o'clock and Catholics would meet at ten. The ladies would get so excited.

Viola was the only Catholic in the group, when she claimed any religion. After her run in with her pastor back in Emporia years ago, she vowed never to step foot in another Baptist church ever again. She would attend church occasionally before moving to Hayfield, but after moving there and with the services being held so close to her room, Viola would go almost every Sunday. She said it was the only way she could get a shot of wine.

Marva and Rose would attend the Baptist service every Sunday without fail. This particular morning Viola's plans seemed to have changed once she found out Javier was going to attend the Baptist service.

"You know, I don't think I've ever attended a Baptist service before. I hear that it's very spiritual," Viola commented.

Marva, knowing what her old friend was up to replied, "Oh it's pretty different than your Catholic service, you probably won't enjoy it, most Catholics don't and besides they don't have wine there, either."

"No wine! What kind of church is that? Well, I don't know, sometimes you want to check out something a little different. It might be very interesting."

"I heard Dr. Chadwick was Catholic so you'd probably see him in there at ten."

"I thought he was Baptist. Where did you hear that he was Catholic?"

"I thought I heard his daughter ask about a Catholic service."

"Hmmm, you know, on second thought, maybe I will go to the ten o'clock service. Maybe you're right, the Baptist service might be a little too radical for me and that communion wine helps relax me."

"You know, I've always wondered what a Catholic service was like," said Rose.

"Oh, they're pretty boring," Viola replied.

"But they seem so structured and classy compared to our get down praise and worship services. Maybe I'll check it out today."

"Actually, now that I think about it, I did hear somebody say that Dr. Chadwick was in fact Baptist. I think it was he himself who told me that," Marva added.

"Is that so?" Viola asked. "You know, Rose I've got a wonderful idea. You go check out the Catholic service and I'll go see how the Baptist folk do it and then we can discuss the differences."

"Naaah, I think I'll just stick with my good 'ole down home folk."

"Bet you miss those fish dinners, huh?"

"I guess about as much as you miss those alcoholic priests."

"Do you miss your Cadillac driving, money swindling Pastor?"

"Probably not as much as you miss your alter boy molesting Priest."

"Ladies, ladies, do you have to argue about everything? Sure, all religions have people who have problems and yes, sometimes it reaches all the way up to the top. They are just people and it doesn't represent what God is about, so please ladies, lets suspend with the religion slamming, Ok?"

Both women retreated and returned to their meals. Al walked over to the ladies' table displaying a huge smile. "How's everything ladies? How's the French toast this morning? Made it special myself."

"It tastes just fine, Al," Marva answered.

"I like it, too," replied Rose

"Oh, I thought it was sugar flavored cardboard, sorry," Viola sarcastically responded.

Al stepped closer to the table and looked down at Viola's plate. "You haven't even tasted it, Miss Vy. How can you say what it tastes like?"

Viola looked over at the potbellied man then cut her eyes quickly away from him.

"Woman, you're as mean as a snake! You were just tryin' to give me a hard time weren't you? See, and I was going to put in a good word for you to my man, Dr. Chadwick. I've seen how you look at him, all of you. He's a nice guy, isn't he? You ladies have been getting all prettied up and for what? He's not thinking about any of you, none of you three anyway. I know. I've seen him with the one he wants."

"What makes you think that we're getting all prettied up for him? He isn't anybody," Viola said trying to conceal her embarrassment. "I do know one thing about Dr. Chadwick that you don't," she continued.

"And what might that be?"

Viola curled her index finger several times gesturing Al over closer to her. She cupped her hand and placed it over his ear to whisper to the young man. Just as she moved her face closer to his she lifted a slice of the sugar covered bread and slapped it violently across the side of his face.

"I know he doesn't like your French toast, either!" Viola yelled.

Al jumped back with his face glazed with sugar and syrup.

"Woman, you are crazy, just plain crazy! I see why he didn't choose you!" he shouted then rushed back toward the kitchen.

"I wonder who he meant when he said he knows the one that he wants," said Viola.

"Yeah, he said he saw them together," Rose added.

"I've never seen him with anybody other than you three," Marva stated as she thumbed through her bible. "Nope, don't know who that could be," she continued.

"Miss Swazi perhaps?" Viola asked.

"Nah, couldn't be his type," Rose replied.

"I've seen a bar of soap shaped like a dog before," Lizzy added.

"Leave it alone ladies obviously Dr. Chadwick has met someone he's interested in, so leave him be," Marva instructed the ladies.

"Leave him be my ass! Not after he led me to believe that I was the one for him," said Viola.

"Did he use those exact words?"

"No, but I sensed it."

"So did I," said Rose. "He said I was a pretty woman and that my size shouldn't matter for any man who had a true respect for beauty."

"Oh Girl, that man acted like he wanted you and you Viola and even Lizzy over here. Maybe he wanted you all but you can't be angry because he found somebody else. He probably told you all nice things. He's a nice man and that's what nice men do. If you're meant to have a man, God will send you one," Marva preached.

"But he sent me that one and somebody took him and I'm gonna find out who," Viola vowed.

Chapter 8 - Winner of the Prize

After breakfast the next morning the ladies gathered in the dayroom. They had already decided during breakfast that they would, in fact, find out who this mystery person was Dr. Chadwick was spending his time. Still flustered and upset from the news she heard from Al on the previous day, Viola, with bags under her eyes, slammed her hand down on the table surface. With a loud thud she shouted, "Girl, I couldn't even sleep last night, I was so mad! I gave that man everything I had and he does this? I've got to know which one of these geriatric tramps stole my man!"

"Your man? I believe he was a bit more interested in me than you. He told me I should be wined and dined in the finest restaurants. He told me about Paris, France and all the wonderful foods they have there. And to think, I was going to eat lettuce for that man!" Rose said then quickly took a puff from her inhaler.

"HE'S MY MAN! I'm going to kill her and then he and I are going to have sex in the kitchen by the stove and if he won't, I'm gonna make him look like a 'Ken' doll," Lizzy said while spreading her index and middle fingers apart then quickly snapping them back together like a pair of scissors.

Viola and Rose both looked at Lizzy then at each other. Viola shook her head while looking down at the floor. "Lord, help us." She looked up at the ladies then held her fist up in the air. "Ok, let's go find the man stealing whore!" She pointed over to Rose, "Rose you're on point. I want you to position yourself strategically and monitor all in and out traffic of the doctor's room. Make note of every woman that enters and exits his room. I want names!" She then pointed over to Lizzy. "Liz, you're on intell. Get as much information as you can from anyone you can. Find out if anybody has seen the doctor with any woman beside one of us or the nurses or aides. On second thought, I want their names too, everybody's suspect! I'll run recon. I'm gonna watch his every move. We'll get to the bottom of this!"

"Woman, you watch far too many spy movies," Rose said.

The ladies all agreed and collected their things and headed to their posts. Rose wheeled herself up to the corner of the hallway which led to the corridor where Javier's room was located. From the bag in her lap, she pulled out her red and white yarn and the partially completed blanket she had been working on for several months. She began to knit and watch the doctor's door. She watched and made notes every time a nurse or an aide entered or left the elderly man's room. Even if Javier left out of his room she remained sitting and waiting to see if someone would step in to leave a note or memento.

She even made a note when his daughter stopped by to drop off his cap that he had left in her car. She sat there for hours, well at least until it was time for her to eat again.

When Javier did leave his room Viola was hot on his trail. She followed him to the physical therapy room, to the administrator's office and inside the dayroom where he and Harvey sat quietly playing chess.

Harvey, with his oxygen mask covering his face, only removed it to say one of two words, "Check…gasp" or

"Damn…gasp". It seems he had not yet had the privilege to utter the words "check mate" as Javier was too good of a player.

Viola followed Javier everywhere he went. She acted as if she were some type of spy running a covert operation. When following him she often found herself humming the theme song to "Mission Impossible".

Lizzy, whenever she could remember, would interrogate every woman that she ran across. She saw Miss Swazi passing the dayroom and stopped her. She grabbed the silver haired woman by the sleeve of her favorite sweater, "Are you making time with my man?" Lizzy asked.

"Pardon me but I'm afraid that I don't quite understand the question that you're asking," Miss Swazi replied confusedly.

"Wait, that's my line. I'm the only one around here that doesn't quite understand what I'm asked so I know you're hiding something. You know exactly what I'm asking you. Let me ask you again, WHERE DOES MILK COME FROM? Wait…no…that's not what I'm supposed to ask you. Uh…wait…did you like your breakfast? No, that's not it either. What did I ask you before?"

"You asked me if I had been making time with your man."

"Oh yeah, that's it!" Lizzy leaned in closer to Miss Swazi's face. She squinted her eyes tightly until they were almost shut. She balled up her fist and whispered through the cracks of her dentures, "Have you been sneaking around with my doctor boyfriend?"

"Doctor Chadwick?" the woman answered. "Heavens no! How dare you ask me such a thing?"

"You look like the type. Yeah, I see you walking around here looking all quiet and stuck up. I bet you had your eye on him though, didn't you?"

"Well, I never!"

"And as long as you wear that raggedy assed sweater, you probably never will either!" Lizzy said and then hurried off.

Every person that she questioned was left in shock. Most of the time she would ask the first thing that came to her mind, but a small percentage of the time she would get it right. She then forgot to whom she should be asking the questions, so as the day progressed, Lizzy began asking everybody questions. She walked up to Miss Jordan and asked, "Have you ever smelled your water?"

She walked over to Mr. Goldberg and asked, "Have you ever seen a circumcised monkey?" She could not seem to get it right and then when she did, she would ask man or woman, "Are you dating my Dr. Chadwick?" You can only imagine just how much confusion that she caused throughout the entire facility on that day.

By the end of the afternoon all three of the ladies were exhausted. Even during lunch they questioned the other ladies and watched all of Javier's interactions. Now sitting back in the dayroom staring at the red deck of cards which lay sprawled across the table, each lady unable to move was blessed by their guardian angel.

Betty walked up to the table and cheerfully asked, "Are you ladies ok, can I get you anything, a cup of tea perhaps?"

Rose barely able to lift her arm, motioned and nodded her head indicating that she would like a hot cup a tea.

Viola nodded and Lizzy looked at her and with a tired, shaky voice mumble, "Do you work for Delta Airlines?"

"I'll bring all three of you a hot cup. You ladies look tired. You all look like you could use some tea, I'll be right back."

As Betty turned to leave, she suddenly stopped and turned back around to face the table which was draped with the slumped over exhausted elderly bodies. "Oh and ladies, I am terribly sorry about Dr. Chadwick. I know how much you ladies tried but I see that he has made a love connection, huh? I just saw them sitting out in the garden. They look so cute together, I had no idea. I've never ever seen them say more than two words to each other. Sorry ladies, I guess you weren't the only ones with your eyes on him, huh? I'll be right back with your tea."

As Betty headed for the door, each of the ladies lifted her head one by one. They all peered around the room to see which of the active lady residents was missing.

"Where's Agnes?" Viola grunted.

"She's sitting over there next to Ben," Rose replied.

"How about Swazi? I don't see her here."

"Yep, there she is over there sitting near the door sniffing her sweater."

The ladies continued their census of the dayroom.

"Wait! Hazel, where is Hazel?" Viola shouted. "That's who it is, it's Hazel!"

"Who's looking for Hazel?" a voice from the adjacent table asked. "She's over at Cape Fear Hospital. They rushed her over last night. I spoke with the doctor and he said that she's feeling much bet..."

"Who in the hell cares!" Viola shouted over to the voice. "Well, she seems to be the only one missing that I can see."

Rose backed her wheelchair up and made a complete sweep of the room, patrolling for absentees. After bringing her chair to its rest she looked over at Viola.

"Everybody seems to be accounted for except for..." Rose said then turned everyone's attention to Marva's empty seat.

"That sneaky, conniving, back-stabbing slut! She has been trying to convince us to leave him alone this entire time because she wanted him for herself. 'He's just a man' she says when all along she was trying to make him HER MAN!" Viola grunted. She cautiously raised her tired frail body and headed for the door.

Lizzy stood and looking as confused as ever, said to Rose, "I thought she was my friend."

"We all did Lizzy. She pulled the wool over all of our eyes. At least you have an excuse, I mean you're half crazy and all, but Vy and I should have seen this coming," Rose said.

"I'm not crazy, Rose."

"I said half crazy."

"Oh, Ok, thanks."

Rose and Lizzy followed Viola out the door and down the hall toward the garden.

"Ladies, don't get in my way because that tramp has an ass whuppin' comin' to her!" Viola grumbled.

"Just hold her down and let me roll over her a few times when you're done," Rose said.

"Yeah and let me fix her some soup!" Lizzy shouted.

The ladies made their way down to the end of the corridor and were just about to turn down the small hall toward the garden doors.

"Hey where are you ladies headed in such a hurry?" It was Stan. Stan was the odd job man around the center. He didn't have any specific job; he did anything and everything that didn't fit anyone else's job description. He was the maintenance man, the driver, the orderly, the courier, the janitor and anything else man. He wore many hats around Hayfield. Viola kept moving and only grunted as she passed the man.

As Lizzy passed she shouted, "We're going to kill Marva."

Stan stood there with a strange look on his face, "Marva?"

"Yes Marva, that lying, back-stabbing, hiding behind her bible, cheating whore!" Rose yelled as she wheeled by.

Stan began to laugh at the ladies then he yelled down to them, "Well do you ladies want to wait to kill Miss Marva after I pull her off the van? I'm just bringing her back from dialysis. She's pretty tired too so she should be pretty easy to kill today, I mean, if that's what you want to do to your friend."

The ladies stopped in their tracks. They made their way back up to Stan. You said that Marva's in the van?" Viola asked.

"Yes ma'am," Stan replied. "I'm about to bring her off the van right now if you want to wait."

"And she's been at dialysis all day?" Rose asked quietly.

"Yes ma'am. I got her there a little late so she had to wait for a chair but she did get in her full time."

"Has she ever had a puppy?" Liz asked curiously.

"I'm not quite sure of that answer, Miss Liz," he replied.

"Well you go on and bring Marva in and we'll check on her after she's settled back in her room because I know she's probably exhausted. Tell her we'll see her later. Oh and Stan, please, don't mention anything about us killing her ok?" Viola instructed the young man.

Stan smiled and returned through the doors to the van to continue with the off loading of his passengers. The ladies now were even more confused than before. Rose looked at Viola in complete bewilderment. "If Marva is out there…then she can't be…but then who is with…I'm confused."

"Let's go, this still isn't over!" said Viola.

"Did he say that she had a puppy or not?" Lizzy asked and followed on.

The ladies charged forward until they reached the double glass doors leading into the garden. They didn't see the couple at first but as they continued down the walk they could see the two sitting on the wooden bench near the fountain. Javier never saw the ladies coming, as his back was to them. As they moved closer their anger grew. It was clear, Javier was sitting on the bench and she was snuggled up against him with her head resting comfortably on his shoulder. The ladies still couldn't quite make out who she was. As they approached the front of the bench all three ladies' mouths flung wide open.

"Oh my God!" Viola blurted.

"No, no, say it isn't so," Rose moaned.

"Two dollars will never make a dime," Lizzy said laughing.

There, cuddled up on the bench, was none other than Dr. Chadwick and the ladies' good friend Simone.

"Good afternoon, Ladies, what a glorious day this is, wouldn't you agree?"

"Damn the day, you're gay?" Viola asked tactlessly.

Dr. Chadwick revved back then began clearing his throat. Simone sat up and looked at the ladies strangely as he rubbed Javier's thighs. "You mean you didn't know? Wait, you ladies thought that he…you didn't know that he and I…Oh my Lord."

"So you're gay and you have a thing for Simone?" Rose asked

"Alternate life style is what we like to call it actually and yes. Yes, I'm gay."

"So you don't like women at all?" Viola grunted.

"Vy I checked and I didn't see fish on his list, sorrys" Simone interjected.

There was nothing more to say. The ladies backed up and slowly made their exit back through the double doors. "Can you believe that?" Viola mumbled. "I know I can't. I wonder if he's always been that way."

"I wonder what he sees in Simone," said Rose.

"I wonder if either one of them knows if Marva used to have a puppy?" Lizzy added.

The ladies headed back to the dayroom where they were met by Betty. "There you are. I brought you ladies some tea but when I got back you had left."

"Yeah, we went to see the flower show in the garden," Rose said.

"Aaaah, you saw those two, huh? You didn't know, I take it? Well you know what they say, '*to each his own*'. I'll just go warm up your tea," Betty said cheerfully then walked back to the kitchen.

The ladies sat there looking only one way…crazy. They were all still in shock by their recent finding. Betty soon returned with the three steaming cups resting on the tray. She placed a hot, red cup in front of each lady, then to their surprise, in rolled Marva being pushed by none other than Stan. He rolled her up to the table, smiled to the ladies and made his exit.

Looking tired and lifeless, the elderly lady produced a warm smile to her friends. "Stan said that you needed to see me."

"Oh, it could have waited, Honey. You look tired. Do you want me to have Betty take you back to your room?" Viola asked.

"No, Stan said that you ladies needed me and that you missed me so it's my duty as your friend to be here. Now are YOU Ok?"

With those heart felt words being spoken by the same woman that each of them was ready to condemn, the women explained to their friend what had happened and that they had observed something that they thought they would never bear witness to. They told Marva how they should have listened to her and how bad they felt.

Then the ladies witnessed yet another first, Viola was weeping! She apologized to Marva for doubting her friendship. She apologized to Rose for every insult that she made against her and to Lizzy for laughing and sometimes ignoring the fact that she was stricken by a very serious illness.

Rose began to cry, too and took Viola by the hand, followed by Marva. Unaware that she was almost a victim of circumstance, Marva's tears flowed greater than any of them.

"I love you, Ladies," Viola mumbled with a very shaky voice.

"I love you, too," said Rose.

"I love you all," joined Marva.

Lizzy raised her tea cup for a toast, "Me too, I love you crazy ladies."

The ladies' cups met in the center. As they clinked them together, Lizzy yelled out, "HOS BEFORE…"

"Lizzy! What did I tell you about that?" Marva said using as much energy as she could muster up to snap at her friend. The ladies looked at each other for a second before they all broke out into laughter. They wiped away their tears and replaced them with smiles. Marva too, began to laugh then looked at Lizzy and raised her cup as high as she could, "Aw what the hell."

The ladies raised their arms and touched cups again as they chuckled and all yelled at the same time at the top of their voices as they toasted to their friendship, "HOS BEFORE BROS!"

"Hey Marva, did you ever have a puppy?"

E.L. RHODES

A FLAMING ROSE

A Novel

E.L. RHODES

CHAPTER 1 THE MAN

"Damn! Damn! Damn, I'm fine. Boy, you should be posin' for Play Girl." Just stepping out of the shower, standing in front of the mirror flexing his hidden muscles and talking to himself, was the hunk of man that all women desired. Okay, maybe not all women, but most. Well, not most, but some. Ah what the hell, maybe just one. You see, in reality, he was big boned, overweight, and extremely obnoxious. He had a gap in his front teeth wide enough to kick a field goal through, short nasty dread locks, and had rolls on the back of his neck that had the appearance of about three unwrapped Vienna Sausages. And regardless of what the temperature was inside or out, he always had at least four beads of sweat on the tip of his nose. At 5' 7" tall and 236 pounds of moist flab, Melvin Dossier was the man; well at least in his mind.

In the mailroom where he was the shift supervisor, Melvin made sure everybody knew that he was in charge. Always reminding his subordinates of extended breaks, lunch, or minor screw-ups, he prided himself on being a tyrant. Oh yeah, he was truly full of himself, the man.

Although he thought he was king of the mailroom, he was known as "The Campbell's Soup Boy" by everyone else. His armpit odor was his trademark. Most of the people who worked there complained about his split pea and onion smell, while others only tolerated it and talked about him behind his back.

He would flirt with every woman in the building, but there was only one that truly had his eye. He adored her. She was Wendy Parker, the administrative assistant on the seventh floor for one of the company's VPs. Wendy was tall, lean, and had the longest, sexiest, bowed legs that she had no problem displaying from underneath the glass table top of her desk. She was a quiet woman by appearance, but had attitude. She was a very confident woman who knew how to handle customers and Melvin. Her dark skin and short hair gave her a kind of boyish look that was attractive to both genders. After his coffee and honey bun, Melvin always made the mail run on the seventh floor just to see those legs and to get in some flirt time. He'd always start by leaning over her desk then blurting out one of his usual suave and sophisticated complimentary lines.

"Damn baby, I'd like to climb up those long ass legs," or "Girl, you know what they say, once you go fat, you'll never go back! Come on let me throw a picnic in that back yard of yours."

Oh yeah, he was smooth, not. Wendy would always listen to his morning greeting, get the mail and then end their brief visit with a sophisticated line of her own.

"Go to hell Melvin, and on your way, stop and hose down those musty arm pits, with your Campbell's soup smellin' ass."

That would be music to Melvin's ears, because in his mind that was just her way of flirting back. As for Wendy, she hated his guts.

Upon his return to the mailroom, he'd always lie about all the women that wanted him and how Wendy couldn't resist him.

"Oh yeah, I can hit that anytime I want!" he'd brag, but everybody in the mailroom knew that he was living in "Fiction City". They knew that he was further from reality than anyone in the building. He couldn't buy a date. The truth of it is, I believe he only approached women because he knew they'd turn him down. Others thought this as well.

One day, as a test, one of the women from the mailroom started flirting back with Melvin. She told him that she would love to go out with him sometime. Everyone could see that this made him a bit nervous, especially since she wasn't one of the dusty swamp rat hussies that he would usually approach.

"So how about it Mel?" she advanced.

Melvin's defense mechanism immediately kicked in.

"Look here girl, uh, you don't want to do that. This here is Melly Mel the Master! I'll rock that world of yours. Turn your ass out! Then you'd do nothin' more than get on my nerves worryin' the hell out of me. Callin' ten times a day just to hear my voice, I don't have time for that. As a matter of fact, do you know why most women use these two fingers to get off?"

Melvin held up his index and middle fingers pressed tightly together up in the air. The woman glared at his two chubby fingers and then back at the other spectators in the office. They too had no clue as to what the answer to Melvin's question was. She looked back over to Melvin and responded.

"Well no, I can't say that I do."

Melvin lowered his fingers down to his mouth. He stuck out his thick wide bumpy tongue and licked them right up the center.

He looked her right in the eye then spoke calmly, "Because, they're mine."

The entire break room erupted in laughter. Melvin had saved himself and his fictional reputation.

After work, Melvin would usually head over to his favorite watering hole, The Sapphire. He would sit and drink with others of the same sort, and talk sports for hours before heading to his cracker box apartment over in the South East section of D.C. His buddy Dave was also one of his scheduled stops on his way home. These two had been friends since GI Joes and pop rocks. They came up through the times together. They were boys back when Chuck Taylors, and red, black, and green sweat socks were the thing. When styling elephant leg bell bottom jeans, bell sleeve shirts with a medallion, and stack heeled shoes labeled you as being hip. They were hanging out when the two-toned, padded shoulder shirts, wide legged "MC Hammer" pants, and run over heeled shoes for some strange reason qualified you as being "down by law". Anyway, yeah, they were a couple of clowns that have been together for quite sometime. Melvin would try to stop in on Dave as much as he could.

Dave's place was like the neighborhood recreation center. Dave had all the important necessities required by the average adult male. He had PlayStation, PlayStation 2, XBOX, the Internet, air hockey, ping pong, a pool table, HD TV with all the cable stations, and satellite television; he even had a damn ATARI. He had beer, chips, porn, and above all, he had weed.

Now weed was one of Melvin's favorite past times. Weed was his best friend that is, next to Dave. In fact, if he had a child, his child would be named "Weed Dossier". Although he had a great love for his child, he never paid support. Meaning, he did love his son "Weed", but always got a free handout from Dave. He'd stop by Dave's and smoke until he couldn't see past his hands and then would leave with a ten dollar bag. Well, a ten dollar bag for most that is. Dave would never charge Melvin and Melvin knew this.

Now Dave was no mailroom clerk, but he wasn't an attorney or a doctor, either. Can you say "drug dealer"? Yep, Dave was a dealer, but let's give him some credit because Dave would only sell weed. No crack, no coke, no crystal meth, and no heroin; just weed, and he wouldn't sell to kids, either. Let's just say he was a dealer with a heart, if there is such a thing.

Seven years ago, Melvin and Dave worked together. They were both runners for Lucas, the neighborhood drug dealer. They used to go everywhere with Lucas until one day Melvin found himself looking down the barrel of a .38 caliber revolver. He was scared shitless. He wasn't alone, either. Both Lucas and Dave were right beside him. It was a drug deal that had gone bad, real bad. Melvin did everything that he could not to look like a little punk by fainting, whereas Lucas was just the opposite. He never stopped cursing the guys and making threats. Dave was just as calm as Lucas, which was just as scary to Melvin. He was on the verge of falling to his knees and crying and begging for his life when Lucas started walking toward the gunman and told him that if he shot him he'd better kill him.

"What kind of monkey bullshit is that?" Melvin thought. He knew right then and there that being a drug dealer was not his intended occupation. He knew a life like this couldn't last very long.

As the argument became even more heated his life had started to pass before his eyes, followed by his bowels. Without hesitation, Melvin turned and ran as fast as he could. He heard gunfire and cursing in the distance and looked back just once.

Melvin woke up the next morning with his head and his right butt cheek wrapped in bandages. He again realized that being a drug dealer was not the life for him. Seems that when he turned to look back, he had gotten shot right in the backside and ran head first into a telephone pole. Go figure. Lucas was killed that night, but Dave had managed to get away. Later that week, the gunman and his accomplice were both found dead in Anacostia Park. Some say it was Dave's doing, but the case was never solved.

Over the next seven years, Dave had become the new Lucas of the neighborhood. He had become the king; the Godfather. Melvin and Dave remained best of friends, but they always knew where to draw the line. Melvin would stop by occasionally and play video games, listen to music, and would always get high with Dave. They'd talk for awhile about the old days. This would occur usually after already having had a few at The Sapphire.

He'd stop by Dave's to take it just a little higher, then he'd go home to think about Wendy and jack himself off to sleep.

BOOKS BY E.L. RHODES

A FLAMING ROSE

THE SERIALIZATION OF DISCONTENT

THE MEETING PLACE

IMPALPABLE (COMING SOON)

www.ingramcontent.com/pod-product-compliance
Lightning Source LLC
LaVergne TN
LVHW091643100826
845152LV00006B/142/J